Rex Stout

REX STOUT, the creator of Nero Wolfe, was born in Nobles-
ville, Indiana, in 1886, the sixth of nine children of John and
Lucetta Todhunter Stout, both Quakers. Shortly after his
birth the family moved to Wakarusa, Kansas. He was educated in a country school, but by the age of nine he was
recognized throughout the state as a prodigy in arithmetic.
Mr. Stout briefly attended the University of Kansas, but he
left to enlist in the Navy and spent the next two years as a
warrant officer on board President Theodore Roosevelt's
yacht. When he left the Navy in 1908, Rex Stout began to
write free-lance articles and worked as a sightseeing guide
and an itinerant bookkeeper. Later he devised and imple-
mented a school banking system which was installed in four
hundred cities and towns throughout the country. In 1927
Mr. Stout retired from the world of finance and, with the
proceeds of his banking scheme, left for Paris to write serious fiction. He wrote three novels that received favorable
reviews before turning to detective fiction. His first Nero
Wolfe novel, *Fer-de-Lance*, appeared in 1934. It was followed
by many others, among them, *Too Many Cooks*, *The Silent
Speaker*, *If Death Ever Slept*, *The Doorbell Rang*, and *Please
Pass the Guilt*, which established Nero Wolfe as a leading
character on a par with Erle Stanley Gardner's famous pro-
tagonist, Perry Mason. During World War II, Rex Stout waged
a personal campaign against Nazism as chairman of the War
Writers' Board, master of ceremonies of the radio program
"Speaking of Liberty," and member of several national com-
mittees. After the war he turned his attention to mobilizing
public opinion against the wartime use of thermonuclear de-
vices, was an active leader in the Authors' Guild, and resumed writing his Nero Wolfe novels. Rex Stout died in 1975
at the age of eighty-eight. A month before his death he published his seventy-second Nero Wolfe mystery, *A Family Affair*. Ten years later, a seventy-third Nero Wolfe mystery was
discovered and published in *Death Times Three*.

The Rex Stout Library

REX STOUT

Double for Death

*Introduction
by Rita Mae Brown*

BANTAM BOOKS
NEW YORK · TORONTO · LONDON · SYDNEY · AUCKLAND

A TECUMSEH FOX
MYSTERY

This book is fiction. No resemblance is intended
between any character herein and any person,
living or dead; any such resemblance is
purely coincidental.

DOUBLE FOR DEATH

A Bantam Crime Line Book / published by arrangement
with the Author

PUBLISHING HISTORY

Farrar and Rinehart edition published 1939
Bantam edition / December 1982
Bantam reissue edition / April 1995

ISBN 978-0-553-76300-3

Published simultaneously in the United States and Canada

Bantam Books are published by Bantam Books, a division of Bantam Double-
day Dell Publishing Group, Inc. Its trademark, consisting of the words "Bantam Books" and the portrayal of a rooster, is Registered in U.S. Patent and
Trademark Office and in other countries. Marca Registrada. Bantam Books,
1540 Broadway, New York, New York 10036.

144915995

Introduction

Mysteries are like cayenne for the brain. The senses *do* pick up. Who was Jack the Ripper? Who killed Judge Crater? How did I burn through my paycheck so fast? Such questions can intrigue or infuriate, but the mind snaps to attention.

How much better if the mystery attaches to someone else! After all, you don't really want to find a body in your library. You probably wouldn't even want to find one in your garage, and it's easier to tidy up in there.

It's much more satifying to read about human carcasses than to see them. Rex Stout understood this fastidiousness in *Double for Death.* The victims are discovered soon after their dispatch from this vale of tears. Actually, the reason they were dispatched might be that for them life wasn't a vale of tears. The living was good until the end, of course. The final moment appeared to make no sense.

That's the fun of the mystery, figuring out why it does make sense. In the fiction of Mr. Stout, murderers do have motives. Given that we exist in a world of aimless violence, having a solid reason for murder makes it somehow less horrifying . . . not less morally reprehensible, just less horrifying. So the key to unraveling the mystery is finding the motive.

Knowing that, Stout sprays motives around like soapsuds at a car wash. It's either that technique or the "he hadn't an enemy in the world" technique. In *Double for Death* we discover that the intended victim, not exactly a prince among men, had enemies enough. At first it appears that whoever the individual or individuals might be, they are woefully stupid: they killed the wrong man.

Imagine going to all the trouble to murder someone and finding out you blew it. Do you succumb to the ravishment of misery or do you try, try again? The author tantalizes us with this information but we still can't unmask the killer.

Whether the detective is the lean and handsome Tecumseh Fox, as in *Double for Death*, or the gargantuan and imperious Nero Wolfe, Rex Stout keeps you on the edge of your seat until the very end.

In Tecumseh Fox, Stout creates a figure as interesting as the mysteries he solves. His country house, dubbed "The Zoo" by neighboring farmers, harbors former criminals trying to straighten up, clients in jeopardy, Mrs. Trimble, the sensitive housekeeper, and Dan Pavey, referred to as Tecumseh's vice president. Set outside New York City in what was then rolling countryside, Tecumseh's house is like camp for adults, only without the mandatory swimming classes. Footsteps tramp up and down the hallways; young men prune large branches out of trees; if someone needs a friend to talk to at three in the morning he can usually find another guest awake or he can rouse one. The police roll in and out, complaining or matching wits with Tecumseh, so there's a dash of animosity to enliven the atmosphere.

We know from the Zoo that Tecumseh, for all his toughness, is softhearted. He can't turn away someone in trouble. He doesn't always get paid, either, and he works on a sliding scale of fees. When the damsel in distress shows up at his farm, one of the first things she tells him is that she doesn't have any money and her uncle, accused of murder and recently fired, doesn't have any money either. He helps her anyway and is soon drawn into a complex web of personalities, one of whom is bound to be the spider.

Tecumseh appreciates ladies, although Nancy Grant, beautiful and in her early twenties, amuses him more than she attracts him. Nancy at times appears to be a quart low, and while airheads appeal to some men, they don't especially appeal to Tecumseh. He likes her, he can't resist her frantic entreaties, but he's not drawn to her. Somehow that makes him far more interesting than if he took the case in a flash of lust. In *Double for Death* he is a man in his mid-thirties, quite capable of exercising all his parts. He's working from a different standard and in his way he mystifies people accustomed to simple men, men driven by lust, money, or even fame. Tecumseh, much more complicated, seeks balance. Redressing a wrong is balance. It's justice, too, but Tecumseh knows better than to pontificate on such subjects as justice, love, and goodness. He lets others blather. He just gets the job done.

How American. Perhaps that's why we like him so much. It's not that Tecumseh Fox doesn't understand the Great Questions. He does. One suspects he's even answered some of them for himself. But he's not going to answer them for you. That's your job. The deepest mysteries are always individual.

One tiny criticism about *Double for Death* from my mystery-writing partner, Sneaky Pie, a tiger cat. There are no cats in this mystery, only sheep. Miss Pie thinks that's awful.

—Rita Mae Brown

Double
for Death

Chapter 1

A man, with brown cheeks smoothly shaven and wearing a clean denim shirt because it was Monday morning, chaperoning his herd of Jerseys across the paved road from the barn side to the pasture side, saw a car coming and cussed. With any driver whatever the car would make his cows nervous; and if bad luck made it a certain kind of weekend driver from New York, which was only fifty miles to the south, there was no telling what might happen. He stood in the middle of the road and glared at the approaching demon, then felt easier as he saw it was slowing down and still easier when it crept, circling for a six-foot clearance past Jennifer's indifferent rump. When it stopped completely, so close alongside that he could have reached out and touched the door handle, the last shred of his irritation was dissolved, for he was by no means so hopelessly committed to cows that he didn't know a pretty girl when he saw one. He even saw, before she spoke, the flecks of ochre that warmed her troubled grey eyes, though she spoke at once.

"Please, am I going right for the Fox place?"

He grunted and crinkles of criticism radiated from

the corners of his eyes. "Oh," he said, "you're bound for The Zoo."

"Yes," she agreed, not smiling. "I've heard that's what they call it in the neighborhood. Am I going right?"

He nodded and jerked a thumb. "On about a mile, big white house set on a knoll with trees around, back from the road a piece."

She thanked him. He saw her lips tighten as she reached for the gearshift and blurted: "What you so mad about this fine summer morning?"

"I'm not mad, I'm worried. Thank you."

He watched the small coupé, not ramshackle but far from elegant, recede until it rounded the bend, then sighed and muttered: "If it's a man worrying her it's not me and never will be," and yelled in fresh irritation: "Hey, Queenie, dern you, move!"

The girl drove the prescribed mile, saw the big white house on the knoll among trees and turned into the private lane which led to it. The pleasant curves of the lane, the little bridge over a brook, the elms and maples which permitted the sunshine to reach only a stingy third of the lawn, even the four or five people scattered around who turned or lifted their heads to watch the coupé pass—these details barely grazed the rim of her attention. There appeared to be no connection between the driveway and the pillared porch, so she followed it around the house to a broad gravelled space, the rear boundary of which was an enormous old barn with one end, judging from the doors, converted into a garage.

She parked at the edge of the gravel and got out. Two big dogs and one little one came loping from behind shrubs, regarded her cynically and rambled off. A rooster crowed without enthusiasm. A man appeared at a small door at the far corner of the barn, decided in one brief glance that the coupé and its cargo were not his affair, and vanished. The girl started for the back entrance of the house, which was all but hidden from view by a riot of yellow climbing roses, and when nearly there was halted by the emergence of a large round-faced woman in a green smock with the impatient eyes of one who has not quite caught up with the urgencies of life and does not expect to. Her voice, too, was husky with impatience, but not unpleasant.

"How do you do?"

"How do you do?" said the girl. "My name is Nancy Grant. I phoned an hour ago. Is Mr. Fox here?"

The woman shook her head. "Mr. Tecumseh Fox hasn't returned. You wait on the front porch unless you want to come in the house this way. I'm busy getting ready to cook dinner."

"I——" The girl bit her lip. "Will he be here soon?"

"Maybe he will, but there's no telling. He was supposed to come home last night. Didn't Mr. Crocker tell you that on the phone?"

"Yes, he did, but I——"

"Well, Mr. Tecumseh Fox'll come some time. He always does. What kind of trouble are you in? Bad?"

"Yes."

"Forget it. You can go and pick flowers. They're all around, pick any kind you want to. I wish I could. I wish I could go to church or sit outdoors or pick flowers a day like this, but I've got to cook dinner." She wheeled abruptly and made for the entrance, but after she had disappeared behind the roses her face showed again for the announcement: "My name is Mrs. Trimble!" and then was gone.

The girl made a face at the roses, pulled her sagging shoulders up straight and started around the house. As she encircled it, again plucking at the fringe of her attention were the multifarious surrounding facts—healthy shrubs and trees, comfortable grass in sun and shadow, beds and borders of flowers—which showed a place cared for but not pampered. Ascending the steps to the pillared front porch, she found it broad and clean and cool, though somewhat unbalanced because its right half sported a dozen summer chairs while its left half had none at all. In one of the chairs sat a man in a striped jacket and grey slacks, with bulbous inflamed blotches disfiguring his face and forehead. One of his eyes was swollen shut; with the other he was gazing intently at something he held in his hand. From somewhere came a sound like sawing wood, though no such process was in view. After one swift glance to the right, the girl turned to the chairless left and perched on the porch rail.

The man's voice came, raised against the sawing noise:

"Sit over here!"

She said she was all right.

"No, you're not! A phoebe has a nest there so we moved the chairs! Sit over here! I'm not mangy; I got stung by bees!"

To avoid argument, she slipped to her feet and moved towards the chairs, while he resumed his scrutiny of the object in his hand, which, she saw as she approached, was a small alarm clock. She was lowering herself into a seat when she jerked erect again, startled by two nearly simultaneous assaults on her ears, first a loud splintering and crashing from beyond the porch and then the jangling of the bell on the alarm clock. She stood there staring at a large dead limb of a maple tree which had hurtled through the lower branches and lay there on the lawn. The sawing noise had stopped. A voice called from above:

"How about it?"

The man the bees had stung yelled: "One second! You win! By God, one second!"

There was a shout of triumph and a sound of scrambling; and a man came sliding down the trunk of the tree and hit the ground. He was young, homely, big and sweaty, and his shirt was torn. He stood at the foot of the steps and commanded:

"Come on, clean it up."

"I'll do it tomorrow. These stings hurt."

"You'll do it now. That was the bet. And first you'll go and make me a drink and bring it to me and I'll sit here and drink it and watch you. You whittled me down to eight minutes and I did it anyway. I want rye——"

He broke off and turned, looking towards the lane. The horn of a car had sounded, one sharp blast, and in a moment the car could be seen, a big black convertible with a chromium hood, noiselessly rolling up the grade this side of the brook.

The man with the alarm clock rose to his feet. "Fox returning," he announced. "Wait till he sees the mess you made on the lawn! I've got to give this clock back to Mrs. Trimble. . . ."

He trotted off into the house. The homely young man bounded up the steps to the porch and strode after him. The convertible rounded the arc of the driveway and disappeared to the rear. Nancy Grant sat down. During the five minutes she still had to wait she turned her head fifty times to glance hopefully at the door, but it was between glances that he finally appeared. She heard light quick steps, twisted her head again and saw a man carrying perhaps fifteen more years than her twenty-two, in a brown Palm Beach suit and without a hat. Her first swift thought, as she rose, was that he looked like a fox, but then she saw, his face towards her, that his chin and nose were not actually pointed and his brown eyes were opened too wide to look sly. The eyes took her in, all of her, with so brief a displacement of their focus into her own that it might have been lightning leaping a gap, and she was disconcerted.

"I'm Tecumseh Fox. Mrs. Trimble says your name is Nancy Grant. You want to see me?"

She nodded, looked left and right, opened her mouth and closed it.

"It's all right out here," he said. "We won't be interrupted or overheard. You look kind of used up. Could I get you a drink?"

"No, thank you."

"No? Sit down." He pulled a chair around to confront hers, sat as she did, reached out suddenly and surprisingly to give the back of her hand three reassuring pats, leaned back and asked: "Well?"

"It's murder." The hand he had patted closed to a fist. "The Thorpe murder."

"Thorpe? Has a Thorpe been murdered?"

"Why, yes." She looked astonished and incredulous. "The papers this morning——"

"I haven't seen them. I apologize. I drove up to Boston yesterday to look at something and just got back. A friend of yours named Thorpe?"

"No, not a friend. Ridley Thorpe, the—you must know. The head of Thorpe Control."

"That one? Murdered?"

"Yes."

"Well?"

"They've arrested my uncle. My Uncle Andy—Andrew. That's why I came to you—he used to know you. Andrew Grant?"

Fox nodded. "Sure. He visited me a while about three years ago. He was going to write something but didn't get started."

A little flush in Nancy's cheeks furnished an idea of what she might look like when not used up. "I know," she said. "He told me all about the people you let stay here as your guests, as long as they want to. I know he was—he was pretty aimless. But when I came to New York to have a career—I think it was on account of me he got a job writing advertising, to be able to help me, though I didn't know that then— anyhow, I admire him and I'm grateful to him and I love him very much and I thought you might be willing to help him—he didn't send me here—though I suppose your opinion of him, since you only knew him when he was . . . well——"

"I wouldn't have picked him for a murderer. Did he kill Thorpe?"

"No!"

"Good. Why was he arrested?"

"He . . . I'll have to tell you all about it."

"Go ahead."

"Will you help him? Will you get him out of it?"

"Go ahead and tell me."

"He was there last night—where Thorpe was murdered."

"Where was that? I apologize again. There are papers in the house. Shall I get one and read it?"

Nancy shook her head. "I'll tell you. I know things that aren't in the papers. He was killed at a place over near Mount Kisco—a little place with a bungalow off in the woods where he went weekends alone. No one ever went there with him, or was invited there, not even his family, except a colored man who was his chauffeur and valet and cook for the weekends. No one else was allowed on the place. Last night somebody sneaked through the woods and shot through an open window and killed him."

"And Andy Grant was there?"

"Yes. It's things about that that I know that aren't in the papers. I drove him there."

"You did. Invited?"

"No. He—Uncle Andy works, writes copy for the Willoughby Advertising Agency. Thorpe Control is their biggest account. He wrote a series for a campaign for a new product they're going to bring out and Thorpe executives turned it down. He thought it was the best thing he had ever done and it should be a big thing for him, and he fought for it too hard and maybe lost his temper, and the agency fired him. That was a week ago. He was sure he could sell the campaign to Ridley Thorpe if he could get to him, but he couldn't get near him. He knew about the bungalow where Thorpe spent secluded weekends, apparently everybody at the agency did, and he decided to try to see Thorpe there. He knew I was . . . he knew . . . I had gone . . ."

Her voice trailed off. She looked apologetically at Tecumseh Fox, then closed her eyes and put her palms to her temples and pressed so hard that he could see the backs of her hands go white. When she opened her eyes again she tried to smile, but all it amounted to was a quivering of her lips. "I guess I'm a softy," she said. "I guess I'll have to have that drink. You see they kept me at the police station, or maybe it was the jail, at White Plains all night, and I didn't get any sleep, and then I got away and phoned——"

"You ran away from the police?"

"Yes, they left me alone in a room and I sneaked out and went down an alley and phoned here and then I stole a car and——"

"You did. You stole a car? The one parked out back?"

"Yes, I had to get here, and I was afraid to try to rent one, even a taxi, for fear——"

"Hold it." Fox was frowning. "Look at me. No, right in the eyes. . . . Uh-huh. How straight are you?"

"I'm pretty straight." Her lips quivered again. "I'm a little stupid sometimes, but I'm reasonably straight."

"Let me see your hand."

Without hesitation she extended it. He took it, inspected the back and palm, the joints and fingertips, the firm little mounds. "Not palmistry," he said curtly. "Nice hand. Is there anything of yours in that car?"

"No."

"Not a thing? Sure?"

"Nothing."

He turned his head and made his voice a baritone bellow:

"Dan!"

After a moment there was the sound of steps, much heavier than Fox's had been, and the screen door opened for a man to come through. He was under forty but not much, in shirt sleeves with no tie, excessively broad-shouldered, and had a swarthy face so remarkably square that its outlines could have been reproduced with a straight rule. Restrained movements of his jaw indicated that he had not quite finished chewing something. He approached and rumbled as from the bottom of a deep cavern:

"Right here, Tec."

"Uh-huh," said Fox, "your shirt's showing. Miss Grant, this is Mr. Pavey, my vice-president. Dan, that coupé out back was driven here by Miss Grant. It's hot. She took it from the curb in White Plains this morning. Tell Bill to take the station wagon and go by the back road towards Carmel, turn left at Miller's Corner and go over the hill towards the lake. You follow him in the coupé and ditch it along there after you top the hill. Take a rag along to wipe the doors and handles and steering wheel. You don't want any audience while you're transferring to the station wagon."

Dan Pavey shook his head. "That's too close by, only four miles from here. Wouldn't it be better if we went down beyond——"

"No."

"Right again," Dan rumbled and tramped off.

"Excuse me," Fox said, and arose and followed his vice-president into the house. Nancy's head fell forward, like a tulip with the sap out of its stem. Again she pressed her palms tight against her temples and was still sitting that way ten minutes later when Tecumseh Fox reappeared, with a newspaper under one arm and, balanced on the other, a tray with chicken sandwiches, a bottle of sherry, a glass and a highball.

"Here," he said, pulling a table over with his foot, "you break your fast while I see what this says."

Chapter 2

Fox refolded the news section of the paper and tossed it aside. All but one of the sandwiches were gone from the plate and the level of the sherry was down two inches.

He frowned at her. "Did your uncle know Luke Wheer?" he demanded.

"Luke? . . ." She frowned back. "Who is that?"

"The colored servant at the bungalow with Thorpe. You said you read a paper this morning."

"I didn't really read it. I stopped on my way here —I think it was Bedford Hills—and bought one, but I didn't read it through, I just looked . . ." Her color was better and so was her voice. "But Uncle Andy couldn't possibly have known that colored man. How could he? What about him?"

"He's gone. Can't be found. You didn't read much if you didn't read that. The paper suggests, dodging libel, that collusion is suspected between Andy and Luke Wheer." Fox emptied his highball glass and put it down. "Other items you may have missed. Thorpe's pockets were empty—no wallet, no keys, no nothing. His wristwatch was gone. Two bullets hit him and none missed him. He has spent every weekend at the bungalow since April. His wife died years ago. His son Jeffrey was found at a roadhouse night club on Long Island and brought to identify the body. His daughter Miranda was notified somewhere in the Adirondacks and is returning by plane. Do you know either of them?"

"Of course not. How could I know people like that?"

"Like what?"

"Why—a millionaire's sons and daughters."

"Oh. The police can't locate Thorpe's confidential secretary, a man named Vaughn Kester. He was weekending at the Green Meadow Club, playing golf, was got out of bed by a phone call at midnight, notifying him of Thorpe's death, and left immediately for the scene. But he seems to have got ditched on the way. Hasn't turned up. Do you know him?"

"No, I don't. I tell you I don't know any Thorpes or any one connected with them and neither does Uncle Andy. It was just like I said. We were at the Bascoms, friends of mine, over near Westport, for the weekend, and he was telling about what he had done and his being fired, and how he had spent a week trying to get to Thorpe, and he mentioned the bungalow where he hides himself weekends, and Della Bascom and I talked him into going there, and Della lent me her car and I drove him over——"

"Why didn't he drive himself?"

"Because he didn't really want to go and I was pushing him. He has plenty of guts, real guts, he really has, but he's not—well, not very aggressive. He didn't know exactly where the place was and we had to drive around and ask, and finally a man at a filling station about three miles out of Mount Kisco told us. We——"

"What time was that?"

"Around eleven o'clock. Maybe not quite. We had left the Bascoms about nine and had spent a lot of time looking for it, and of course it was some distance to Mount Kisco. The filling station man told us the place was fenced and the gate would be locked, and it was, so we couldn't drive in. We couldn't see the bungalow from the road on account of the trees and apparently it was quite a ways in or he had gone to bed, because we couldn't even see any sign of lights. We parked the car at the edge of the road near the gate and Uncle Andy climbed the fence. I wanted to too, but he wouldn't let me; he said there might be a savage dog."

Fox observed: "I wouldn't have picked Andy Grant to climb fences at night in the direction of savage dogs."

"He's not a coward!"

"Okay. But he's not—as you say—not very aggressive."

"Don't I know it?" Nancy demanded. "I had—that's why it's all my fault! Don't you understand that? I persuaded him—I hounded him into it!"

"And now you want me to pull him out. Go ahead."

"You will! Won't you?"

"Go ahead. He climbed the fence. What did you do, wait in the car?"

"Yes. I sat and waited, I suppose fifteen minutes, and I was feeling satisfied with myself because I thought he must have got in to see Thorpe or he would have been back, when I heard someone scrambling over the fence and he called to me to turn on the car lights. He came and got in and I asked him what happened, and he said to drive on and he would tell me on the way, but I sat tight and made him tell me.

He said he had followed a winding drive about three hundred yards to the bungalow and instead of going to the door had gone around to the side where light was coming from a window. The window was open, and he stood behind a tree only a few feet away and looked in. Thorpe was there in a chair, leaning back comfortably smoking a cigar, listening to the radio playing a piece of band music——"

"Could you hear the radio out at the road?"

"Yes, I heard it plainly, it must have been turned up high. I looked at the dashboard clock and my wrist-watch too, and it was ten minutes past eleven and I decided it must be Al Rickett's orchestra at the Regency on WRK, and I turned on the car radio, low, and it was. Uncle Andy said it was playing very loud. He stood there a minute or two, watching Thorpe through the window, and then went back around the corner and into an enclosed terrace to the door. He stood on the terrace for two or three minutes, waiting for a rest in the radio so his knock would be heard and that's where he was when he heard the shots fired."

"Uh-huh," Fox grunted. "Did he tell you that at that time, sitting there?"

"Of course. He said he heard two shots. That's where it was my fault again. I said he had got cold feet and was using that for an excuse, that it must have been something on the radio. I had heard something myself that had sounded like shots, but had taken it for granted it was a trick of Al Rickett's. I—I made fun of him. He wanted to drive on and get away from there, but he never had wanted to go. We argued about it and we both got worked up, and I said things I'm darned sorry for now. I finally got out of the car and said he could drive on alone if he wanted to, and we went on arguing. We were still at it when we saw the lights of a car inside on the drive coming our way. It stopped the other side of the gate and in a minute the gate swung open, and then the car came out in a rush, swerving sharp into the road. I was standing there and had to jump for my life, and by the time I got straightened up again the car had gone and its rear bumper had hooked into our left front tire and torn a gash in it and pulled it half off."

"Your lights were on."

"Uncle Andy had turned them off."

"Did you see who was in the car?"

"I was too busy jumping and Uncle Andy was too busy yelling at me. Naturally I was so furious I was trembling. He got out and looked at the tire and swore some, and began looking for tools. I walked through the gate and on up the drive to the bungalow. He called after me, but I didn't answer. I felt I had ample excuse to knock on Thorpe's door myself."

"After hearing shots fired? Brave girl?"

"Oh, no, I wasn't brave, I was mad. I hadn't thought they were shots, anyway. You'll see how brave I was in a minute. The door of the bungalow was wide open and at the end of the entrance hall another open door showed a lighted room. I stood on the terrace and called a few times and got no answer, and then went in, entered the lighted room, and saw a body on the floor. One look was enough to tell you it was a body and not a man. I turned and ran, ran as hard as I could back down the drive, and told Uncle Andy and said he must get the spare tire on as quick as he could so we could get away from there."

"I take back the brave. Nor was it bright."

"That's what Uncle Andy said. He said the man might not be dead and we should find out, and be- sides, everybody at Bascoms' knew where we had

gone and we had asked half a dozen people the way to
Thorpe's place, so if we bolted we might be in the
soup. He took a flashlight and trotted back up the
drive with me behind him. I wasn't brave then either;
I trembled all over while I stood watching him kneel-
ing to look at the body. He got up and said it was
Ridley Thorpe and he was dead, and went to the
phone and called the police. Pretty soon a car came
with state troopers and then some others came. They
kept us there a long while and then took us to White
Plains and put us in separate rooms and asked me
questions the rest of the night, and I suppose Uncle
Andy too—"

"Did you send for a lawyer?"

"I don't know any. I don't think Uncle Andy does
either. Why would he know a lawyer?"

"He might. Lots of people know lawyers. Go
ahead."

"That's all." Nancy upturned the palms of her nice
hands. "They left me alone in the room, and I climbed
out a window and hung on the ledge and dropped and
went down an alley and phoned and took that car and
came here."

"You left by a window?"

"I had to because the door was locked."

Fox grunted. "Didn't you know you had the right
to insist on making a phone call?"

"I only wanted to phone to ask if you were here.
You were the only person I could think of that might
help him and I had to persuade you, and I was afraid I
couldn't on the phone. You see, I haven't got any
money and neither has he. I guess I could scrape up
about a hundred dollars and I could borrow——"

"What have you left out?"

"Left out?" She frowned. "You mean about money?"

"I mean facts. What have you left out?"

"Why, nothing. Honestly I haven't. Didn't I admit I stole the car?"

"Not the car. The murder. What happened last night and what led up to it. What have you left out about that?"

"Not one thing." Her lips quivered again for a smile. "You see why I had to come instead of just phoning you? With me here like this looking at you and you looking at me, you can't possibly think I'm lying about anything. Won't you—please? It's all my fault . . . the whole thing is entirely my fault——"

"Excuse me," Fox said abruptly, and got up and left her to finish her plea to the air.

Within the screen door was a wide hall with a waxed wooden floor, a stairway, tan wallpaper with gold stripes, pretty bad, and six doors, all of them standing open except two which were for closets. In the room to the left, which was very large and very full of books, chairs, shotguns, tennis rackets, gerani-ums, guitars, binoculars, parrots and so forth, Fox paused to put his hand on the shoulder of the man with the bee stings, who sat with a drink in his hand watching the homely young man stalk a fly with a swatter.

Fox asked: "Did you put soda on them?"

"No, I——"

"Put soda on them."

Through the room beyond, which contained a table that could have seated twenty and also chairs for that number, and he was in the kitchen—huge, clean, hot and aromatic. He intercepted Mrs. Trimble on a trip from the range to the sink.

"Well, darling, how goes it?"

A man washing red radishes at the sink snorted. "I'm glad to hear she's somebody's darling."

"I'm sure, Bill, all you did was marry her. I'm free to adore her. I'm going out on business."

Mrs. Trimble glared at him. "Back for dinner?"

"I'll try."

"You won't. Starve."

Fox went out the back door and stuck his head around the roses to see Dan Pavey rubbing a chamois over the polish of the black convertible.

"Dan! All right?"

Dan tramped over to him, which seemed a long way to come for the one word he growled: "Right."

"You left it the other side of the hill?"

"Right."

"Put things away and get a coat on. We're going over to White Plains and maybe around a little. On business."

"Wouldn't it be better if we took the station——"

"No."

"Right again." Dan turned, flipping the chamois, then suddenly turned again and stood hesitant.

"Well?" Fox inquired.

"Nothing. Only I remembered something. I remembered the time that good-looking Bennett woman came here to get you to help her, and after we'd had a talk with her we put her in the car and took her to New York and turned her over to the cops for poisoning her husband."

Fox shook his head. "It didn't happen that way. You've garbled it. Anyway, this is different. Miss Grant hasn't poisoned anyone."

"Thorpe wasn't poisoned, he was shot. According to the paper."

"She hasn't shot any one either. Do you agree?"

"I do."

"Good. If I change my mind I'll let you know."

Fox left him. Re-entering the house, he went upstairs to a large corner apartment which, in addition to the usual furnishings of a bedroom, contained a desk, a safe that reached the ceiling and filing cabinets. Nine minutes later, having washed his face and hands, cleaned his nails, brushed his hair and changed his shirt, tie and suit, he trotted down to the front porch and said to Nancy Grant:

"Come on, let's go."

Chapter 3

The husky heavy man in a blue suit and black shoes with his chair tilted back against the wall was Ben Cook, the White Plains chief of police. The one at the big desk, in tailored grey summer worsted with slick hair and quick eyes was P. L. Derwin, the Westchester County district attorney. The younger one, incongruous in white dinner jacket and black trousers, with tousled hair and bloodshot eyes, was Jeffrey Thorpe; and the impeccably arrayed and arranged young woman with sleepy lids half down was his sister Miranda.

Miranda, whose name was Pemberton and not Thorpe because that was the one vestigial remain of a divorced husband, said: "I couldn't even offer a guess."

"Neither could I," her brother declared. "Luke has been with Father over twenty years, almost ever since I was born. I don't say he was devoted to him, but—hell, you know. He was square and straight and easy-going, and I would have bet Father had more confidence in him than any one else in the world. Anyway, why would he? He had a good job for life and an easy one. All he had to do was valet, which with Father was a cinch. He cooked and chauffeured only in that damn' weekend hideout."

"It's ridiculous," said Miranda.

The district attorney put his fingertips together. "I accept your opinion, of course," he stated, in the tone of politic patience which an elected person has always in stock for such citizens as bereaved millionaires. "But the fact remains that Luke Wheer has disappeared. If we are to believe Grant and his niece, he went precipitately, in your father's car, within a few minutes after the shooting, and your father's pockets had been emptied. No one knows what money or valuables he may have had with him or in the bungalow."

"Luke never did it," said Jeffrey Thorpe with conviction and rubbed his eyes with his knuckles.

"Someone did," Ben Cook rasped and scowled unimpressed at the district attorney's admonitory glance.

"I doubt it myself." Derwin was judicious. "I doubt if he—uh—fired the shots, but he may have—uh—taken advantage of the situation. I'm satisfied in my own mind that Grant did the shooting. It's unfortunate—yes, Bolan?"

The man who had entered reported nasally: "Grant says he's perfectly willing, sir, but nothing doing on any more questions."

"I don't want to ask him any. Bring him in." The man went and Derwin turned to Miranda. "I dislike asking this of you, Mrs. Pemberton. I know it's a painful thing——"

"I don't mind." She compressed her lips and released them. "I mean it's all pretty painful. To look at the man who did it won't make it any worse."

They all turned their heads as the door opened. The man who entered, ushered in, was near forty, one side or the other. In spite of looking unwashed, extremely weary and disarranged as to clothing, there was an air of efficacy and distinction about him. Under the circumstances, which he understood, it must have been difficult not to make too much either of defiance or contempt, but his face and attitude displayed only a composed resentment. He walked in nearly up to the desk, stopped and turned to confront the young man, and then wheeled to face the young woman, looking down straight at her.

"I didn't kill your father," he said in a voice strained with fatigue. "That's nonsense. I'm sorry anybody did. I needed to get my job back and he was my only chance of getting it. You look more intelligent than any of these idiots around here. Are you? If you are, for God's sake tell them to quit bullying me and start looking for the damn murderer. They brought me in here to see if you would recognize me as someone who has been prowling around the basement door. Do you?"

"No."

"Have you looked at me long enough?"

"Yes, thank you."

He walked out.

Miranda's eyes followed him to the door, then her face returned to the district attorney. "I——" She bit it off and compressed her lips.

"Yes, Mrs. Pemberton?"

"I believe him."

"Rot." Her brother snorted. "You have no reason to believe him or disbelieve him either. Maybe he's a good liar. He certainly knows how to look into a girl's eyes and hand it out, Sis dear." He looked at Derwin. "But one thing, I've never seen him before."

"Have you, Mrs. Pemberton?"

"No. Never."

"Why do you say you believe him?"

"I do, that's all." She shrugged. "And I think——"

She stopped and he prodded her. "Yes, Mrs. Pemberton?"

"I think you're going to find things that will make it more painful than it is now. If I didn't think you'd find them eventually, I wouldn't say this, but I think you will. I know you have the impression that I'm cold-blooded about my father's sudden death, but Ridley Thorpe wasn't much of a father. He was too busy being a financier and a philanthropist and a great man. The fact is that since Mother died, when I was ten years old, my brother and I have been orphans except that we have had our bills paid. But I knew my father a good deal better than he knew me, because I was interested in him—at least I used to be—and he was never interested in me. And what I think you're going to find out eventually, if a murder is investigated the way it's supposed to be, is that he didn't have that bungalow for seclusion with Luke and his thoughts. He had it for—I mustn't shock you, I suppose—for secret female companionship."

"Good lord!" her brother blurted incredulously. "Him?"

"Yes, Jeff, him," she declared imperturbably. "I knew him a lot better than you did and I'm a woman myself. He didn't want to be bound by marriage again, because he was too selfish to be bound by anything, and open philandering would have been bad for his reputation as a national ornament, but he was by no means devoid of carnality. I'm not saying tritely find the woman; I just predict you'll find out things about that bungalow if you really try, instead of putting it on to this Grant man because by bad luck the poor devil——"

"Excuse me," Derwin put in a little less patiently. "I assure you, Mrs. Pemberton, we're not putting it on to any one. Every angle is being thoroughly investigated. The New York police are cooperating from that end. An intensive search is being made for the three people who have disappeared: Luke Wheer, Nancy Grant, this man's niece, and Vaughn Kester, your father's confidential secretary. We're not putting it on to Grant, though I repeat that the evidence against him is strong. He was there, right there when the shots were fired. There is no evidence that any one else was, except Luke Wheer. He was a disgruntled employee, fired from his job. And he has been caught in a lie regarding the time he got there. The servants at the New York residence, and others, have corroborated what you and your brother told me about your father's invariable custom of listening to Dick Barry's broadcast every evening from eleven to eleven-thirty. So Grant lied and his niece, too. But we're not neglecting other angles. For one thing and perhaps the most important, where's Vaughn Kester? Possibly he could tell us things about Grant that we don't know. And where the devil is he? Has he been murdered too? Colonel Brissenden thinks so. Regarding your surmise about your father's—uh—his weekends in that bungalow—yes, Bolan?"

The man who talked nasally closed the door behind him, approached, stopped and cleared his throat. "Excuse me," he said, "I don't know. He insisted on it."

"Who insisted on what?"

"Tecumseh Fox. He wants to see you."

"What does he want?"

"All he says is he wants to see you."

"Tell him I'm engaged. I can see him in an hour."

"Yes, sir." The man turned to go.

Miranda touched his sleeve to stop him. "Is it Tecumseh Fox the detective?"

"Yes, ma'am. I guess that's the only one there is."

"Then couldn't . . . I'd like to see him." She transferred to Derwin. "When I was collecting celebrities and notorieties I invited him to dine at my house three times and he declined—and I had good dinners, too."

"I don't know what he wants, Mrs. Pemberton."

"Send for him and ask him."

Derwin frowned, but took it. "Send him in, Bolan."

Jeffrey said: "Randa dear, you'll stop your own funeral to get out and ask a man about a dog," and rubbed his bloodshot eyes with his knuckles again.

Ben Cook rasped: "If it's this one it'll be a fox."

The door opened, quick light steps sounded, and that one was there at the desk before they knew it. Passing, his eyes swiftly took in all of the brother and sister; now, amiably, they were for the district attorney. "Good morning, Mr. Derwin. I apologize."

"Good morning. What can I do for you?"

"I'd like to see Andrew Grant. The fellow that found Ridley Thorpe's body and reported it. You've got him around here, haven't you?"

"What do you want to see him about?"

"I'm working for him."

Derwin tightened his lips, folded his arms and hunched his shoulders. The impression he produced was one of shrinkage. "Since when have you been working for him? He has made no communication that I know of."

"Oh, yes, excuse me, he has. Through his niece Nancy. She came to see me."

"His niece . . ." Derwin stared. "She went to see you?"

"Yes."

"She is a fugitive! Where is she?"

"She's available. I didn't know she was a fugitive. I apologize. I didn't know she had been charged."

"She was being held for questioning."

"Well, she's available. No charge, was there?" Fox, conciliatory, smiled. "By the way, she borrowed a dollar from one of your men. Would you mind finding out which one and returning it?" He handed across a dollar bill. "Thanks. She had left her purse in her friend's car that had the tire ripped off and she wanted to make a phone call. No commitment, was there? Just holding her without one. That's risky sometimes. I request permission to see Andrew Grant."

The district attorney, with his head tilted back, scowled up into the brown eyes which Nancy Grant had decided were too wide open to be called sly. He lowered his chin, turned his head, saw a speck on his desk blotter and flipped at it with his finger four times before he got it off. His glance went sidewise in the direction of Ben Cook, and the chief of police's head all but imperceptibly moved to the left and then to the right. Derwin brought his around and up again and said:

"You can't see him."

"Has he been charged with murder, Mr. Derwin?"

"Not—no."

"Or with anything?"

"No."

"May I ask, did you find a gun on him? Or find one anywhere? Or evidence that he had one?"

"Not yet."

"You've had him here nearly twelve hours and he's not under arrest. I'm afraid I'll have to insist on his right and mine——"

"I said you can't see him. That's that." Derwin had a fist on the desk. "And I want the girl, his niece, back here as quick as she can get here."

Fox wheeled as if to go, but he stayed on his spot. He glanced at the two seated there and spoke to the young man. "I'm sorry to interrupt you folks. I apologize. I expected just to make a request and have it granted and get out, but now I guess there'll have to be a discussion——"

"No discussion at all," Derwin snapped. "I want to know where the Grant girl is——"

Miranda's voice cut in, her sleepy lids lifted for a focus up at Tecumseh Fox. "I'm Miranda Pemberton, Ridley Thorpe's daughter. A couple of years ago I invited you to dinner three times and you didn't come. This is my brother Jeffrey."

"I don't like to dress." Fox stepped to her, took the offered hand and bowed over it. Jeffrey got halfway up from his chair for the handshake and then dropped back again.

"Go on and discuss it," Miranda said.

"Thanks." Fox turned to the district attorney and his eyes, not more sly, were less conciliatory. "It's like this, Mr. Derwin. I could have Nat Collins here in less than an hour, I've already phoned him, and you'd have to let Grant's lawyer see him. Collins would be sore to begin with, called away for suburban penny ante, and he'd be in a mood to make all the trouble he could. You know how that would be, especially if you're not ready to charge Grant with murder and I don't think you are. It's just possible he won't need a lawyer at all and, in that case, it would be a pity to give Nat Collins the kind of retainer he's accustomed to. Wouldn't it be simpler all around to let me have a little talk with Grant?"

"Nat Collins wouldn't touch it."

"I said I had phoned him. I don't lie on Monday."

Derwin regarded Fox for a moment and then turned for a look at Ben Cook. Cook pursed his lips and raised his shoulders and refused the office. Derwin arose and beckoned to him, and led him to a far corner of the room, where they held a whispered conference. Miranda said:

"Mr. Fox. I don't believe that man Grant killed my father."

"Don't be a goof, Sis," Jeffrey blurted. "This bird is a detective working for Grant."

Fox ignored him. "Why do you not believe it, Mrs. Pemberton?"

"Because he was in here in a while ago and I saw him and he said something to me."

Fox smiled down at her. "That's the kind of reason I like."

"I say don't be a goof," Jeffrey repeated.

"Shut up, laddie," said his sister; and then they looked at Derwin resuming his chair. He slanted his gaze up at Fox and demanded:

"How long would it take to get Nancy Grant here?"

"Not long."

"All right. Bring her. Then you can talk to Grant for ten minutes in the presence of a police officer."

Fox shook his head. "No, thank you. I'll deliver Miss Grant if there is really something you want to ask her, but she has already told you fellows everything she knows upside and down, and when I leave here she's going with me. And ten minutes with Grant isn't enough, and I won't need any help with him."

Derwin shrugged. "Take it or leave it."

"I'll leave it. My request was reasonable." Fox put his hands behind his back and stood rigid, and two faint spots of color showed on his tanned cheeks. "Now you've got *me* sore. You did that once before. How did you like it?"

He whirled, and was nearly to the door with steps quicker and lighter than before when a rasp came from Ben Cook: "Hey, Fox, come back here!" Fox whirled again. Cook looked at Derwin and said: "Suit yourself. I'd as soon be a Nazzy Dutchman with Joe Louis after me."

Derwin sat a moment, with a fist on the desk again, and then snapped: "All right. But first I want to see Miss Grant."

Fox snapped back: "I stated fair conditions. She will be with me when I see her uncle."

"Bring her. I'll allow it."

"The talk with Grant will be private."

"All right, all right, bring the girl."

Fox left. In the anteroom there was a collection of three county detectives in plain clothes and two state troopers in uniform, and along the corridors of the courthouse there was more bustle than usual. As he descended the steps to the sidewalk he met, coming up, another in uniform, with the collar insignia of a colonel and with a sternly preoccupied face that took no notice of the encounter. Fox walked briskly to the corner and turned right, proceeded a block and turned left, and down a hundred yards opened the door of the black convertible. With a foot on the running board he stopped short, finding himself confronted by empty seats front and rear. Frowning, he banged the door shut and sent his eyes on a quick survey of the street buildings, on both sides and in both directions. Apparently something expected was in view, for he strode down the sidewalk some fifty paces, opened a screen door for admission to a tiled floor and the buzz of electric fans, marched half the length of a soda fountain stretching for infinity, and stopped.

Dan Pavey twisted around on his stool and announced: "Miss Grant is trying a Westchester Delight."

"A super-soda," said Nancy, abandoning her straw. "Colossal." She saw Fox's compressed lips. "Did . . . did you see Uncle Andy?"

"No. We'll see him together. You're going in with me to the district attorney. Remember what I told you and behave yourself." Fox looked at a hunk of pink ice cream consigned to the interior of the vice-president. "When we're on business and I say wait here, I mean here. I've told you that a thousand times."

"Right," Dan agreed in low thunder. He swallowed the hunk. "My responsibility. Miss Grant accepted my invitation. She was about to go to sleep. She had no sleep last night. In my opinion she is in no condition to scrap with a district attorney. Wouldn't it be better——"

"No."

Dan did not say "Right." What was even more startling, he scowled at his Westchester Delight and pushed the glass away without finishing it. He and Nancy descended from their stools and followed Fox out to the sidewalk and along to the convertible.

Fox started the engine and engaged the clutch and the car rolled to retrace the route he had taken from the courthouse. He parked in front and told Dan to stay in the car and Nancy to hop out. In the anteroom of the district attorney's office one of the state troopers started across with an evident intention of intercepting them, but he was too slow. They were at the door and through it.

Their entrance interrupted an oration. Its loud and uncompromising tone issued from the mouth of the colonel of state police, who stood erect at one end of the desk glaring in all directions at once and who chopped it abruptly off at the approach of the newcomers. Fox started to speak and so did Derwin, but they were both forestalled by Jeffrey Thorpe, who sprang to his feet with an amazed ejaculation:

"I'll be damned!" He was staring at Nancy Grant. "Of all the—got you! By God, got you!"

She drew back, stiffened and returned his stare. Hers was intended for freezing. "You have not got me," she declared disdainfully, "you—you——"

"No? Ha! Got you!" Jeffrey took a step, stopped and jerked around. "Say! Is this—what? Is she Nancy Grant? My God!"

"Yes," said Derwin. "Andrew Grant's niece. You seem to know her."

"He does not know me," said Nancy icily.

"Are you drunk, laddie?" Miranda demanded.

Jeffrey looked befuddled, staring at Nancy again. "I will be damned," he muttered. "I've been hunting you—I've had a detective looking for you——"

Derwin asked: "Was the detective Tecumseh Fox?"

"Nuts." Jeffrey looked at him, at his sister, at Fox. "Double nuts," he said shortly. "I'm making a jackass of myself. It was a . . . shock." He looked at Nancy again. "I beg your pardon. I seem to meet you only under peculiar and difficult circumstances. The present ones being that your uncle appears to have murdered my father——"

"That's a lie!" Nancy's eyes were blazing. "He didn't!"

"All right, he didn't. He did, he didn't. One way or the other——" He stopped abruptly and turned to survey the others. "Gentlemen. That's a trick I copied from my sister. You say the name of the person addressed, or of persons, a collective designation, like that, with a stop. Gentlemen. Period. My former association with her—with Miss Grant, has no connection whatever with the crime you are investigating. It was a purely personal affair. Forget it. Proceed." He sat down.

"Nevertheless, Mr. Thorpe," said Derwin with an edge to his voice, "an important part of our investigation is the—uh—background of Grant and his niece. I'm afraid we'll have to ask you—"

"You're damn right we will," Colonel Brissenden barked. "There's been entirely too much——"

"Bowwow!" Jeffrey cut him off. "There are a lot of disadvantages to being a millionaire's son, but there are also some advantages and one of them is that I can tell you to go to hell."

Ben Cook cackled and then swallowed it.

"Excuse me," Tecumseh Fox said pleasantly, "but I have work to do. If you want to question Miss Grant after I've had a talk with her uncle—"

"That's out," Derwin blurted.

Fox gazed at him in astonishment. "But you agreed if I brought Miss Grant—"

"It's out. I've consulted Colonel Brissenden and he completely disapproves——"

"Oh. He does. I thought the district attorney was the chief investigating officer——"

"Think again," Brissenden spluttered, in the tone of a colonel who has just been told to go to hell. "And go somewhere else to do it! Derwin says you threatened to get Nat Collins. Go ahead, get ten of him! Get out! The trouble with you is that your head's got swelled to the point where you presume to interfere with the processes of law——"

Fox said in a voice so strained through tensed throat muscles that it was nearly a squeak: "I haven't interfered——"

"All right, don't."

"I have requested permission to see Andrew Grant."

"We heard you. On out."

Fox took two steps and got Nancy by the elbow. "Come on, Miss Grant."

"No you don't." Brissenden moved towards them. "She stays here. We want her."

"So do I. Don't touch her." Fox was in between, expanded to cover her. "Don't touch me either. I'm telling you. Have you got a commitment? No. Touch her and I'll give you a lesson in the processes of law."

"Why, you damned insolent——"

"Easy, Colonel." Derwin was there. "This is my office and I won't stand for——"

"Come on, Miss Grant," Fox said, and took her elbow again and steered her out.

Chapter 4

They left the building and gained the sidewalk, but were not to get away without interference. As they climbed into the car, with Nancy protesting and demanding to know what was going to be done, Dan Pavey rumbled from the back seat:

"Hey, you didn't pay your check. Here comes a waiter after you."

The next moment Jeffrey Thorpe in his white dinner jacket, hatless, his eyes more bloodshot than ever from the rubbing, was standing on the running board and poking his head in and blurting:

"Miss Grant, I want you to understand——"

Nancy, clutching Fox's sleeve, pleaded: "Go ahead! Please!"

Dan, leaning over from the back, asked: "Shall I push him off?"

"No." Fox eyed Jeffrey. "Have you got a car around here?"

"Yes, that Wethersill Special across the street. I just want to tell her——"

"You can't tell her anything here. Give——"

"He can't tell me anything anywhere!"

"Miss Grant, you talk too much, too often and too

soon. Mr. Thorpe, the man in the back seat is Mr. Pavey, my vice-president. Give him the key to your car, and take his place. Dan, take the Wethersill and follow us. Nothing fancy, just follow us."

"But I just——"

"We're leaving now."

Jeffrey fished in his pocket for the key and handed it to Dan. Dan scrambled out and headed for the Wethersill, and Jeffrey took his place. As soon as Dan had got the Wethersill turned around ready to follow, Fox started the car rolling and spoke to Nancy.

"First, if you don't mind, I'd like to catch up. You told me you didn't know any Thorpes or any one connected with them. Your words."

"I don't!"

"You don't. Does he know you?"

The back seat put in: "Let me tell——"

"No, Mr. Thorpe, I'm working for Miss Grant, I'd rather have it from her. Does he know you?"

"No, and he never will. He's an arrogant fool. It was just—disagreeable. Last winter at the Metropolitan Opera House he accused me of stealing an ermine thing from his wife or fiancée."

The back seat protested: "I'm not married and it wasn't my fiancée! It was a girl I had——"

"Hold it," Fox told him. "Please don't do that any more. What were you doing at the Metropolitan Opera House?"

"Listening to an opera. I was a standee, of course, and dressed accordingly—I told you I came to New York to have a career—I was going to be a prima donna and was taking lessons—which Uncle Andy helped me pay for—but I finally found out that some of the notes are missing from my voice and now I'm modelling at Hartlespoon's and earning my bread and butter. It happened in the refreshment room. She had carelessly left it on a table and I had a perfect right to move it—are standees people?—and the stupid disagreeable—he was actually going to have me arrested——"

"I was not! She was! She's an imbecile——"

"Arbitrate it," Fox suggested, bringing the car to a stop at the curb in front of a drugstore at the edge of town. "I have a phone call to make."

He got out, entered the store and sought a phone booth. After a five-minute conversation he came out again and slid into his seat. "Get it settled?" he inquired as the car moved on.

"There's nothing to settle," said Nancy curtly.

"Uh-huh," he grunted. "I called Nat Collins and he'll be at the courthouse in half an hour. He may not be able to get a writ without an argument, but there'll be fur flying."

"Why didn't we wait there for him?"

"Because I didn't want to call him from there and we couldn't help him anyway, and I can't stand around or sit down when I'm sore. Also I wanted you out of there."

"What the devil good am I, there or anywhere else? I can't even pay the lawyer his retainer. You're being—oh, damn——"

"Look here." Jeffrey was leaning forward to her over the back of the seat. "Let me pay the lawyer— now wait! Say I'm an ape. Say I'm loathsome and repellent. Okay. But I owe you something. You could probably have collected colossal damages. That imbecile girl—she was my aunt's husband's partner's daughter—she started it, but I admit I joined in and I'll tell you why. I had been roped in. I hate opera and I thought if there was a row it might develop into our getting out of there. Then I got a good look at you with your eyes flashing and I'm here to tell you it was an experience. Right then and there it aroused—well, it was an experience. Then the excitement made that girl sick at her stomach and she insisted on leaving when I had decided I wanted to stay. I took her home and scooted back and got there before the show ended, but you had gone too—at least I couldn't find you. I hunted you. The next day I got a detective. I advertised. I kept hoping I'd hear from a lawyer that you were suing for damages, but I never did. You should have. So it would merely be paying a legal debt if I pay a lawyer for defending your uncle—granting that he's guilty, a guilty man has a right to a law-yer——"

"Make him shut up," Nancy said savagely, "or I'll open the door and jump out!"

"Another thing." Jeffrey leaned farther forward. "I spoke of the exper——"

Nancy grabbed the door handle and pushed it down. Fox lifted his foot from the accelerator and snapped: "Don't do that!"

"But I will! I swear I will——"

The car left the concrete, bumped a few feet along the wide grassy shoulder and stopped. Fox reached across Nancy to pull the door to, twisted around to face the back seat, saw that the Wethersill was stopping a dozen yards behind and spoke to Jeffrey.

"Will you quit talking to her?"

"But my God, I've just begun——"

"You'll have to swallow it. She'll jump out and break her neck. Or there's your car waiting for you."

"I like it here."

"You can't talk to her."

"All right, I won't. I'll sit and look at the back of her head."

"I see no profit in that—for me. I'm paying for the gas."

"Well, hell's bells, what do you want me to do? Talk to you?"

"You might."

"What about?"

"Oh . . . tell me about Luke Wheer, your father's valet. Have the police found him?"

"No."

"What's he like?"

"He's dark brown, tall and skinny, and a little pop-eyed. As I just told what's-his-name back there, he's square and straight and easy-going, and Father had complete confidence in him. He's been with Father over twenty years."

"Have they found your father's car—the one Luke went away in?"

"No."

"Where did they take you to identify the body— was it still in the bungalow?"

"No. They didn't find me till after two o'clock, out on Long Island and he—they had taken it to White Plains for the autopsy. I went there."

"Have you ever been in that bungalow?"

"No. Nobody has."

"Nobody at all?"

"No one that I know of. Of course, there might have been dozens and I wouldn't have known it. All I knew about my father was what I read in the papers. I happen to know, though, that Kester had been in the bungalow."

"Vaughn Kester, your father's confidential secretary?"

"Yes. He mentioned it only last night. He said he was up there a couple of weeks ago to arrange about some repairs——"

"Wait for me. I must have skipped something. I thought Kester was at Green Meadow, near Pleasantville, last night, and it was after he was notified of the murder and left there for the bungalow that he disappeared."

"That's right."

"And you were on Long Island?" Fox was frowning. "Where did you see Kester?"

"At Green Meadow. My sister and I had dinner there with him, and I went to Long Island afterwards."

Fox's frown gathered another wrinkle. "I guess I'll quit reading the papers. I read that your sister was in the Adirondacks."

"She was, but she flew down yesterday afternoon for the meeting I had arranged with Kester. He was our liaison officer with headquarters, meaning our parent. I'm not revealing secrets. All our best friends love to talk about it. When we needed to undertake financial negotiations we went to Kester. When I decided to be a Communist a few years ago it was Kester I notified."

"Oh. Are you a Communist?"

"Not any more. I tried it a couple of months. I was so damn bored and useless. I ought to have a job, but I don't seem to find anything. How about being a detective? Have you got an opening?"

"Not right this minute." Fox's tone had no banter. "I'll consider it. After dining with Kester, did your sister go to Long Island with you?"

"Nuts." Jeffrey scowled. "Mr. Fox, my sister didn't kill my father and neither did I. That what's-his-name back there had me convinced that Andrew Grant did, but now that I know who his niece is I hope he's a fathead. I mean what's-his-name."

"Your hope seems reasonable," Fox declared. "He has no evidence that Grant had a gun. The only motive that can be imputed to him, resentment at being fired from his job, is puerile. Beyond that, Derwin has nothing whatever except that Grant was there."

"Oh, yes, he has. Grant lied."

"Lied? What about?"

"About the time he got there, or maybe—anyway, he lied. He said when he looked in at the window Father was sitting there smoking a cigar and listening to the radio play band music, and it was a little after eleven o'clock. That's impossible. If it was between eleven and eleven-thirty, Father was listening to Dick Barry. He hasn't missed it once in three years."

Fox made a noise of contempt. "As thin as that? Maybe he couldn't get that station, or maybe in the bungalow his tastes changed, or maybe someone else turned on the radio—that's as close to nothing——"

"No, really," Jeffrey protested. "I tell you it's a point. Grant must be lying. Ask anybody that knows my father. A year ago, when Dick Barry changed from seven to eleven o'clock, Father changed his bedtime. I don't say he would have lost a leg to avoid missing it, but it's a million to one that if he was in a room where a radio was at eleven o'clock, and he was conscious and free to act, he dialed WLX and got Dick Barry. Ten million to one. I suppose I shouldn't tell you how what's-his-name dopes it, but I will. He thinks Grant was in the room, covering Father with the gun, and Grant turned on the band music to smother the sound of the shots. Then of course he had to say the band music was playing because someone might have heard it. I hate to say it, but it sounds to me—what are you staring at?"

"Excuse me," said Fox softly. "I apologize, Mr. Thorpe. I also apologize for a sudden decision I've made. I'm going somewhere in a hurry. So if you'll kindly take possession of your car——" He stuck his head out the window and called: "Dan! Come here! Step on it!"

"But my God," Jeffrey complained, "I was doing my best—"

"I know you were. I appreciate it. Thank you. Why don't you write Miss Grant a letter? Get in, Dan, get in! If you don't mind, Mr. Thorpe—thanks—women always read letters before they return them un-opened. See you again. Look out, I'm——"

The convertible moved, regained the concrete, was at 20 in second, at 40 in high, at 60. Fox's baritone was approximating the tune of "The Parade of the Wooden Soldiers":

"Lah-de-dah,   dum   dum,   lah-de-dah,   dum dum . . ."

The back seat, Dan's bass again, demanded: "Why, are we getting hot?"

"Dee-dee-dee—no! We're taking a flyer on a ten-million-to-one shot!"

Nancy spoke loud to his ear: "But you're turning south! I don't—where are we going?"

"Going to work, Miss Grant. Heigh-ho! We're go-ing to New York to find someone who knows someone who knows Dick Barry."

Two hours later Dan and Nancy were seated at a table in a corner of an enormous air-conditioned room on Madison Avenue near 60th Street. She was sipping an orangeade and he was finishing a Perisphere Float.

Dan was telling her not to worry. "He'll find him all right," he assured her. "If he's buried he'll dig him up. Don't worry about your uncle either. That'll work out. If you've got to worry, worry about me. I'm supposed to keep you awake. You might think it wouldn't matter where you were awake or not, but you heard me trying to suggest—huh. Here he comes again. Find him, Tec?"

Tecumseh Fox, his hat in his hand, stopped at their table, and shook his head. "Not yet. Some day you're going to get a stomach-ache. Come on."

Two hours still later Dan and Nancy were facing each other in a booth of the fountain grill of the Hotel Churchill. She was sipping iced pineapple juice and he was working on a Strawberry Dream.

"You're dead wrong," Dan was saying earnestly. "I mean in my opinion. The right age for a man to marry is between fifty and fifty-five. I can give you a dozen good reasons, but I won't do it now because you're not wide enough awake to appreciate them and anyway you're too young. I expect to get married in about fifteen years. Say I had got married when I was twenty-five. Where would I be now? A fellow I know named Pokorny was saying the other day—here he comes again. Find him, Tec?"

"No." Fox was there. "Come on."

In the summer dusk Dan and Nancy were at a table on the raised terrace of the Eskimo Village at the New York World's Fair. In front of him a Caramel

Iceberg was slowly melting into slush; Nancy was cooling her fingers around a glass of iced tea with lemon.

Dan grunted. "I can stand it if you can," he declared.

Nancy looked at him in surprise. "Stand what?"

"Now now." He grunted again. "I'll bet you'd never guess."

"I'm too hot and tired to guess. And this certainly seems like a wild-goose chase to me, the celebrated Tecumseh Fox chasing all over five boroughs for hours trying to find a radio gossip and dragging us with him. I don't feel like guessing."

"Right. I repeat, I can stand it if you can."

She gestured in weary exasperation. "Stand what?" she demanded. "What on earth are you talking about?"

"I am referring to that camel at the table by the pillar that keeps staring at you."

"Oh." Nancy darted a sidewise glance. "I hadn't noticed him."

"Sure you hadn't."

"Well, I hadn't. And what if I had?" She shot another glance. "What's wrong with him?"

"I didn't say anything was wrong with him. But since you ask, have you noticed the outfit on the chair by him? It looks professional. If you felt like guessing, you might guess he's a news photographer."

"What if he is?"

"Well, you're news, aren't you?"

"Why . . . but he . . ." Nancy looked startled. "He couldn't know that."

"He could if he reads the tabloids and his eyes are good." Dan scowled across the slush of his Caramel Iceberg. "I admit it's possible you hadn't noticed him gazing at you. Naturally you're used to it. You've had whole audiences gazing at you. It's your job to put on clothes and walk around so people can look at you. Also it's obvious that you're perfectly aware that your face and figure are stareogenic, so you wouldn't——"

"What does stareogenic mean?"

"Genic is a suffix which means generating or producing. Therefore stareogenic means 'generating stares.'"

"Then you're trying to say that it's obvious that I'm aware that my face and figure generate stares."

"That was the idea."

"Like the bearded lady, for instance, or Albertelle the What-is-it, man or woman, only a dime ten cents——"

"I said nothing about beards or what-is-its, I merely said that you——"

"Miss Grant!"

Their argument had removed their attention from the camel at the table by the pillar, so his deft and speedy manipulation of his outfit had been unobserved. Now, as he suddenly shouted Nancy's name and they both turned to face him, they blinked simultaneously at the blinding glare of the flashlight bulb. Dan, as he blinked, also leaped. Then the camel blinked, as Dan's fist caught him on the side of the jaw and toppled him among chairs and tables, his camera bouncing on the floor. There were screams, and movements, and waiters came rushing.

An authoritative voice sounded: "May I ask what that was for?"

Dan, turning, frowned at Tecumseh Fox. He shook his head. "I think I've got a stomach-ache."

"I hope you have." Fox got Nancy by the arm. "Come on, let's get out of here."

Following them, Dan had the appearance of a man who could be detained only with considerable effort and difficulty, so no one tried.

At eleven o'clock that Monday night Nancy Grant was in an upstairs room at the Fox place, sound asleep. The soundness of her sleep was due partly to her healthy youth, partly to the extremity of her fatigue and partly to a tablet which Mrs. Trimble had dissolved in water for her; and her presence at the Fox place was due to the fact that it was closer to White Plains than was the little flat in New York which she shared with a Hartlespoon co-worker. Her Uncle Andy was sleeping, or not sleeping, somewhere in White Plains, just where she didn't know. He was being held as a material witness and bail could not be arranged until Tuesday morning, in spite of the fur Nat Collins had started flying; and if he were charged with murder, as seemed likely, there would of course be no bail. But for the three good reasons cited, she slept.

Downstairs, the large room which was full of things contained also half a dozen people. Dan Pavey and the man with the bee stings were playing backgammon; the homely youth and a man with a short neck and a long grey mustache were arguing over a crossword puzzle; Tecumseh Fox was playing a guitar duet with a black-haired little Latin with narrow slanting eyes. But at 10:58 Fox put down the guitar, went to the radio and switched it on, dialed for a station, moderated the volume and stood frowning down at it. It spoke:

". . . so I introduce myself because the last time the announcer did it he said Du Barry by mistake and I had to talk falsetto for thirty minutes, and not only that, I had to do it in French which I can't play without music. So here is Dick Barry saying hallo. . . ."

The homely youth called across: "I never knew your curiosity to get you down that low before."

He got no retort. Fox stood for ten minutes.

". . . I was sitting in the lobby of the Hotel Churchill and a bellboy came along singing: 'Calling Dick Barry, calling Dick Barry, calling Dick Barry,' and I told him from force of habit: 'Take the pot, my straight's still open in the middle.' . . ."

The homely youth arose and left the room. Fox stood another ten minutes,

". . . And now for tomorrow's and next week's news. My challenge as usual, check it as it happens and see if I'm wrong. The Brooklyn grand jury will indict a man who parts his hair on the side, eats at the Flamingo Club and answers if you say Leslie or just Les. 'Hope Chest,' opening Wednesday night at the Knickerbocker Roof, will be a flop. Tom Booker will plead guilty to the charge of smuggling and take what he gets. Tecumseh Fox, the super-sleuth, knows why the radio at the Thorpe bungalow was playing band music last night instead of Dick Barry, your favorite broadcaster and mine as was to be expected, and will inform the police if necessary to protect Andrew Grant, who is being held as a material witness and may be charged with murder tomorrow. Three women who . . ."

Fox turned the radio off, gave every one a good night and left the room. He was halfway up the stairs when Dan Pavey's rumble came from below:

"Hey, Tec! Anything stirring tonight?"

"I don't know. I may have laid an egg. I said ten million to one." Fox turned to continue up and then turned again. "But I'm getting a bet down. Do you want a slice?"

"What are the chances?"

"You might triple it."

"I'll ride for a hundred."

"You're on. Good night."

Fox ascended, went down the hall to the large room with a desk and a safe, seated himself and pulled the telephone across. He got the man he wanted and spoke:

"How are you, Harry? Family all right? Good. I'm sorry to bother you at home like this, but I may be moving around too fast in the morning to get you at the office. I'm developing a sort of an interest in the Ridley Thorpe murder. Of course. No, I'm working in a side show. What I wanted to ask, I notice that Thorpe Control Corporation closed at 89 Saturday and dropped to 30 today. Is that because the Thorpe enterprises were dominated by Thorpe and he was responsible for their success? No other reason? Holy smoke. Oh, you think it will. He was as good as that, was he? I suppose so. Let's see—buy me a thousand shares when you think it's around bottom tomorrow morning. Even if you think it may drop again in the afternoon, get it before twelve o'clock. Wait a minute —get it before *eleven* o'clock. That's important. No, I can't, but I never bet on a sure thing. Suit yourself. . . ."

He hung up, tiptoed back down the hall to listen for a minute at the door of Nancy's room, returned and undressed, and went to bed and to sleep.

Thunder awakened him. It was low thunder issuing from the throat of Dan Pavey. Fox recognized it and stayed on the pillow.

"What?"

"Derwin and a state trooper."

"What time is it?"

"Ten minutes to one."

"Did you let them in?"

"No, they're on the porch."

Fox turned on the bed light, hopped out, donned a linen robe and slipped his toes into mules, went downstairs with Dan at his heels and opened the front door the width of his shoulders. Two faces were there.

"Well?"

Derwin spoke. "I want a talk with you."

"Well?"

"Not through a crack. I want to know what information you have that will protect Andrew Grant."

"I don't—— Oh, sure. You've been listening to the radio."

"And now I'm going to listen to you."

"I haven't got a thing to tell you, Mr. Derwin. Sorry."

The trooper muttered something to Derwin. Derwin muttered back and showed his face again, twenty inches from Fox's nose. "Look here, Fox, what's the use of stunting it like this? Just to be cute? You know damn well we don't want to pin it on Grant unless he's guilty. If he can prove he didn't lie—if you can explain why the radio was playing band music—I'll turn him loose right now. I've got him out here in the car.

Damn it all, this thing is worse than dynamite—the murder of a man like Ridley Thorpe——"

Fox shook his head. "Sorry, nothing to tell. Radio muck. Dick Barry trying to start a sensation. But I'll give you a hot tip, buy Thorpe Control on the drop in the morning. That's an insult to your intelligence— see if you can figure out why. Good night."

He shut the door. Shoulders were against it and explosive protests came, but Dan's bulk was with him and the door clicked shut as the lock caught. Fox thanked Dan, went back up to the corner room, heard a car retreating down the drive and was asleep again in three minutes.

It was not thunder, but clangor, that roused him the second time—the telephone bell. He switched on the light, bounced to the floor and trotted to the desk. As he lifted the receiver, a glance at the clock told him it was a quarter past three.

"Hallo."

"Hallo." The voice in his ear was low and blurred from lips too close to a transmitter. "I want to speak to Tecumseh Fox."

"This is Fox."

"I . . ." A pause. "I must speak to Fox himself."

"You are. I'm Fox. Who is this, please?"

"I'm calling on account of the statement made by Dick Barry on the radio. Was that authorized by you and what basis did you have for it?"

"You'd like to know. Don't be silly. Is your last name——"

"Don't say it on the phone!"

"I won't. Is your last name Teutonic and does it mean *from the village*?"

"No."

"Is your first name Old English and does it mean *from the red field*?"

"No. But that's enough . . ." The voice was agitated and even more blurred than before. "That tells me you do know——"

"Wait a minute. What does your last name mean?"

"It doesn't mean anything. It was——"

"What does your first name mean?"

"It's Celtic and means *small* or *little*."

"Hold the wire a minute."

Fox went to the shelves and pulled out a book bearing the title, "What Shall We Name the Baby?" flipped to a page, got what he wanted in a glance and returned to the phone.

"Fox again. Go ahead."

"Do you know who I am?"

"Yes."

"I'm talking from a booth in an all-night lunch place at Golden's Bridge. We want——"

"Is he with you?"

"Yes. Not in here—he's in the car around the corner. We want to see you."

"Come to my place."

"No, there are people there."

"Go north on Route 22, six and two-tenths miles from where you are. Turn left on to Route 39 and follow it three and four-tenths miles. Turn right on to a dirt road, go one mile and stop. You'll get there before I do. Wait for me. Have you got the directions?"

The voice repeated them. "But you must be alone. We absolutely insist on that——"

"I won't be. My vice-president will be with me."

"Your what?"

"Never mind. You're in no position to dictate terms, are you, Mr. *small* or *little*? I'll handle my part. You be there."

Fox slipped out and down the hall, entered a room, grasped a massive shoulder and shook it, said: "Come on, Dan, work to do," trotted back to his room, dressed in four minutes, put an automatic in a shoulder holster under his arm and another smaller one in his hip pocket, tiptoed back to Dan's door and whispered explosively: "Come on!"

"Right," Dan yawned.

Three dogs met them in the dark in front of the garage door and saw them off. Fox took the wheel, wound along the drive and was on the highway. The headlights split the summer night at seventy miles an hour; and since it was only fifteen miles or so to the spot on Route 39 where the dirt road offered its narrower and dustier track, the ride wasn't as long as it was fast. Fox slowed down and swung around the sharp turn on to the dirt. It was uphill the first thousand yards, then leveled out and narrowed still more as the leaves of the trees on either side reached out for space.

Rounding a bend, there was a car, a long sedan, parked at the roadside in the entrance to a disused wood lane, a branch from a tree scraping its top. Fox drew up behind it, turned off the lights, told Dan to stay there and got out. A man emerged from the sedan and moved towards him in the darkness, all but impenetrable there in the woods. The man spoke:

"Who are you?"

"Tecumseh Fox."

"I'm Kester. Who's in your car?"

Instead of answering, Fox swept past him, found the handle of the rear door of the sedan and flung it open, sent the ray of a flashlight darting within, focused it on a face and uttered a cordial greeting:

"Good evening, Mr. Ridley Thorpe."

Chapter 5

The mouth of the face opened to blurt a command: "Turn that thing off!"

Fox bent his wrist to aim the light at the front seat and saw a dark-brown face with black eyes popping out. He switched the light off, observed: "Luke Wheer too, pretty good fishing, three on one hook," climbed in the tonneau and plumped on to the seat. The man outside muttered an ejaculation and was going to follow him in, but Fox pulled the door shut.

"You can talk through the window, Mr. Kester. I like elbow room. Even though there's no occasion to use my gun—not to mention the fact that there's company in my car——"

"Who is it?"

"A man that works for me named Dan Pavey. That's my affair. Think what Dick Barry *might* have said on the radio."

A grunt came from Ridley Thorpe. "Does Dick Barry know?"

"No."

"Who knows besides you?"

"Nobody. But don't get silly notions. I carry the

gun from force of habit. Dan's back there and if you try any tricks——"

"We have no intention of trying tricks. How did you know?"

"I didn't. I played a probability." Fox's eyes were adjusted now for the darkness and he could see faces and hands. "Do you know Andrew Grant?"

"No. I've read the papers."

"Of course. Grant said that he looked through the window of the bungalow at ten minutes past eleven and saw you smoking a cigar and listening to the radio play band music. Your son said that was impossible. The most obvious explanation was that Grant was lying, but I had reasons for putting that last. Among other explanations, the one I liked best was that it wasn't you he saw. It presented difficulties, for instance that your son identified your remains, but I liked it anyway and went fishing with it. I'd call it——"

"I thought so," came bitterly from Kester's face at the window. "It was nothing but a bluff."

"Quiet, Vaughn." It was his master's voice. "We didn't dare risk it."

"Correct, Mr. Thorpe," Fox agreed. "If I hadn't heard from you by noon tomorrow—today—your dentist would have been at White Plains examining teeth and in two minutes——"

"Yes. Just so. Certainly. And what are you—what do you intend to——"

"I'm going to inform the police. I have to, to clear Andrew Grant. Their chief ground of suspicion against him is that they think he's lying about the radio."

"You'll tell the police about our phoning—about our meeting you here——"

"Certainly."

"Why do you want to clear Grant?"

"I'm working for him. I don't know whether you happen to know that I'm a private detective——"

"Oh, yes, yes indeed, I've heard of you." Thorpe's voice came smoothed with oil of compliment. "Of your private life too—your generous hospitality for unfortunate persons—yes, indeed—that seems to be a point of resemblance between us—not that my philanthropies have the charming personal touch that you— and by the way, that's a coincidence, that only last week I made my annual contribution to the Society for Preserving the Culture of the American Indian— I've heard that you are part Indian—of course, your name——"

"I'm not." Fox was curt. "My elder brother was named William McKinley Fox. I was named William Tecumseh Sherman Fox. Too many Williams. And I graduated from kindergarten, Mr. Thorpe. I am aware that you are an able, shrewd and ruthless manipulator. If the tears were running down your face I wouldn't lend you my handkerchief. As for telling the police about this meeting——"

"You can't do that," said Thorpe with the oil gone.

"Well, I'll try."

"I say you can't. You've got me hooked, I admit it. Your silence is worth fifty thousand dollars. Cash."

Kester put in: "We'd have to have satisfactory——"

"Forget it," Fox snapped. "Nothing doing."

"How much do you want?"

"A billion. More than you've got, for that. Forget it."

"Then why—what did you come here for?"

"To establish a fact—you, Kester, watch your

hand. What have you got in your pocket, the gun that shot a man in Thorpe's bungalow? Don't try——"

"Nonsense," Kester said. "Chief, he'll hang on for life. We should never——"

"Quiet," said Thorpe testily. "Was there any alternative? Mr. Fox, do you mean that your purpose in—coming here to establish a fact was not to blackmail me?"

"That's right. Thank you."

"You're not demanding money and you don't intend to?"

"That's right."

Kester blurted: "Then why the devil——"

"Quiet, Vaughn—I repeat my offer of fifty thousand dollars, this time to do a job for me. Five thousand in advance and the remainder when the job is successfully completed. Do you want it?"

"Certainly I want it, but it depends on the job."

"I'll explain it. It will soon be daylight and daylight will be dangerous. The man who was killed last night—Sunday night——"

"Chief, don't! You're putting——"

"Vaughn, get in the front seat with Luke and be quiet. What have we accomplished in twenty-four hours? Nothing. The man who was killed in my bungalow was named Corey Arnold. He was my stand-in."

Fox grunted. "Oh, you had a stand-in."

"I did. Three years ago certain activities of mine which I wished to keep secret seemed in danger of being exposed. They were not illegal activities, but for personal reasons I did not care to have them known. I saw pictures in a magazine of the stand-ins of various motion picture actors and that gave me an idea. At the cost of a great deal of time and trouble, on account of the necessary caution, I found a man who was very nearly my twin. I found others who resembled me, but I needed other qualities too, for instance trustworthiness; this one seemed to meet every requirement. I had already had that bungalow for some time. I arranged for Arnold, impersonating me, to go there weekends with my valet—you see I was thorough. It was a great inconvenience for me to be without Luke, but he had been going to that bungalow with me and so I had him continue to go with Arnold."

"While you followed certain activities elsewhere?"

"Yes. There had been attempts—but that's irrelevant. There seemed to be not the slightest chance of discovery. Arnold was well paid and was absolutely reliable. Luke was always there with him. No one except Kester was ever permitted to go there—never had been. When I had spent weekends there I had refused to talk on the telephone; all communications, if any were necessary, were through Kester. There appeared to be no chance whatever of its being known. And now this! Now the front page of every newspaper in America says that I've been murdered!"

"But you haven't," said Fox dryly. "You can prove that easy enough. Only what about the certain activities you were following?"

"That's exactly it! They must not be known!"

"But if you suddenly appear and announce: 'Here I am!' a great many people, including a lot of newspapers and police who are investigating your murder, will want to know: 'Where were you?'"

"Yes. They will."

"They sure will. And I'm afraid you'll have to tell, for under the peculiar circumstances—even though you're Ridley Thorpe—any explanation you give is going to be run through a meat grinder."

Kester offered from the front seat: "My advice has been to refuse to give any explanation."

Fox shook his head. "You might try it, but." Enough dawn had sifted through the leaves so that he could easily have recognized all three faces from the pictures in the newspapers. "Very doubtful. The police are after a murderer. Not to mention such items as the angry clamor of the folks who have dumped Thorpe Control at 30 in the effort to keep a shirt, and the fact that you've waited a day and two nights to reveal yourself. If you were going to do that you should have done it immediately."

"I advised it first thing——"

"Quiet, Vaughn! It wouldn't have worked! Fox agrees that it wouldn't have worked! Don't you?"

"I do. If the police hadn't traced you, the papers would. Now you'll have to tell all about it."

"I can't do that."

"I wouldn't say 'can't.' Like the woman on a horse who said: 'I can't get off.' The horse reared and she fell off. So she was wrong. So are you."

"No, I'm not wrong." Thorpe was peering at him. "That's the job I have for you. I want you to arrange an explanation for me that will stand investigation. I want an alibi that will stand up. Kester and Luke and I have been discussing it all day and got nowhere. We're handicapped because none of us dares to make an appearance, even on the telephone. That's the job I'll pay you fifty thousand dollars for, and it has to be done in a hurry. I want it done before the stock market opens in the morning. Will you do it? Can you do it?"

"I'm working for Andrew Grant."

"This won't interfere. You said yourself that Grant will be clear as soon as I reappear."

"But there will still be a murder. To arrange a false alibi——"

"Not for a murder. I had nothing to do with that. I was . . . nowhere near the bungalow."

"That's good. Where were you?"

"I was in the woods, walking. The pinewoods in New Jersey. I often do that, with a rucksack, alone, and sleep on the needles, under the stars, the summer nights——"

"Don't waste it." Fox sounded disgusted. "Where were you?"

"I tell you I was in the woods, walking——"

"No, no. That must be one of the explanations you and Kester invented and discarded; and it sounds like the poorest of the bunch. Don't forget, Mr. Thorpe, that your activity was one which you were, and are, determined to keep secret. I have to know what it was and you have to satisfy me on it. Don't waste time like that. Where were you?"

Silence, except for a faint noise the source of which was now visible in the unfolding light. It came from the suction of the gums of the colored man against his teeth as he nervously and monotonously worked his lips. Vaughn Kester's lips, thin anyway, made a tight straight line as he sat twisted around in the front seat for a level gaze of his pale hostile eyes at Tecumseh Fox. Ridley Thorpe, disheveled and unornamental with a streak of dirt slanting across his unshaven cheek, ground his right palm against his left, as if with that mortar and pestle he expected to pulverize all obstacles.

Fox said impatiently: "You understand it has to be the truth. Depending on how it sounds, I'll either accept it for the time being or I won't. I'll check up on it as soon as I can, and if it's phony I'll turn it loose. I must be satisfied that I'm not establishing an alibi for a man who might be a murderer."

Thorpe sputtered: "But I tell you——"

"Don't do that. It will soon be sunup. Tell me where you were."

"If I do that, Mr. Fox, I'll be putting myself completely in your power——"

"No more than you are now." Fox frowned at him. "Must I diagram it for you? I could trace you down. Any competent man could and a lot of them will, if they are given a suspicion to start on. That's why you have to furnish an alibi that will exclude all suspicion, which is a big order to fill. It is also why I must have the truth and all of it or you can count me out."

Thorpe gazed at him, and suddenly abandoned the mortar and pestle to make a gesture of decision. "Very well. Quiet, Vaughn. I never supposed—very well. I was in a cottage at Triangle Beach, New Jersey. I arrived there Friday evening and remained continuously. Shortly before midnight Sunday—I was in bed—the phone rang and it was Luke. He said someone had shot through the window and killed Arnold——"

"Did he phone from the bungalow?"

"No. Luke is no fool. He had left in the car and phoned from a booth in Mount Kisco without being observed. He asked what to do and I told him to come to the cottage. He arrived there around two o'clock; it's over ninety miles. In the meantime Kester had phoned, having been notified of the murder at the Green Meadow Club. I told him also to come to the cottage and he got there about an hour after Luke did. We began a discussion of the situation and we've been discussing it ever since. Luke and Kester are the only people on earth who know of that cottage. Except you. Now."

"The only ones?"

"Yes."

Fox shook his head. "It won't do. It sets up the conclusion that you were alone there and that——"

"I didn't say I was alone there. I was . . . I had a companion."

"What's her name?"

"I don't think you need that." Thorpe was scowling. "This is very embarrassing to me. Very. If my reputation with the American public which I have so scrupulously earned—if I have chosen to safeguard it by maintaining a decent privacy for certain activities which are natural and normal——"

"I'm not the American public, Mr. Thorpe, I'm only a man you want to hire to manufacture an alibi for you. If this lady felt like it, she could make both it and me look silly. What's her name?"

"Her name . . . is Dorothy Duke."

"How long have you known her?"

"Five years."

"She used to spend weekends at the bungalow with you before you got your stand-in?"

"Yes."

"How thoroughly do you trust her?"

"I trust no one alive thoroughly except Luke. I trust Kester because it is to his advantage to remain loyal to my interests. With Miss Duke other—ah—considerations are involved, but I rely on her discretion for the same reason that I rely on Kester's loyalty. Quiet, Vaughn."

"Is she at the cottage now?"

"No, she's there only for weekends. She returned

to her New York apartment. I instructed her to stay there in case it was necessary to communicate."

"Do you ever call at her apartment?"

"Never. I never see her in New York."

"What's the address of the cottage at Triangle Beach?"

"It hasn't any. It's remote, two miles south of the village, with five hundred yards of private water front. Its name is Sweet Wilderness. My name there is George Byron."

Fox rubbed his nose to camouflage a grimace. "Where's the car Luke drove there?"

"In the pinewoods back of the cottage. My property."

"That's bad."

"We had to leave it somewhere."

"You should—never mind. Where's the one Kester drove?"

"This is it."

"What about servants at the cottage?"

"A local woman cleaned during the week. There was no one there weekends. Miss Duke did the cooking. There's nothing to fear there." Thorpe pointed. "What's that—that pink——"

"That's the sun. Or it soon will be. I'm willing to have a try at your job, Mr. Thorpe, but I'm afraid it's impossible. I'm afraid the American public is destined to see the name of that cottage in big type. Sweet Wilderness. The requirements are too drastic. It has to be plausible enough to allay suspicion. We can't say you were alone, anywhere at all, from Friday evening until now; they wouldn't swallow it. We must have corroboration. So we must find a man who will fill this bill:

"One. He must be a friend of yours, or at least an

acquaintance on friendly terms. Two. He must be willing to lie, either for friendship or for money. Three. He must have a cool head and adequate intelligence and discretion. Four. He must accept your word that you want an alibi not to protect you from a charge of murder, but merely from the disclosure of certain non-criminal activities which you wish to keep secret. Five. He must have been alone, in some place where you might conceivably have been with him, either for pleasure or for profit, from Friday evening until the time we find him; or if not alone, with another person or persons who can meet the other requirements along with him." Fox grunted. "That's a minimum. Without that it would be foolish to try."

Thorpe, sitting with his mouth open, muttered hopelessly: "Good gracious!"

Chapter 6

While the morning breeze danced in at the window and birds sang in the trees, they discussed it and sank more deeply into hopelessness. A dozen, three dozen, names were suggested: a man who was at his cabin in the Adirondacks, one whose hobby was an amateur research laboratory at his estate on the Hudson, one who fished a privately stocked stream somewhere north of Pawling, many others; but there were insuperable objections to each and all. Thorpe proposed that Fox should himself furnish a reliable man whose testimony could be bought, but that was only the blabber of despair; he agreed that it would be too risky. Finally, into a glum silence Luke Wheer blurted a name:

"Mistah Henry Jordan?"

Thorpe glowered at his valet. "What made you think of him?"

"Well, sir, I was running through my head persons who might be alone, and his name has been in and out all the time, because once I heard Miss Duke say he was away most of the time alone on his boat and once she sent me to take something to him, and he was away then on his boat——"

"Who is he?" Fox demanded.

"He's a stubborn old fool. It's out of the question."

"A friend of Miss Duke's?"

"He is Miss Duke's father. Dorothy Duke is the name she used on the stage."

"Oh. Do you—does his daughter support him?"

"No. He has a little income from capital—his savings. He's a retired ship's officer—purser. I have only met him once—no, twice."

"As Ridley Thorpe or as George Byron?"

"He knows who I am."

Fox frowned. "You said no one knew of that cottage except Luke and Kester."

"Jordan wasn't in my mind."

"And I suppose he's disaffected? You being the companion of his daughter's weekends?"

"I don't think so. I don't think he's affected one way or the other. Miss Duke is not a child. Jordan doesn't like me, but very few people like me. I called him a stubborn fool on account of his obstinate pride. He won't accept presents from his daughter. A year ago she told me that the only thing in the world he wanted was a new boat of a certain design and I offered—through her—the necessary twenty thousand dollars to buy it, but he wouldn't take it. Also I have given him some good market tips, but I doubt if he has profited by them."

"Is it generally known that you have an aversion to water—as something to float in—and boats?"

"Certainly not. I like the water. I used to sail, years ago. Later I had a yacht."

"So there would be nothing implausible about your enjoying a weekend cruise with your friend Jordan?"

"No." Thorpe tasted vinegar. "But to ask that man——"

"He sounds good to me," Fox declared. "Obviously he's not a chiseler. He must be discreet, since your relations with his daughter have remained a secret. He can probably be persuaded to lie, if not for money, then to avoid unpleasant publicity for his daughter. He can't suspect you of wanting an alibi for a murder, since his own daughter supports your real alibi. If he can meet the fifth requirement on my list, he's better than good, he's perfect."

"I don't like it."

"Of course you don't! If you're going to sit here and wait for something you like——"

Vaughn Kester put it urgently: "He's right, Chief. I could kick myself for not thinking of Jordan——"

"Quiet, Vaughn." Thorpe swallowed the vinegar. "All right." He looked at Fox. "I haven't a blank check with me——"

"I'll collect if I earn it." Fox opened the door and stepped out. "But it's my job and I'm in command. My instructions are to be followed without question and if they're not I drop it. Understood? You too, Kester. Understood?"

"Of course."

"Good." Fox turned. "Dan!"

The vice-president emerged from the door of the convertible, trod the roadside grass and was there. Fox told him: "This is Ridley Thorpe, Vaughn Kester and Luke Wheer. You saw their pictures in the paper. We're going to run their car into that wood lane out of sight and wait there. You drive home and get Bill, and then go to the Excelsior Market in Brewster and offer Sam Scott twenty dollars for the use of one of his closed delivery cars. He has two. He'll let you have it. Drive it back here and have Bill follow you in the convertible. Stop here, but don't start blowing horns. I'll see you."

Dan turned.

"Wait. Tell Miss Grant to sit tight and do nothing, that I'm making progress and will soon have her uncle out. That will be enough. Don't invite her to go to Brewster with you for an ice-cream soda."

"Right." Dan went.

That was the initial maneuvre of an extraordinarily complex and critical operation by land and sea, during which Fox had to contend with mutiny, bad luck and acts of God. The mutiny, or a threat of it, was recurrent; it first confronted him as, waiting in the shelter of the woods, he detailed the next step of the operation. Thorpe vetoed it. Fox stated bluntly that he would not proceed until he saw Miss Duke; he would not leave so unknown and dangerous a factor in the rear without a reconnoitre; Thorpe surrendered and gave the address. The threat of mutiny recurred when Dan arrived with the closed delivery truck, EXCELSIOR MARKET painted in red on its shiny white side, and the trio were instructed to climb in at the back and dispose themselves on the piles of gunny sacks which Dan had thoughtfully furnished. Thorpe demurred again and again Fox was blunt. Kester's car was left concealed in the woods; Bill Trimble was sent home with the convertible; and it was not yet six o'clock of a sultry summer morning when the truck headed south, with Fox driving, Dan beside him on the seat, and Luke Wheer the valet, Vaughn Kester the secretary, and Ridley Thorpe the national ornament, inside bouncing on the burlap.

In spite of the fact that with a commercial car the restricted boulevards had to be avoided, it was only twenty minutes past seven when the truck stopped at the curb on East 67th Street and Fox jumped to the sidewalk, walked around the corner to Park Avenue and entered an apartment palace, and asked to be announced to Miss Duke. The functionary stared in amazement at a creature who called on people in the middle of the night, but used the phone; and since Fox had already telephoned en route and so was expected, in a moment he was motioned to the elevator.

To the woman who opened the door of Apartment H on the twelfth floor he said with his hat off: "Good morning, Miss Duke, I'm Tecumseh Fox. Here's the note."

Without saying anything she took the sheet of paper, a page torn from Kester's memo book bearing Thorpe's scribble, read it twice, held it an angle for better light to inspect the writing and said huskily: "Come in."

The door closed, she was starting to lead the way to an inner room when Fox's voice stopped her. "This will do, Miss Duke. I'm in a hurry." He had already seen what there was to see: a woman of thirty and something got out of bed too early, distress and anxiety pulling at her face to make wrinkles, but displaying to a penetrating eye characteristics which might conceivably render a wilderness, if not sweet, at least tolerable. Under more favorable circumstances, he thought, homage might have needed no lift from charity.

"Where is Mr. . . . Mr. Byron?" she demanded.

"Mr. Thorpe's all right," Fox said. "You told me on the phone you're alone here?"

"I am."

"Good. I'd destroy that note if I were you. I'd like to know, when did Mr. Thorpe arrive at the cottage at Triangle Beach for the weekend?"

"Friday evening. So did I."

"When did he leave?"

"I don't know. I came—he sent me away yesterday morning. He was still there when I left."

"Were Luke Wheer and Vaughn Kester there?"

"Yes. They came late Sunday night, to tell him——" Her hand fluttered in appeal. "But where is he? What's going to happen? For God's sake——"

"He's all right. Don't worry, Miss Duke. We'll handle it. Was Thorpe with you at the cottage continuously from Friday evening until Sunday midnight?"

"Yes, he——" She stopped and her eyes narrowed. "Why do you ask a question like that if——"

"If I'm working for him? Because no matter who I'm working for I have to be sure of the facts. Don't waste valuable time suspecting me. Was he?"

"Yes."

"He didn't go away at all?"

"We went for a ride and to the movies at the village. He didn't go away from me, not for five minutes."

"Thank you. Now what I really came for, do you know where your father is?"

"My father?" She gawked at him. "My *father*?"

Fox nodded. "Mr. Henry Jordan. Now take it easy, you're jumpy. Thorpe says in that note that you are to answer my questions. We want to find your father because we need his help. Thorpe will explain when he sees you—or you'll read it in the papers—I haven't time now. Do you know where he is?"

"But, good Lord——"

"Do you?"

"No."

"Do you know whether he spent the weekend on his boat?"

"No. I know he's on it most of the time. Weekends are the same as week-middles to him since he retired. I expect he was——"

"Where does he go on the boat?"

"Lord, I don't know. Around on the water."

"Where does he keep it?"

"I don't know that either, but I suppose somewhere near his house. He lives in a little house at City Island. I suppose somewhere on the ocean——"

"City Island isn't on the ocean, it's on the sound."

"Well, then, on the sound. That's all I know—but I can give you the address of his house. Wait a minute, I'll get it."

She disappeared within, and in a few moments came back and handed Fox a slip of paper. "That's the address. He hasn't any phone."

"Thank you very much. No, Miss Duke, I can't tell you a thing. But don't worry. Go to bed. I interrupted your sleep. I apologize."

He left her, left the building, walked around the corner to the truck, got a key from his pocket and unlocked the rear door, poked his head in and spoke to the dark interior:

"I saw her. She doesn't know where he is or where he was over the weekend. He lives at City Island and we're bound for there."

"This is insuf——"

"I told you not to talk," Fox snapped and banged the door.

North on Third Avenue, on the car tracks under the elevated, the truck bumpety-bumped along, back through the city; darted deviously through the vastness of the Bronx and finally straightened its course on Central Avenue. The sun was beginning to assert itself and obviously it meant to make a day of it. On a stretch where no sidewalk offered a risk of curious pedestrians and the bedlam of passing traffic smothered lesser sounds, Fox steered off the through lanes, stopped the truck, got out and unlocked the rear door again, and inquired:

"All right?"

"No!" Thorpe yapped. "It's unbearable! It's an oven in here! We can't——"

"Sorry, you'll have to take it. Quit banging on that partition, or I'll park this thing and take a taxi home and you can play the hand out. You even banged after I stopped. How did you know where I was stopping?"

He swung the door to and trotted back to the front. As they eased back into the swift current, he observed to Dan, with his eyes on the road and his face straight: "Good gracious, it's hot in there."

"It's even hotter where his stand-in is," Dan rumbled. "Anyhow, people pay three or four dollars for a Turkish bath. The same thing."

Ten minutes later they turned off of Central Avenue at a busy intersection, rounded another corner and parked at the curb. Fox opened the rear door enough to poke his head in, stated that he was leaving Dan on the seat and there was no telling whether he would be gone forty minutes or four hours, walked back to the intersection and found a taxi, and gave the driver the address he had got from Miss Duke. As the taxi headed east towards the causeway to City Island, Fox was on the edge of the seat, gripping the strap, frowning and not singing. If he found Henry Jordan at home, his boat at its mooring, the operation was defeated, done, and he might as well drive the truck straight to the courthouse at White Plains.

But the little house at 914 Island Street, perched, like its companions in the row winding with the shore of the sound, with its rear on stilts to lift it above the tide, had no occupant. Fox, having found both front and back doors locked, and having got no response to his knocking, stood on the little elevated porch and looked out across the water. Boats of all sizes and descriptions tugged at their moorings; and bobbing dots here and there—one a hundred yards straight out from where he stood—were moorings without boats. He was saved the trouble of deciding on the next step by the sound of a voice.

"He's not there!"

Fox turned and saw the head of a woman with frowsy hair protruding from the window of the house next door, thirty paces off.

"Good morning!" he called. "I'm looking for Henry Jordan!"

"Yeah, I see you are. He's out on his boat."

"Thanks. When did he go?"

"Oh, I think . . . yeah, I think Thursday."

"Hasn't been back?"

"No, he often stays out a week or more."

"Where does he go, anywhere in particular?"

"No, nowhere particular. He likes flounder. There's more of them down the Long Island side. Once my husband and I caught——"

"Excuse me. What's the name of his boat?"

"*Armada.* Funny name, don't you think?"

"Very. What's it like a cruiser?"

"Yeah, it's thirty foot, nine-foot beam, high out of the water and an awful roller, white all over with the cabin trimmed in brown, though he was telling my husband not long ago——"

"Thank you very much."

"Who shall I tell him——"

"Don't bother." Fox was on his way. "Thanks!"

That, of course, was the best of luck. The bad luck was waiting for him when he got back to the truck—a flat tire; and there was no spare. Fox glared at it; this would not only cause delay, but would call attention to a conspicuous vehicle far from its haunt; but there was no help for it. He drove back to the intersection and found a garage, and told the mechanic:

"Fix it as quick as you can, will you, brother? I've got meat in there that's going to spoil on a day like this."

That cost a dollar and thirty-five minutes. Then he headed north again and at a favorable spot halted to report progress to his inside passengers. Again north.

His wristwatch said half-past ten and the heavy oppressive air said ninety in the shade, when he parked the truck once more, this time on the main street of South Norwalk. Before he left the seat and left the truck for good, he told Dan:

"Remember, my part's easy. I'm taking it because I can find it from the water and you can't. You've got the job and it's up to you. Don't let them out until I'm beached and don't let them out if there's any one in sight close enough to see faces. They're not to run or do anything but act natural—walk across the beach to me—and they're not to do that if there's any one within three hundred yards, even if it means waiting all day. As soon as they're on board and the boat's under way, take the truck home, get the convertible, drive to South Norwalk, park outside Carter's place and wait. You may wait an hour and you may wait twenty. Stay with the car."

"Wouldn't it be better if I parked——"

"No."

Dan's "Right again" reached Tecumseh Fox, if at all, through the back of his head, for he was off. A block away, at the railroad station, he entered a taxi and left it again five minutes later at the entrance to an enormous barnlike wooden building at the water-side with an inscription painted across the front: DON CARTER BOATS & EQUIPMENT. He went in and traversed its length, dodging construction scaffoldings and jumping blocks and timbers, emerged on to a platform from which piers jutted over the water, went up to a man who was watching two others scrape the side of a cabin cruiser and accosted him:

"Hello, Don. Is the tide still with you?"

"Hello there!" The man extended a hand. "Well, well! Where did you come from?"

"Oh, places. I'm in a hurry this time, I have to make a little trip. Can I have the Express Forty?"

"Sure! Sure you can. She's all tuned up." The man's crinkled eyes laughed at him. "I don't suppose you're bound for foreign shores? After that on the radio last night and then the papers this morn-ing——"

"I haven't had time to look at a paper. No, I'll bring her back all right, but I can't say when. While you're warming her up I'll step across the street and get a sandwich."

In a quarter of an hour he was back, with a large package under his arm and a bundle of newspapers. At the end of one of the piers a long narrow power-boat, with seats for six in a glassed-in cockpit, was purring smoothly. Fox hopped in and got behind the wheel, the engine swelled to a roar and then purred again, a man holding her to the pier gently eased her off and she glided away, with Don Carter watching her with pride in his eyes. Fox took her out beyond the last marker, turned her north and opened up the

throttle. She reared, lifted up her long narrow aristo-
cratic nose and scooted.

In twenty minutes he went ten miles. He throttled
down the engine, aimed for a desolate-looking stretch
of beach strewn with rocks and old seaweed; a hundred yards offshore he reversed to stop her, left the
seat and catfooted it to the bow, and dropped an anchor. Peering inshore, he caught through scraggly
trees a glimpse of a white object with a splotch of red
on its side. A survey of the beach showed him no sign
of life. He hopped to the stern, unlashed a dinghy that
lay athwart, lowered it into the water, got the oars
and rowed to the beach. Jumping out, he stood and
surveyed the scene again, and in a moment saw activity around the white object, and soon three men
emerged from among the trees and stumbled towards
him over the stones. They looked unmistakably like
men running away from something and Fox scowled
fiercely as they approached, but when they reached
him he said only:

"Get in. Thorpe and Luke in the stern, Kester in
the bow. Get in!"

With that weight in the little dinghy, he had to
wade in to his knees to get her free; then he hopped
over the gunwale and took the oars. Back alongside
the boat, he got them transhipped, pulled the dinghy
to the stern and lashed it, and issued instructions:

"You are all to lie low. No faces showing. It would
be a shame to spoil it now. There are sandwiches and
beer in that package, and help yourselves to the
newspapers. We've taken a trick. Jordan left Thursday on his boat and hasn't returned. I won't describe
it or tell you the name of it, or you'd be sticking your
faces up to help me look for it."

Ridley Thorpe growled faintly: "My stomach hurts and I think I'm going to vom——"

"Lie down and take it easy. Open that window, Luke, and he'll soon get enough air. Now remember, keep down."

He went to the bow and upped the anchor, climbed into the seat and started the engine, reversed and nosed her around for open water, and the search for the *Armada* was on.

By four o'clock that afternoon Tecumseh Fox would have given ten to one that there were fifty million boats on Long Island Sound and that a high percentage of them were white cruisers with brown cabin trim. The Carter Express Forty had poked its nose in at a hundred coves, inlets and harbours, all the way from Norwalk to Niantic on the Connecticut shore, and back from Plum Island as far as Wading River on the Long Island side. It was at four o'clock that an act of God came perilously close to terminating the operation by the conclusive process of sinking the entire outfit. Fox saw it coming around three-thirty and he knew that prudence dictated a flight for shelter, but he decided the boat could take it with proper handling. It came swooping and swirling from the west, a savage wind lashing with a thousand staggering blows, the recently placid water swelling, rushing, breaking, careening like a maniac, the summer day darkened into night. Fox throttled down, took it three-quarters on and prayed that the gear was good. The boat quivered, lunged and plunged, turned on its side, righted and tried the other side for a change, fought desperately to keep its nose into the danger. The act ended almost as abruptly as it had begun; and when he could, Fox turned for a look at his passengers. Vaughn Kester was trembling and as white as a sheet; Luke Wheer was not white but he was trembling; Ridley Thorpe nodded at Fox and declared, "You did that very well! Gracious, that was a blow! You handled it just right!"

Fox nodded back at him and returned to his steering, muttering to himself, "One more proof that no man is a total loss. Never forget that."

Ten minutes later, not far beyond Shoreham, a tiny cove no bigger than a hollow tooth came into view and planted in the middle of it was a white cruiser with brown cabin trim. Apparently it was well anchored, for there was no sign that the storm had torn it loose. Fox circled inshore and in a minute made out the name on the stern: *Armada.* He throttled down and floated up to it, alongside, reversed, grabbed the cruiser's gunwale to hold off and killed his engine. In the cockpit, mopping water which the storm had blown in, was a man around sixty, brown as leather, small but not puny, with jutting cheekbones guarding deep-set grey eyes.

Fox asked him, "Are you Henry Jordan?"

"I am," said the man. "Who are you?"

Chapter 7

That was at 4:40 p.m.

Across Long Island Sound and some miles west, Dan Pavey slouched in the front seat of the convertible, parked in front of Don Carter's place at South Norwalk. He was motionless and his eyes were closed. Suddenly his right leg twitched, then his left arm; his eyes opened; he jerked himself upright, stared around, blinked at his wristwatch and saw that it said 4:40.

"Well!" he told himself, in a rolling rumble of shocked incredulity.

He stared fixedly at space for three minutes.

"Well!" he repeated, still incredulous. "Mrs. Pavey's boy Dan dreaming about a girl. Don't deny it. Wake up. Is your boy running a fever, Mrs. Pavey? Perhaps he has acute cerebral flimmuxosis. What a pity. Flush out his skull and let it dry in the sun. How far can he spit? Phut!"

He got out, walked along the sidewalk to a door with a sign, BAR & GRILL, entered and ordered a double Scotch.

He downed it in a gulp, frowned around the place and ordered another. It went the way of the first. He ordered a third, sent it after its predecessors and ordered another one. The man behind the bar demurred.

"Right," Dan growled. "It's a waste of money. You might as well try to fill a gas tank with a teaspoon."

He picked up his change from the bar, returned to the street, walked a block and a half to a drugstore, climbed on to a stool at the fountain and told the boy:

"Westchester Delight with nuts."

He muttered to himself, as the boy started the complex operation.

"Yes, sir, nuts."

In the late afternoon, a little after six o'clock, District Attorney P. L. Derwin sat at his desk in his office at White Plains, wearily mopping his face with a damp handkerchief. Not only was he harassed by the impacts and exigencies of the most spectacular murder case Westchester County had enjoyed during his term of office, but also the weather was getting him; the thunderstorm that had raged across the city on its way to the sound in midafternoon had brought only ephemeral relief; it was now hotter and more humid than ever. Derwin looked at the man and girl in chairs facing him, let his handkerchief drop to the desk and spoke irritably:

"I may need to question you further at any time. I can't say when or how long or how often. Mr. Collins is of course correct when he says that it is your right to refuse to answer questions, but if you do so, the law has a right to make inferences from that refusal. You have both been released under bond as material witnesses." Perspiration showed on his forehead again. "You are bound, under severe penalty, to be available when needed. That publicity stunt of Tecumseh Fox's —that radio broadcast—has no bearing whatever on your status. As you know, Fox disappeared from his home during the night, has not returned and cannot be found."

He shifted to a man standing between two chairs —a large healthy-looking man in a white linen suit, with an amused mouth and sharply watchful dark eyes. "I resent your last remark, Mr. Collins. I'm not an infant. I'm well aware that you are acquainted with the law. I merely ask that you keep me informed of the whereabouts of Grant and his niece, so that in case——"

"Refused." Nat Collins was brusque. "I'm under no obligation to keep you informed. If you want to see them at any reasonable hour I'll produce them and I'll be with them." He put his hand on Andrew Grant's shoulder. "Come on, my boy." He must have been at least four years older than Uncle Andy. "Come, Miss Grant."

They left Derwin wearily mopping his face again. As they traversed the anteroom, the faces of four or five men sitting there, one a trooper in uniform, were turned to escort them across. Nearing the exit, Grant, who was in the lead, halted abruptly to avoid head-on collision with the door, which was being opened from without. The trio stepped aside to make gangway and were face to face with the pair who were entering.

Jeffrey Thorpe, red-faced from the heat, but no longer sartorially incongruous, confronted Nancy, blocked her off and demanded:

"Why wouldn't you see me?"

Nancy's look should have been cooling. "I don't know you. Let me——"

"The name is Jeff Thorpe. Not only do you know me, I am in your thoughts. You hate me. That's why you looked out of the upstairs window both times when I was leaving the Fox place today after you refused to see me. You couldn't help looking out of the window because I fascinate you like a snake. You fascinate me too, damn it! Did you get my letter? What did you—Randa, let go of me!"

His sister pulled him around. "Behave yourself, Jeff. It's picturesque to be headstrong, but it's an open season on Thorpes—oh, I didn't mean that, that was brutal—well, maybe I am brutal—" She tilted her face for her handsome eyes to slant up at Andrew Grant. "You're picturesque too, Mr. Grant, much more subtly than my brother, but I doubt if you're headstrong. That was quite effective—what you said to me yesterday in there—and the way you said it."

Andrew's eyes, gloomily withdrawn, met hers. "Was it?"

She nodded. "Very. Impressive. I told Mr. Derwin immediately that I believed you. I'm sorry—I speak as the daughter of Ridley Thorpe, surely with as much right to speak as an outsider, even a district attorney—I am sorry that you are innocently involved in the tragedy of my father's death. Shall we shake hands?"

"Why . . ." Grant's lips twisted a little. "I think not. I don't want to be doggish, but in such a situation as this a handshake would be so extremely . . . personal . . ."

"I suppose it would." She shrugged. "Will you introduce me to your niece?"

He did so. Each of the two women, one beginning her twenties and the other ending them, extended a hand and there was a clasp as Nancy said:

"Of course he's innocent! We're both under bond as material witnesses, but you can't help that."

"No, I'm afraid I can't, Miss Grant. You're very

lovely. Exactly the type that makes me look like a frump. I hope you'll go on hating my brother; it will do him good. If you're under bond . . ." She glanced at Nat Collins. "So this man isn't a policeman?"

"No, this is Mr. Collins, our lawyer. Mrs. Pemberton. Mr.——" Nancy stopped short and bit her lip.

"Thorpe," said Jeffrey, giving Collins a hand. "She doesn't know me. If anybody wants to make a study of headstrength or headstrongness, whichever it is——"

"Don't get started again, Jeff. Come, we're late." Miranda nodded to the others and turned to the room. "I believe Mr. Derwin is expecting us?"

A man said yes, he was waiting for them, and got up to open the inner door. Collins and his clients departed.

Derwin arose to greet the visitors, saw them disposed in the chairs recently vacated by the Grants and sat down again.

"Thank you for coming," he said. "It was next to impossible to get away from here to see you. I appreciate it very much——"

"Oh no, please," said Miranda. "It would be shabby of us not to remove difficulties for you if we can. Not that I would lift my finger for—well, for vengeance—and I'm sure my brother wouldn't either. But after all, we're his offspring, his family, and we inherit his wealth——"

"Of course," Derwin agreed. "Anyhow, I appreciate it. Colonel Brissenden wanted to be here, but he's busy on another angle of it in New York and couldn't get away. You must excuse me if I'm blunt and frank. Apropos of a new theory that is being considered. I want to ask some questions. You first, Mrs. Pemberton. Yesterday you suggested the possibility that your father used the bungalow for the purpose of—uh —female companionship."

"I did more than suggest it as a possibility. I said you'd find it to be a fact."

"Just so. I'd like to know, if you don't mind, on what information—on what grounds you based that statement."

"I told you." Miranda frowned. "On my knowledge of my father. I knew him better than he thought I did. Better than any one else, I'm pretty sure, except possibly Luke. It wasn't like him to seek solitary secluded weekends with his valet. And as I said, he was by no means as austere——"

She stopped because of a knock at the door. Derwin called come in and a man entered and approached the desk.

"Well?"

"I thought I'd better tell you, sir, though of course there's nothing to it. The Chief of Police over at Port Jefferson, Long Island, just called up. He's got a nut that claims he's Ridley Thorpe."

Derwin gestured irritably. "Why do you bother me about it? I have enough nuts to contend with as it is."

"Yes, sir, I know, but he says that this one is absolutely a dead ringer for Thorpe and the way he talks, and he's corroboration, a man that says his name is Henry Jordan—he says, this nut, he says he was out on the sound with his friend Jordan in his boat ever since Friday night and it wasn't until they went ashore for supplies at Port Jefferson this afternoon that he heard about the murder—of course that's goofy, hearing about his own murder—anyhow, the chief and a trooper are on the way here with him——"

"Bosh! I haven't time—let Ben Cook see him."

"Yes, sir."

The man went. Derwin mopped his face and neck. "You see, Mrs. Pemberton, the kind of vexations that interrupt us constantly. You were giving me the reasons for that statement you made."

"I have done so."

"You had no other reason?"

"No."

"It was only a surmise? You had no facts, no actual knowledge of—uh—a woman or women——"

Miranda shook her head. "No facts, but it was more than a surmise. It was a conclusion from premises."

"A logical deduction. I see. It should gratify you to learn that a fact has turned up to support it."

"I suppose it should. What is it?"

"I'll tell you in a moment. First I'd like to ask your brother something." The district attorney turned his regard to Jeffrey. "Mr. Thorpe, I want to say that I understand perfectly your reaction to Colonel Brissenden in this office yesterday. I even sympathize with it. The colonel's manner is sometimes—uh—brusque. Nevertheless, the question that was asked you is an important one and I would greatly appreciate it if you would give me the information. I refer to the circumstances of your previous acquaintance with Nancy Grant. I may tell you that I have good reason to suspect—come in! Damn it! Excuse me, Mrs. Pemberton."

The door burst open and the same man entered as before, but this time his eyes were shining with excitement.

"They've got Vaughn Kester and Luke Wheer!"

Apparently Derwin had heard that one before too, for he demanded dryly, "Who has?"

"No, they've really got 'em! A boat tied up to a dock at Southport and Tecumseh Fox went in the clubhouse to use a phone——"

"What!" Derwin goggled at him. "Fox?"

"Yes, he was with 'em! A cop happened to be on the dock and recognized Fox, and he got curious and thought he'd take a look in the boat while Fox was inside phoning and there were two guys that looked like the pictures of Kester and Wheer, and he pulled a gun and took 'em, and when Fox came out he took him too——"

"Where are they?"

"They're on the way, they'll be here in less than an hour."

Derwin scowled. He picked up his handkerchief and mopped his face, and then scowled some more. "It sounds screwy to me," he said finally, in slow bewilderment. "Tying up at a dock and leaving them there in plain sight—that doesn't sound like Tecumseh Fox to me, not for one second."

Miranda sighed. "Darn that Fox man anyway," she muttered. "Refusing *three* invitations to dinner——"

"He'll dine on the county tonight," said Derwin grimly.

Chapter 8

Jeffrey Thorpe crossed one knee over the other and observed, "That's a good example of it."

"Of what?" The district attorney shifted the scowl to him.

"Of authority. The insolence of it. My father had it too; that's why I only lasted in his office a couple of weeks when I was started in there to learn the tricks. Here you are saying Fox will dine on the county before you even see him. How do you know but what he found Luke and Kester hiding on a desert island, and was bringing them in to you?"

"I don't, Mr. Thorpe. But I think I am justified in making the tentative assumption, since Fox had not communicated——"

"All right, forget it." Jeffrey waved it away. "Anyhow, this ought to lift a lot of fog for you, since Luke was apparently right there when it happened. I might suggest that you don't try to bully Luke. I got on to Luke when I was knee-high to him and wanted little favors. Get him sympathetic and you can have his shirt, but he won't take bluster. Kester—do you know Kester?"

"No, I've never met him."

"Well, there's one that was made to order for an authoritative bird like you. You can twist him around your little finger—provided you limber him up first with a few good blows with a sledge hammer. How the devil he happens to be with Luke, or Luke with him—can you figure that one, Sis? How come?"

"I have no idea, Jiffy."

"So have I." He returned to authority. "You were telling me that you have good reason to suspect something."

Derwin nodded. "Yes, Mr. Thorpe, I have. It appears, in the first place, that Grant's niece was not as complete a stranger to your father as she pretends and secondly, that she has not told the truth regarding her movements at the bungalow Sunday evening. I assure you I am not exercising the insolence of authority; I am stating facts; or at least inferences weighted by a preponderance of likelihood. In view of that, in view of my earnest conviction that any and every detail of Nancy Grant's previous contacts with any member of your family may be relevant to the murder of your father and should be disclosed to the author—uh—to those conducting the investigation, I strongly urge you to tell me——"

"About her previous contacts with this member of the family. Little Jeff."

"Yes. I strongly advise——"

"I heard you." Jeffrey uncrossed his knees and leaned forward. "Now here. You heard what my sister told you yesterday. Down in our hearts, taking it for granted that we've got hearts, I guess she and I are both a little bitter about our father. That is, we were. Not that he was cruel or anything romantic like that; he just didn't fill the bill. To look at me now, sophisticated, blasé, hard-boiled, on speaking terms with the headwaiter at Rusterman's, you would never suppose that I once wept tears because Johnny Holcomb's father—you see, by God, to this day I remember his name—spent a whole afternoon at the zoo with him, whereas my father not only wouldn't take me to the zoo, he wouldn't even take time to let me tell him what I saw when I was taken by the assistant governess, who had the teeth of a gnawing rodent, such as a beaver. Her name was Miss Jandorf."

"Lefcourt," said Miranda.

"No, damn it, it was Jandorf. Lefcourt took me to the aquarium—My sister was correct yesterday when she said that we have batted close to a thousand as orphans since our mother died. The murder of our father was deplorable and naturally it gave us a jolt, but to say it made our hearts heavy with grief—still taking it for granted that we've got hearts—that would be bunk. Nor are we out yelling for blood, because we don't happen to be the vindictive type. In spite of which, I hope you catch the bird who did it and if I had any information that could possibly help you, I'd hand it over. I told you so yesterday morning. Which brings me to the point, namely, that if a million G-men investigated a million years they wouldn't find any connection between my father's death and my previous brief contact with Miss Grant. So it's none of your business. Q.E.D. I knew I'd find a use for my geometry some day."

Derwin dropped his damp handkerchief to the desk. "I think you should tell me about it anyway," he insisted. "If it is completely irrelevant and innocuous——"

"I didn't say it was innocuous, I said it had no connection with murder. It wasn't innocuous. I made an ass of myself and earned her venomous hatred."

"Ah! hatred——"

"No no, no like that." Jeffrey waved it off again. "I mean the kind of hate that's just the opposite on the other side. All you have to do is turn it over, like flipping a pancake, but it's one hard trick."

"You said venomous."

"Cross it out."

Derwin screwed up his lips. "Let me ask you this, Mr. Thorpe. Do you—no, I'll put it this way. Is your attitude towards Miss Grant such that you would not want her to suffer the legal penalty for killing your father if she were guilty?"

Jeffrey stared a second, then snorted contemptuously. "It's not the heat, it's the humidity," he stated.

The district attorney pulled open a drawer of his desk, got out a large rectangle of pasteboard, glanced at it and handed it across. "Did you ever see that before?"

Jeffrey looked at it and Miranda stretched from her chair to look with him. It was a portrait photograph of Nancy Grant, her lips parted a little and her eyes laughing. At the lower right was an inscription in a round bold hand generous with space and ink: "I'll never forget!" Beneath it was the signature, "Nancy Grant."

"Is that for sale?" Jeffrey demanded.

"No. Did you ever see it before?"

"No."

"Did you, Mrs. Pemberton?"

"No. Where did it come from?"

"It was found in a drawer in a cabinet in your father's dressing-room in the New York residence."

Miranda's eyes widened. Jeffrey's mouth fell open. He closed it, looked at the photograph again, glared at Derwin and stated, "That's a goddam lie."

"No, it isn't, Mr. Thorpe." Derwin met his glare. "Neither is this." He opened the drawer again. "Here are two gloves. As you see, they are of yellow cotton, good quality, well-made, the kind that women wear in the summer. One of them was found on the grass back of a shrub twenty feet from the window through which Andrew Grant says he saw your father smoking a cigar and listening to the radio Sunday night. The other was found on the running board of the car which Nancy Grant parked near the gate when she drove her uncle there. We have found——"

Miranda exclaimed, "But these are both for the right hand!"

"That's correct, Mrs. Pemberton. We have found no proof that they belong to Nancy Grant. They were bought, as the label shows, at Hartlespoon's and they have sold several hundred dozen pairs of them this season. I do not pretend that the fact that she works at Hartlespoon's has any important significance. But she was at the bungalow Sunday night and so far there is no reason to suspect that any other woman was anywhere near there. According to her story, she was never on that side of the bungalow where the window is; she went straight in at the terrace entrance upon her arrival. One of the gloves was found on the running board of the car she was driving. So while there is no proof, there is a strong presumption that the gloves are her property and that she dropped one of them outside that window where it was found; in which case, she is lying about her movements. She also says that prior to Sunday evening she had never met, or even seen, your father. Again, the photograph furnishes a strong presumption, if not proof, that she is lying."

"Good heavens," Miranda muttered.

Jeffrey stood up.

"Where are you going, Mr. Thorpe?"

"I'm going to find Miss Grant."

"Take in the slack, Jeff dear," Miranda advised. "She won't speak to you."

"But this bunch of crap——" He confronted her trembling with fury. "Do you realize that this poisonous cream puff is actually suggesting——"

"Perfectly." Her tone was sharp. "I also realize that he actually wants to find out who murdered our father and I expect he will before it's over, and if it turns out that it was the lovely Nancy—which I do not believe—you are in for a piece of hell. But it isn't going to help any to double up your fists and call him names——"

Derwin interposed, his tone also sharp. "Thank you, Mrs. Pemberton. You're right, that won't help any. If you'll sit down again, Mr. Thorpe, I have some more explaining to do. I told you about the photograph and the gloves for a specific purpose. I thought it possible that your reluctance to tell about your previous meeting with Nancy Grant was because she was in the company of your father and if I showed you that I already know——"

"You don't know a damn thing! About her!"

"Well—I have grounds for inference. Was she with your father when you met her?"

"No!"

"Will you tell me about it—now?"

"No."

Miranda put in, "What does she say about the photograph and the gloves?"

"I haven't asked her about the photograph. It wasn't found until this morning and by the time I got her here Nat Collins was present as her counsel, and he was advising her to answer no questions except those pertaining to the events at the bungalow Sunday evening. Her denial that she had ever seen or met Ridley Thorpe is on record. Also her denial that the gloves are her property or that she had any knowledge of them."

"It's strange that the gloves are both for the right hand. Do you suppose there could have been two women, wearing the same kind of gloves, and each happened to lose the right one?"

"No. It's possible, but very unlikely. If one of them was Nancy Grant and she lost hers on the running board of her car, why should she deny knowledge of it? If she lost it by that shrub outside the window, she's lying about her movements. And to suppose there were two women there besides her—that's a little too much, since there's no evidence that there was even one. It is more likely that both gloves belong to a woman who had taken two right-hand ones by mistake."

Derwin picked up his handkerchief and mopped his face. "But that's a police job, tracing those gloves. I mentioned them and the photograph only—for the purpose I stated. There's another subject I have to ask you to discuss with me: your father's will. Won't you sit down, Mr. Thorpe? Thank you. You know, of course, that you two are the residuary legatees. There are various bequests: Luke Wheer gets a life annuity of three thousand dollars . . ."

They discussed that at some length. Then Derwin wanted to know more about their meeting with Vaughn Kester on Sunday evening, for dinner at the Green Meadow Club. He was suave and deferential again on that subject—as suave, at least, as a man can manage with sweat trickling down his neck two minutes after he has wiped it off. The discussion of Kester eventually brought him back to the will again, to that clause in it which left the confidential secretary a handsome legacy, and the possible ramifications of that were being considered when there was a tap at the door and a man entered. It was Ben Cook, the chief of police, with his mind too engaged to take notice of the presence of the Thorpes.

"Something new?" Derwin demanded.

"I don't know how new it is," Cook said, "but it's worse than a horsefly. It's that specimen that they brought over from Port Jefferson that says he's Ridley Thorpe——"

"I gave instructions for you to take care of him."

"I know you did, but you ought to hear him. He sure *thinks* he's Ridley Thorpe. I thought the easiest way to get rid of him would be to bring him in here and let the son and daughter see him——"

"Nonsense! Lock him up and find out who he is."

"But I tell you . . ." Cook stood his ground. "It'd only take a second. Would you mind, Mrs. Pemberton?"

"Not at all."

"Would you, Mr. Thorpe?"

"No."

"Okay, Phil?"

Derwin growled assent. Cook lost no time going and very little coming back. The door opened again and he marched in, standing aside to make passage for two men, both around sixty, one small but not puny and as brown as leather, the other bigger, more deliberate, more commanding. The latter stopped in the middle of the room and boomed:

"Well children?"

Miranda was slowly rising from her chair and gazing at him with wide and startled eyes. Jeffrey sat transfixed, staring, the color drained from his face.

"Well?" he boomed again.

Without moving her eyes, Miranda approached, unhurried, got within three feet of him, gazing another five seconds and said in a tight, thin, quiet voice, "We were just discussing your will with Mr. Derwin."

"What——" Derwin came bounding. "What the— what do you——"

"This is my father, Mr. Derwin. Or his ghost."

"Ghost——"

Jeffrey, with his white face, was there. He looked directly into the big man's eyes and said harshly, "Yes. It's you."

"Yes, my boy, it is."

"Ghost! I . . . what . . ." The district attorney was incoherent. He appealed to Miranda. "You're mistaken . . . this is some——"

"They are not mistaken," the big man declared. "I am Ridley Thorpe. This is my friend, Henry Jordan. Henry, I believe you've never met my son and daughter. Shake hands with them; Miranda; Jeffrey. I'm tired and I want to sit down."

Chapter 9

They sat around the desk, except Ben Cook who was against the wall with his chair tilted back and Derwin who was standing, wary and incredulous; and Ridley Thorpe was in command. Unshaven and disheveled and battered as he was, he had not dominated stormy directors' meetings for twenty years for nothing.

"First," he told Derwin, "get on the phone and stop meddling at once. Everyone prying into my papers and affairs and belongings. Call them off."

Derwin shook his head. "Oh, no. That's not first. First you satisfy me. Do you think I'm going——"

"All right. I'll satisfy you. I'm Ridley Thorpe. My son and daughter——"

"Your son recognized the remains——"

"Quit interrupting me! My son and daughter recognize me. I used to spend weekends at that bungalow in order to get some privacy, but it became too widely known that I did so and I was annoyed. Three years ago I found a man who closely resembled me and hired him to spend weekends at the bungalow, impersonating me, leaving me free to enjoy genuine privacy at such places and in such activities as might

appeal to me. I have done so. I have devoted my
weekends to various relaxations and mild amuse-
ments, my identity never suspected because it was
generally believed that I was at the bungalow—and
thanks to my stand-in, I was. Frequently I have taken
little trips with my friend Henry Jordan on his boat. I
did so last Friday evening. Ordinarily I return Sunday evening or Monday morning, but this time I was
worn out and it was hot and I stayed on the water. We
anchored at various spots on the sound, fishing, talking, sleeping——"

"Didn't you go ashore?"

"No. On that boat I can forget the world and give
my nerves a rest. We didn't leave the boat until this
afternoon, after the thunderstorm. We were anchored
in a little cove on Long Island. When the storm was
over we chugged down to Port Jefferson and went
ashore—I was intending to get back to business—and
the first thing I saw was big headlines about the investigation of my murder. I would have had to wait an
hour for a train, so I got the police and told them I
wanted a fast car. They didn't want to believe me and
I suppose I can't blame them. Here I am."

He looked at his children. "I'm sorry you had this
shock, Miranda. You too, Jeffrey. But you've had the
advantage of reading my will. It treats you fairly,
doesn't it?"

"Perfectly." Miranda's gaze hadn't left him once.
"But I knew it would. More than one shock, though.
Two. The first one was—shocking. This is shattering."

"Of course it is. You were a multimillionaire in
your own right. Now you have to go back to pestering
Vaughn to watch for a good moment to get my con-
sent to an extra twenty thous——"

"I didn't mean that, Father. I only meant it's a shattering surprise."

"It is. Yes," Jeffrey muttered.

"Yes, my boy, you too. Shattering. Well, I'm not dead. By the way, where in the name of heaven is Vaughn? I read a paper on the way here. And you're District Attorney Derwin, investigating my murder. Good gracious, it's a fantastic mess! Have the meddling stopped at once. I don't want an army of people —Here, give me that phone."

"Just a minute." Derwin dropped into his chair and got his hand on the phone. He turned: "Is your name Henry Jordan?"

"Yes, sir." Jordan's deep-set grey eyes were level and his tone quiet and composed.

"What's your occupation?"

"I'm a retired ship's officer."

"Where do you live?"

"914 Island Street, City Island."

"How long have you lived there?"

"Five years. Ever since I retired."

"Do you corroborate what this man has said?"

"I do."

"Is he Ridley Thorpe, the financier and corporation executive?"

"He is."

"How long have you known him?"

"Seven years. I first met him when I was purser on the *Cedric* and he was a passenger."

Derwin snapped at Ben Cook, "Send a man to City Island to check it. Got the address?" Cook nodded and tramped out. Derwin turned to Miranda:

"How sure are you that this man is your father?"

"Completely. Of course he is."

He shifted to Jeffrey. "Are you sure too?"

Jeffrey nodded without taking his eyes from the ghost.

"You are?" Derwin insisted.

"Certainly I am. Wouldn't I be?"

"I'm asking. You were sure that the body you saw was your father's."

"I wasn't asked if I was sure. I didn't—there was no reason to doubt it. It looked like him—only—it was a body. This is my father, alive."

The district attorney regarded him glumly, then slowly transferred the regard, first to his sister, then to Henry Jordan and last to his ghost.

"I would say," he growled, "that fantastic mess is a damn mild term for it. I'll want a signed statement from you, Mr. Thorpe, and copies of it will be furnished to the press. From you also, Mr. Jordan. God, what an uproar——" He looked at the phone, his hand still clutching it, in sour distaste, lifted it and clapped it to his ear, and told the transmitter:

"Get Colonel Brissenden. He's somewhere in New York, probably at the Thorpe residence. Find him. Send in a couple of men, whoever's out there. As soon as I'm through with Colonel Brissenden I want Joe Bradley. . . ."

Nine minutes later the radio had it. Long waves, short waves, old-fashioned sound waves, undulated and quivering with it. City editors shouted it and telephone wires let it pass, and swift rumor distorted it. From different spots in New York, three newsreel trucks headed north almost simultaneously. At a water-front dock at Port Jefferson a policeman on guard arrested a man for swiping a cushion from the cockpit of the *Armada* for a souvenir. . . .

In the district attorney's office at White Plains, Derwin was desperately mopping his face with a wet handkerchief and trying to handle with official calm an utterly preposterous situation, Ridley Thorpe, with his friend Henry Jordan at his elbow, was carefully dictating a statement to a stenographer whose hand was trembling with excitement, Miranda was deliberately and effectively using a compact, and Jeffrey was sunk in his chair, scowling with compressed lips, when the door opened for a state trooper to usher in three men. Vaughn Kester, in front, looked pale, exhausted and tense; Luke Wheer's eyes were threatening to pop entirely out; Tecumseh Fox's apparel was untidy and his face exasperated, but his step was still quick and light and might even have been called jaunty.

Derwin jumped up and started to bark at the trooper, "Didn't I tell—take them outside and——"

But that was beyond his handling too. Bedlam intervened, everyone joining in. Luke and Kester saw their employer and made for him. Miranda exclaimed something at Kester. Jeffrey leaped for Luke and got him by the arm and shouted at him. Fox stood aside, taking it in. Derwin abandoned official calm completely and barked helplessly.

Ridley Thorpe's voice finally emerged from the confusion: "I tell you we were on the Long Island shore all the time! You should have found us Monday! Inexcusable incompetence——"

Miranda: "But Vaughn, why didn't you——"

Jeffrey: "What happened, Luke, damn it? What——"

Kester: "I did my very best, sir——"

Luke: "I told Mr. Kester we ought——"

Derwin: "I tell you I want——"

A baritone claimed the air and got it: "Everybody,

please!" Tecumseh Fox, among them, got Kester's arm and turned him. "Is this Mr. Thorpe?"

"Yes, I'm trying to tell him——"

"Quiet, Vaughn. Who are you?"

"I'm Tecumseh Fox. Kester hired me to help him find you. The district attorney——"

"I want——"

"I know you do, Mr. Derwin. You'll have to take what you get. From me would be the quickest. Did you take my tip and buy Thorpe Control on the drop?"

"What the devil——"

"All right, I'll rub it in some other time. Andrew Grant's statement that he saw Ridley Thorpe listening to band music on the radio at the Dick Barry hour suggested to you that Grant was lying. To me it suggested that it wasn't Ridley Thorpe he saw, neither then alive nor later dead. I got an item relayed to Dick Barry for his broadcast last night, as bait. I got a nibble from Vaughn Kester. Has Mr. Thorpe explained to you where he was and about his stand-in?"

"I have," Thorpe cut in, "and you're not——"

"I'm at bat, Mr. Thorpe—Kester phoned me at three o'clock this morning and I met him, and Luke Wheer was with him. Luke, entrusted with guarding the secret that the man at the bungalow was not really Thorpe, got panicky when the man was murdered and ran. He didn't even know where Thorpe was. He got in touch with Kester and they hid out to get time to consider the situation. Kester did know that Thorpe was supposed to be somewhere, probably on Long Island Sound, with Henry Jordan in his boat. But he didn't know precisely where. He didn't even know positively that it wasn't Thorpe who had been killed, in spite of Luke's assurance that it was the stand-in; Kester wasn't absolutely sure of what had happened and couldn't be sure until he found Thorpe. He and Luke tried it; they were afraid to hire a boat, so they worked along the shore. Late last night they were on a pier at Huntington when they heard, on a radio on a boat anchored nearby, Dick Barry broadcasting the item I had got to him. That scared them and Kester phoned me, and I met them."

"All the time——"

"I'll finish first, Mr. Thorpe. Kester engaged me to help in the search. I hired a boat from Don Carter in South Norwalk and took Luke and Kester on board from a strip of deserted beach. That was around eleven o'clock this morning. All day long we searched the sound, both shores——"

Thorpe snorted. "All afternoon we were anchored in a little cove not far east of Port Jefferson, in plain view——"

"Then we must have missed you in the storm. I apologize. The storm nearly sank us. At six-thirty we tied up at a dock at Southport because I wanted to phone a man who was waiting with my car at South Norwalk. By bad luck a cop spotted me, and then Luke and Kester, and took us."

"Took you," Derwin rasped, "in the act of concealing and harboring fugitives from justice!"

"Oh, for God's sake," said Fox, disgusted. "Gathering sea shells with a tidal wave headed for you. Luke and Kester are not fugitives from justice. They were frantically trying to find Thorpe, which you might have been doing yourself if you had made a good guess about the radio instead of a bum one. I only wish I had found him myself and brought him here to you; that would have been a real pleasure. But apparently—what did you do, Mr. Thorpe, go ashore somewhere?"

"Yes, at Port Jefferson. And saw a headline—good gracious, what's that?"

They all jerked around, startled; and as they jerked, it was over. A noise at one of the open windows, a face leering at them, a man's arm thrust within the room, the hand clutching something that flashed and glittered like a reflection from polished glass—and then the explosion and the blinding glare. Miranda stifled a scream. Luke bounded towards the window. Tecumseh Fox laughed. Derwin shouted at the trooper in fury, "Go out and catch him! Put a man out there! By God, news photographers climbing up the sides of the building like monkeys! Or maybe the fire department lent him a ladder!"

"You're nervous," said Fox sympathetically. "You jumped three feet——"

"Oh, I am? I'm nervous, am I?"

"You are and I don't blame you. You're going to get a universal horse laugh because you were busy investigating a murder and the murdered man walks into your office. Think how much happier you'd be if you hadn't got me sore yesterday. Where's the man I'm working for, Andrew Grant? This frees him doesn't it?"

"He's free already. He's out on bond." Derwin circled his desk, seated himself, surveyed the group of faces and settled his regard on the perturbed visage of Ridley Thorpe. His jaw muscles twitched; he controlled it. "Mr. Thorpe," he said, "you are a man of large affairs, of nation-wide—uh—renown. I don't need to say that I have full respect for your position, your—elevated position. Your sudden appearance here has created an unprecedented situation—as you yourself said, a fantastic mess, but you cannot be held accountable for that. In engaging a man to impersonate you at your bungalow, and yourself seeking privacy and diversion elsewhere as you saw fit, certainly you committed no wrong. I want you to understand that I take full cognizance of your rights and of your eminence in the community. But though I am glad—I am delighted—that you are alive and unharmed, the fact remains that a man has been murdered in the county under my jurisdiction, and as it stands now, I don't even know the man's name."

Thorpe was frowning. "His name was Corey Arnold."

"Who was he?"

"He was an architect." Thorpe glanced at the stenographer who had been shorthanding his statement. "You'd better take this down. I investigated Arnold thoroughly when I engaged him three years ago. He was fifty-eight, two years older than me. Born in Zanesville, Ohio. Graduate of Stevens. Father and mother dead. Two brothers, one a druggist in Columbus, Ohio, the other an insurance man in San Francisco. No sisters. Married in Boston in 1909; wife died in 1932. One daughter, married and living in Atlanta; no sons. He lived in a boardinghouse at 643 Archer Street, Brooklyn, when I found him; I paid him well, and for two years he has been living in an apartment at 406 East 38th Street, Manhattan. I got him by advertising for a man to sit for a bust of Gladstone; my skull and facial structure bear a strong resemblance to Gladstone's. Apparently he was a pretty good architect, but he had had one little job in two years and he needed the money. He was down in weight when I found him, but after a month of proper diet my clothes fitted him almost perfectly. He smoked cigarettes but changed to cigars when impersonating me, drank moderately, was sober-minded, read a great deal of biography and American history—do you want any more?"

"That will do for the moment, thank you." Derwin screwed up his lips. "What did he do when he wasn't impersonating you?"

"Enjoyed himself. As I say, I paid him well. He gave me a report each week detailing his activities— naturally I wanted to keep tabs on him. Music and plays in the winter, golf in the summer——"

"Thank you." Derwin screwed up his lips again. "You see, of course, the first knot in this tangle to be untied. If not the first one, at least a vital one. The person who fired a gun through the window of that bungalow Sunday night—who did he think he was shooting at, Ridley Thorpe or Corey Arnold?"

Thorpe stared. "Why, he thought it was me."

"I hope so. In that case we have the enormous advantage of being able to consult with the man who was murdered. You realize, Mr. Thorpe, that what I am concerned with, as the district attorney of this county, is the murder. Though naturally you regret the tragic fate of Corey Arnold, with you, and possibly with everyone in this room except me, other aspects of this sensational affair may be paramount— since the victim was only an unsuccessful architect hired by you as a stand-in—but I am chiefly, and in fact exclusively, concerned with the murder. I want to find the guilty man and bring him to justice."

"Good gracious, so do I."

"Of course you do. I appreciate—excuse me." He reached for the phone to answer it. It was a long conversation, his part consisting mostly of grunts, and during it there was talk among the others in low tones. It was continuing after Derwin hung up, but he stopped it:

"Please! I was saying, what I want is the murderer. That's my job. I want to question your valet, Luke Wheer——"

"So do I," Thorpe declared. "I read a paper on the way over here and that's all I know about it. What in the name of heaven—what happened, Luke?"

"No," Derwin snapped. "I'll do the questioning, Mr. Thorpe." He fastened his eyes on the colored man. "Where were you when the shots were fired?"

Chapter 10

L uke sat, stiff and erect, on a chair back of his
employer's shoulder making faint sucking
noises with his tongue and teeth.

"Move your chair over," said Derwin irritably, "so
I can see you better. Where were you when the shots
were fired?"

Luke lifted himself an inch, moved his chair six
inches, and went on making the noises.

"Are you dumb?" Derwin demanded.

Luke shook his head. "No, sir," he said in a low but
firm tone. "I am not dumb in the vocal sense. I am
being careful what I say because I realize the preponderance——"

"Oh, spill it, Luke," Jeffrey blurted.

"Yes, Mr. Jeffrey. At the time the shots were fired
I was in my room writing a letter to the editor of the
Harlem *Courier.*"

Derwin nodded. "I've read it. You left it there.
Your room is the one at the right of the kitchen?"

"Yes, sir."

"What did you do when you heard the shots? How
many did you hear?"

"I heard two shots, almost simultaneously consecutive. At first I thought they were shots, then I thought they were a part of the radio program which was turned up very loud, but after an interval of three or four minutes, according to my judgment, I became dissatisfied with that thought and went to look through the door into the living room. The sight that met my eyes was the worst I have ever seen. I ran over to him and saw it was the end. My blood ran cold. The psychology——"

"What did you do?"

"Yes, sir. My blood ran cold. On account of psychology, I was imbued with the impression that Mr. Thorpe, for whom I have worked more than twenty years, had been murdered. That impression was because I had strictly trained myself for three years to speak of him and think of him as Mr. Thorpe when he was there in the bungalow. Then I realized it was not Mr. Thorpe, it was him. Then I realized the only thing to do was obey my orders to never cause or permit any suspicion that he was not Mr. Thorpe. Then I realized that if I did that the news would get out that Mr. Thorpe was dead, and that would be inconvenient because he was dead. Not knowing where Mr. Thorpe was, I thought the only thing I could do was telephone Mr. Kester, but then I thought that would be bad because everything that happened in that bungalow was going to be taken into consideration. So I realized I couldn't use the telephone and I couldn't conveniently be there when anybody came if they had heard the shots, and I went out and got the car and drove away."

"Did you see a car parked on the road outside the gate?"

"Yes, sir. That increased my desire to get away. My rear fender hooked it as I swung into the road and

I would have run over a woman if she hadn't jumped, because I didn't see her until I was right on her. I have been worried about her, provided she wasn't the murderer, because I have never struck a living creature——"

"She's all right. Where did you go?"

"I turned west before I got to Mount Kisco and then went on through Millwood to Chappaqua. I stopped the car there and sat in it a while, thinking it over, and then went in a drugstore and telephoned Mr. Kester at the Green Meadow Club. He had just been notified by the police and was up dressing. I drove to Pine's Bridge and he met me there, and we had a talk and decided to find Mr. Thorpe. First we decided to try——"

"Let's go back to the bungalow. You were in your room when the shots were fired?"

"Yes, sir."

"Did you see anyone, hear anyone, hear any noise?"

"No, sir, the radio was on so loud——"

"Had anyone called to see Arnold during the weekend?"

"No, sir, no one was ever let in. The gate to the drive was kept locked. Not anyone for deliveries even —I brought everything from Mount Kisco."

"Had there been a phone call for Arnold?"

"No, sir, there couldn't be. When he was there he was Mr. Thorpe. We never forgot that for a second, neither of us. If the phone rang I answered it. It was never anybody but Mr. Kester with instructions."

"Had Mr. Kester phoned this weekend?"

"No, sir. Usually he only phoned to tell us when to leave because Mr. Thorpe was returning to his home or his office."

"What had you and Arnold been fighting about?"

Luke blinked. "Me? Fighting with him?"

"That's what I said. What was it about?"

Ridley Thorpe snapped, "Bosh! If you're cooking up a theory that Luke——"

"I'm not cooking up a theory," Derwin snapped back. "God knows there are plenty of theories without trying to cook one up. Would you like to hear a few of them?"

"I'd like to hear all there are. I want this thing cleared up."

"So do I." Derwin met his gaze. "I'll state some of them briefly and bluntly. One. Luke Wheer had a quarrel with Arnold and killed him. Two. Vaughn Kester, knowing it was Arnold and not you, killed him for financial profit—No, let me finish, Mr. Thorpe wants to hear them. Three. Andrew Grant, thinking it was you, killed him for revenge or some other undisclosed motive. Four. Nancy Grant, thinking it was you, killed him for revenge or some other undisclosed motive. Five. Jeffrey Thorpe, thinking it was you, killed him to inherit a fortune. Six. Miranda Pemberton, thinking it was you, killed him to inherit a fortune. Seven. You yourself, knowing it was Arnold, killed him for financial profit. Eight. Some enemy of Arnold's knowing he was there, killed him. Nine. Some enemy of yours, thinking it was you, killed him. That's all. At this moment they're all possible. I can ignore none of them."

"You might explain a couple of them, though," Vaughn Kester said dryly. "How would Mr. Thorpe or I have profited financially by killing Arnold?"

Derwin looked at the secretary's pale cold eyes. "I can answer that, Mr. Kester, by repeating a piece of information I got on the telephone a little while ago.

Over a hundred thousand shares of Thorpe Control were sold on the exchange yesterday and today, at prices ranging from 29 to 40. If they were sold, somebody bought them. With Mr. Thorpe alive and well, it will jump back around 80 tomorrow. Whoever bought them will have a nice profit."

Ridley Thorpe inquired quietly, "Are you daring to intimate——"

"I'm not intimating anything. You asked for the theories. I hardly need to say that such an accusation against a man of your standing would not be remotely considered without conclusive evidence and I have no evidence at all. Until an hour ago—two hours ago—I thought you were dead. But that theory applies to Mr. Kester as well as you. The theory which formerly applied to him——"

"May I ask what that was?" Kester sneered.

"For the record, if you want it. It no longer applies, since you knew the man in the bungalow was not Thorpe. It was simply that investigation had disclosed that you aspired to marry Thorpe's daughter and if she inherited millions—the theory embraced the possibility of a conspiracy——"

"Also the possibility that I hired him to do it, or Jeffrey and I both did while we were dining with him Sunday evening," said Miranda calmly. "For shame, Mr. Derwin! That's plain nasty."

"He asked for it, Mrs. Pemberton. You often find nasty things back of a murder."

"You will permit me," said Kester icily, "a comment on your statement that I aspire to marry Mr. Thorpe's daughter. It is true that at one time——"

Derwin cut him off. "It's no longer relevant. I would like to say that most of the theories I proposed are at present no better than moonshine. Obviously those applying to the Grants, both uncle and niece——"

"More moonshine," Ridley Thorpe said impatiently. "All that stuff in the paper—just because he happened to go there——"

"Don't you know them, Mr. Thorpe?"

"No. Not from Adam. Apparently the man works for an advertising agency that does copy for some of my companies——"

"Have you never met either of them?"

"Never."

"That's curious." Derwin pulled open a drawer of his desk. "Would you mind telling me how this happened to be in a drawer of a cabinet in your dressing room in your New York residence?"

Thorpe took the photograph of Nancy Grant, gave it one sharp glance, let a near-by hand, which happened to be that of Tecumseh Fox, take it from him and arose. He put his fists on the desk and leaned on them, towards the district attorney.

"Do you mean to say—" he demanded in a voice trembling with outraged indignation, "are you telling me that men have ransacked my private apartments in my private residence?" He thumped the desk. "That you have actually had the effrontery——"

"But my God, we thought you were murdered!"

"I wasn't! I'm not! If anything, anything whatever has been removed from my belongings, I want it returned at once! You understand that? Where's that picture? What did I do with it?"

"I have it," said Fox.

"Keep it!" He pointed a finger at the drawer. "What else have you got in there that belongs to me?"

"Nothing. That was taken because—really, Mr.

Thorpe, this is ridiculous. We were investigating a murder. We still are. This is childish——"

"Oh, I'm childish, am I? What about you?" Thorpe thumped the desk again. "With your imbecile theories about my son and daughter and secretary and valet and people named Grant that I have never seen! Wasting time having me make signed statements about a trip on a boat and asking Luke what he was fighting about! You're a fool. Why don't you ask me who killed me—who killed Arnold? *Good* gracious! Do you want me to tell you or not? I will!" He reached in his pocket for something and tossed it on the desk. "There! Whoever sent me that killed Corey Arnold! You and your half-witted theories!"

Derwin picked it up, an envelope that had been slit open, and removed from it a piece of paper. The others sat watching him, except Thorpe and Fox, who stood, as he unfolded the paper and read it, first rapidly, then a second time slowly.

Fox put out a hand. "May I see it?"

"No," said Derwin shortly. He raised his eyes to Thorpe. "When did you——"

"Give it to him."

"But I want——"

"I said give it to him! It's mine!"

Fox got it and with the same swoop of his hand collected the envelope from the desk.

Thorpe faced him: "Keep it. I want to see you about it. Your name is Tecumseh Fox? I've heard of you. Apparently your head works, since you seem to have deduced for yourself that it wasn't me that was killed. A head's going to be needed——"

Derwin blurted, "I want that paper. It's vital——"

"Quiet," Thorpe snapped. "Stop interrupting me— Where's your office? New York?"

"I haven't any office. I live up south of Brewster."

"Can you be at my New York office at nine in the morning?"

"Yes."

"Good. Ask for Kester and he'll get you in to me. Vaughn, bring him in at once. I'm tired and hungry. You'd better come and spend the night at Maple Hill. What about you children? Where are you bound for?"

"I was in bed at Maple Hill last—Sunday night, when this news came," said Miranda. "I slept there last night. So did Jeff."

"Then we'll all go there. Have you got a car? Good." Thorpe wheeled to the stenographer. "Is there any good reason why you aren't getting those statements typed so we can sign them and go?"

The stenographer flushed, arose and trotted out. Derwin said firmly:

"I want that paper. I am not through with Luke Wheer. Also I want to question Mr. Kester——"

"That paper is mine." Thorpe looked as if he might begin thumping again. "I'll send you a photostat of it tomorrow. Fox, remember that. We'll keep the original or turn it over to the New York police. I suppose I should have done that when I got it, but I was too busy. Luke is my valet and I need him—look at me! If you insist on heckling him, you can see him at Maple Hill tomorrow. You can see Kester at my New York office, but you'd better phone for an appointment. In case you want an appointment with me, make it through my counsel Buchanan, Fuller, McPartland and Jones—Yes, Henry? You saying something?"

"I've been trying to." The wiry little man had to tilt his head back to meet the eyes of the taller one. "I'm worrying a little about my boat. I'd like to get back over there and I don't know about a bus or a ferry from Bridgeport——"

"Excuse me," Tecumseh Fox interposed. "You're Henry Jordan, aren't you? The owner of the boat Mr. Thorpe was on?"

"I am."

"Well, if I were you I wouldn't try to get back there tonight. You and your boat are objects of great romantic interest. The Hermit of the *Armada*, they'll probably call you. They'll interview you and photograph you all night and all day. You couldn't keep them off with a machine gun. It wouldn't be any better if you went home. You'd better come and spend the night with me; there's plenty of room at my place."

"I'm worried about the boat."

"The police will take care of it."

"He's right, Henry," Thorpe asserted. "You'd better spend the night with him, or you can come with us to Maple Hill."

Jordan shook his head doubtfully. "I don't know——"

He was kept from finishing it by an interruption almost as startling as the former one at the window, only this came from the anteroom. There were scuffling noises and the door burst violently open, and the floor shook under their feet as a man came bounding through. Bounding after him, clutching for him, tripping each other up in their eagerness, were four others, two state troopers and two in plain clothes. The hare kept coming without deceleration clear to the desk, the hounds at his heels, greeted by exclamations from the group as it scattered to avoid being trampled underfoot. Derwin was up barking again.

The man looked at Tecumseh Fox, ignoring the

hands reaching and grabbed him, and said in a deep rumble of relief, "Oh, there you are."

"What in the devil is this?" Derwin shouted.

A trooper panted, "Chased him all the way upstairs—a mob outside and we're guarding the entrance—said he wanted to find Tecumseh Fox—wouldn't let him in—he tore through and got in and up the stairs——"

"You're out of breath," said the man. "Let loose of me." He looked at Fox. "I know you told me to stay in the car, but I heard they had pinched you and I thought it would be better——"

"No."

"Right again."

"I apologize," Fox said to everybody. "Let me present Mr. Pavey, my vice-president. Mr. Derwin, Mr. Thorpe, Mrs. Pemberton, Mr. Kester, Mr. Jeffrey Thorpe, Mr. Wheer, Mr. Jordan. I'm going home and take a bath and eat something. I'll see you in the morning, Mr. Thorpe. Come on, Dan. Come, Mr. Jordan——"

"Wait! He hasn't signed that statement!"

They waited for it. Derwin was summoned by the phone. Ridley Thorpe spoke with his son and daughter. The troopers and the other two left. Kester approached Fox and muttered at him in an undertone, and got nods but no words in reply. Finally the stenographer entered, and Henry Jordan was given a chair and a pen, and the statement was read and signed. He departed, looking stubborn and a little bewildered, with Fox at one elbow and Dan Pavey at the other.

In that formation they fought their way through the street mob at the entrance to the building and walked two blocks to where Dan had parked the convertible. There, when he was invited to climb in, Jordan's stubbornness found words.

"I'm much obliged," he said, hanging back, "but I'm worried about the boat. I have no doubt I can find a bus——"

"I expect you can," Fox agreed, "but you won't. The fact is, Mr. Jordan, I want you around. You're an extremely important person, since you're in on the secret of our little dodge. Frankly, you strike me as a man to be trusted, and I admire you and respect you for refusing to take pay for this. But a bunch of newspaper reporters are quick to take a hint and you might let one out inadvertently. If you did and they got a nose on the trail, a day's hard work would be spoiled. Not only that, you'd have all your trouble for nothing, since you're doing this to prevent a blaze of publicity on your daughter. Get in."

"I can keep my mouth shut."

"You can do it a lot easier if you stick with me. I insist on it, really. It's the only way to do it. I like to play safe when I've got a choice."

Jordan, grumbling about the boat, climbed in the rear with Dan and Fox took the wheel.

It was dark, after nine o'clock, when they got home. In spite of the fact that Mrs. Trimble greeted him with the news that Andrew Grant and his niece were up in the room that had been assigned to Nancy, waiting for him, Fox did not go there when he proceeded upstairs, but to his own room. After a bath and shave he returned below, joined Dan and Jordan in the dining room, and helped them dispose of cold roast beef, bread and butter, a mixed salad, iced tea, pot cheese, home-made sponge cake and strawberries and cream, while Mr. and Mrs. Trimble and various guests sat around and listened to a recital of such of

the day's activities as he cared to recite. He liked that
and so did they.

That over, he went back upstairs, stopped in his
room a moment, proceeded to Nancy's room and entered after knocking, greeted her and her uncle,
handed her a large rectangle of pasteboard and inquired:

"What was that doing in a drawer in a cabinet in
Ridley Thorpe's dressing room in his New York residence?"

Chapter 11

Nancy looked at it, saw what it was and looked up at Fox in astonishment.

"What kind of a crazy trick is this?" she demanded. "Did you say—say it again."

"That photograph of you, bearing the inscription, was found by the police when they searched Ridley Thorpe's rooms in his New York residence, in a drawer in a cabinet."

Grant, having peered at the pasteboard over his niece's shoulder, snorted incredulously. "Who says it was?"

"Derwin. He had it. He must have got it somewhere. But also, he put it up to Ridley Thorpe himself and all Thorpe did was hit the ceiling because the cops had invaded his home. He didn't deny the picture had been there." Fox's eyes were on Nancy. "What about it?"

"Nothing about it." She looked dazed. "But I can't —do people actually do things like this? I've heard of frame-ups, but I never—I can't believe——"

"It's—why, it's too damned funny!" Grant stared at the picture in helpless and indignant bewilderment.

"You say Thorpe—it wasn't him that was killed, was it?"

"No. You've heard about it?"

"Yes. Crocker got it on the radio and came up and told us. He's alive?"

"He is. Alive and kicking. Especially kicking. But, Miss Grant, while it may be incredible that the photograph was where the police say they found it, it is still more incredible that it's a frame-up. No one but a lunatic would think of trying——"

"Then it's a lunatic," said Nancy firmly. "Those pictures were taken more than two years ago, when I was going to try a concert. I only got six. I sent one to my mother and gave one to Uncle Andy, and two went to the newspapers and—Oh!" Her eyes widened in horrified disbelief, and she lifted her fists and pushed them into her cheeks. "My God! Uncle Andy! Do you know——" She was speechless.

"Do I know what?" Grant demanded irritably.

Fox, gazing at her, said nothing.

"Oh—it's awful!" she cried. It was the bleat of a camel whose back is bending under the last straw. "Of all the people in the world—did it have to be Ridley Thorpe? Did it?"

"I don't know," said Fox shortly. "Apparently it was."

Grant shook her shoulder in a rough grasp. "What the hell are you talking about? Do you mean to say you wrote that on that picture and gave it to Ridley Thorpe?"

Nancy wriggled free, looked up at him, nodded and burst into laughter. She kept on nodding, bent over, laughing louder—high-pitched and half hysterical. Her uncle got her shoulder again and straightened her up.

"Cut it out," he ordered. "This isn't——"

"But it's funny!" She gasped. "It's a scream! It *is* funny!"

"Good," said Fox. "Let's hear it."

Grant shook the shoulder he held. She pulled free again and told him with spirit, "Quit that! It hurts!" She looked at Fox. "It must have been—I suppose— Ridley Thorpe. And I say it's funny. But I swear I don't remember the name, not even now. Uncle Andy was helping me all he could, paying for my lessons, and my teacher said I should have a recital, but it would cost a lot of money and I couldn't afford it—or rather, I just didn't have it. My teacher was sure I was going to have a big career on account of my per- sonality—I didn't have sense enough to know I was being played for a sucker—and he said he could get a thousand dollars to finance the concert from a million- aire who was a well-known philanthropist and patron of the arts and I told him to go ahead. I suppose he must have told me the name of the millionaire, but if he did it glanced off because at that time I didn't hear anything that wasn't about me and my voice and my personality and my career. It was one of those. If you think I'm off the key now, you should have known me then. Having those pictures taken was one of the things I did with the thousand dollars and my teacher said it would be nice to autograph one for the million- aire, and I did so and gave it to my teacher to give to him. I'll bet I thought he was getting more than his money's worth, having that picture. That's the way young geniuses feel about the rich boobs that stake them. And now—it was Ridley Thorpe! It must have been! Do you say that isn't funny?"

Her uncle was scowling at her. "You never told me anything about a millionaire."

"Certainly not. I was afraid to. I let you think enough tickets were sold to cover expenses. I guess eight or ten tickets actually were sold. The rest was paper." She touched Grant's sleeve. "Now don't get huffy. You darned sweet old Puritan."

"I'm not a Puritan."

"Yes, you are, Andy, I've told you that myself." Fox tossed the photograph on the bureau, pulled a chair around and sat. He smiled at Nancy. "I like you very much. Every time evidence turns up that you're a liar, you dissolve it with a story out of your past so improbable that no liar could invent it. And you can't be much over twenty. You should have a marvelous future."

"Are you kidding me?" Nancy wrinkled her brows at him. "You believe me, don't you? About the picture?"

"Of course I believe you. I doubt if you could be trained to lie, you're too conceited—No, we'll argue that some other time. I want to ask you—I understand that you're under bond as a material witness?"

"Yes. Mr. Collins——"

"Both of us are," Grant put in. "Collins arranged it. He drove us here—he suggested it. He said if we went to New York we'd be pestered . . . we took the liberty of coming here . . ." He hesitated with embarrassment. "I don't think I ever properly thanked you for letting me stay here—as your guest—so long that time . . . and now you're doing this just because Nancy came and asked you——"

"Forget it." Fox waved a hand. "I do what everyone else does who can afford it, I do what I like to do. I suppose you've heard me say that what keeps my spring wound up is curiosity. I've never seen or heard of anything yet that I wasn't curious about. The things that move are more interesting than the things that stand still and the most interesting moving things that I've seen so far are people. All I'm saying, I'm just relieving your mind of the notion that you have anything to thank me for. The fact is, I ought to be thanking you, because I'm collecting a big fat fee out of this. I can't tell you who from or what for, but I wanted to mention it and tell you that it won't conflict with the job I undertook——"

There was a knock at the door. He looked at Nancy. She said, "Come in," and the door swung wide to make room for the broad shoulders of Dan Pavey. To Fox's inquiring glance he said:

"Mr. Thorpe calling. The young one."

"On the phone?"

"No, he's down on the porch. His sister's with him."

"Tell them I'll be down in a few minutes."

Dan shook his head. "I think it's just a social call. He asked to see Miss Grant."

Nancy blurted, "Why—of all the unbelievable nerve——"

"I told him I'd see if you were still up." Dan eyed her with gloomy scepticism. "He'll wait if you want to take time to think it over. Now that his old man's alive and well and his cash has reverted to prospects, if you want to play it different——"

"Play what different?" Nancy demanded. "I'm not playing anything."

Dan grunted. "Call it work then. I suppose it's a kind of work at that. Providing for the future—okay, call it work. You can ask Fox and your uncle what they think, but my advice is to stay on that horse. His old man won't live forever, even if nobody shoots him. You've already got him blinded with dust. How would this be? I'll go down and tell him you refuse to see him, and I'll keep him there talking, and pretty soon you can come down, pretending you thought he had gone——"

"Are you intimating—" Nancy choked with indignation. "Are you daring to intimate——"

Dan nodded imperturbably. "I sure am. What's that to get sore about? I'm only being practical. The question is whether it's time to begin to reel him in, whether I ought to go down and tell him——"

Nancy turned her back on the vice-president, as offensively as possible, and her eyes flashed at Fox. "Will you please tell Mr. Pavey," she began scathingly, "to tell Mr. Thorpe that unless he stops annoying——"

"No," said Fox brusquely. "You'll have to control your personal reactions. If you want me to help your uncle you'll have to help me too. In the job you asked me to do, getting you people out of a difficulty, Jeffrey Thorpe's eagerness to converse with—may I say us— is a valuable asset. Hate him and despise him if you want to, that's all right, but you can do it with him present as well as in his absence. Even better, I should think." He turned to Dan. "Anyone else on the porch?"

"Oh, just two or three."

"Anyone in the living room?"

"Leo and Wallenstein are playing chess."

"Dining room?"

"Crocker's reading poetry to Mrs. Trimble. Some of his."

Fox grimaced. "That's the disadvantage . . ."

He looked around. "This is a little small and anyway I doubt if Miss Grant would let him in her room. Will you please bring him up to my room?"

Dan said he would and went. Fox invited the Grants to accompany him. Nancy muttered mutinously, but went through the door when it was opened for her and again through another door into the large corner room. Fox got the lights on and some chairs moved, and then returned to the hall to receive the visitors. In a few moments he was back with them. Grant stood up and bowed and answered greetings: Nancy was absorbed in a bulletin of the United States Department of Agriculture which she had picked up from Fox's desk. That position was untenable, for she would unquestionably have to speak to Miranda, who had been quite decent at the encounter in the courthouse; but before she had worked out a solution of the problem Jeffrey Thorpe marched over, planted himself in front of her and demanded hoarsely:

"Will you marry me?"

"Good heavens," gasped Miranda and dropped into a chair.

Jeffrey ignored that. "I'm asking you, will you marry me?" He was hunched over at Nancy. "Of course you won't, not now you won't, but I wanted to ask that first to get things clear. Next, I want to ask when did you give your photograph to my father and why, and under what circum—hey, now don't——"

But, popping out of her chair, Nancy slid past him, avoiding his hand outstretched to stop her, circled around Fox like a breeze around a bush, and only after she had the door open turned on the threshold to say to Miranda:

"Good evening, Mrs. Pemberton. I'm glad your father wasn't murdered."

Then she went out and pulled the door to behind her.

She headed for her room. At the top of the stairs she paused irresolutely, thinking that outdoor air might cool her off a little, but faint voices came to her from below, evidently from the porch, so she resumed her course along the hall. Because the composition soles of her sport shoes made no noise on the hall floor, postponing the warning of her approach until she flung the door of her room open, her surprised glance showed her not only Dan Pavey sitting in a chair, but also her photograph which he held in both hands as if it were a book he was reading.

"Excuse me," Nancy said in an astonished voice, leaving the door open and standing there.

"Sure," Dan nodded. He arose, without haste, facing her. "Mrs. Trimble asked me to come up and see about towels."

"That's curious. She told me where to get towels from the cupboard."

"Oh." Dan cleared his throat. "Then I guess she didn't ask me to come up and see about towels."

"You ought to know."

"Yes, I ought," Dan agreed. He tapped the photograph with his finger. "You see, this thing is important evidence. Fox shouldn't leave it around like this. I happened to remember he had left it in here——"

"It is not evidence," Nancy asserted stiffly. "I have given Mr. Fox a satisfactory explanation of how Mr. Thorpe got it. Am I supposed to explain to you too?"

"You're not supposed to, but you can if you want to."

"I don't want to."

"Right."

"Are you prepared to maintain that Mr. Thorpe's having my photograph is any of your business?"

"No."

"Especially since my explanation satisfied Mr. Fox completely?"

"Right."

Nancy stamped her foot. "Don't stand there and say 'Right' like a robot!"

"Okay."

"And Mrs. Trimble did not send you to my room to see about towels!"

"I've conceded that point."

"So," Nancy swept on scornfully, "why didn't you say you sneaked in just for the thrill of looking at my picture? That would have flattered me! That would have made me tremble with delight!"

"You're trembling anyhow."

"I am not trembling! If I am, I assure you it isn't with delight! And even if you came in here to snoop for what you regard as evidence, I'm glad you did because it gives me a chance to make a polite request. I would greatly appreciate it if in future you will confine your conversation to things you know something about. I am referring to the remarks you made a while ago about my—my purely private affairs——"

"I was only offering a suggestion," Dan declared. "It struck me you were overplaying your hand. If you handle it right, I don't think there's any question that he's all set to ask you to marry him——"

"He has already asked me to marry him. In Mr. Fox's room just now."

"Then you *were* trembling with delight. Congratulations."

"Thank you very much."

"I said, congratulations."

"I said, thank you very much."

"Then you——" Dan stopped.

"I what?"

"Nothing. I guess my suggestion wasn't necessary. Congratulations."

"You're repeating yourself. You have already congratulated me."

"So I have." Dan got up. He tapped the picture again with his fingers. "I'll give this to Fox." He moved, detouring not to brush against her on his way to the door, and with his hand on the knob turned to say:

"I'll wish you happiness some day. At present I hope you choke."

He was gone before she got a retort out, though apparently one was on its way, for her mouth was open as she stood gazing at the closed door. "That's what comes," she muttered at it, "of eating six ice-cream sodas in five hours. The nerve of some bassos!"

She crossed to the mirror, decided her face was too red, went to the washbowl and started the faucet running, and when the water was cold enough took a cloth and dabbed her forehead and cheeks and neck. She was engaged at the mirror with her compact when there was a tap at the door. It opened as she turned, to admit Andrew Grant.

"Well?" Nancy demanded.

"More complications," said her uncle wearily. "Fox wants to ask you something."

"I'm not going back where that——"

"Oh, forget it, Nan. Let him yap. What's the difference? We're in Fox's house and he's trying to help us. Come on."

Nancy compressed her lips, and after a moment said, "All right, I'll come in a minute."

She finished with the compact, made a couple of passes at her hair with a comb, marched into the hall and along it to Fox's room, and entered. Her uncle was back in his chair between Miranda and Jeff.

"Sit down," Fox told her curtly. He looked and sounded exasperated. "You bounce around too much. I would like to discuss ladies' gloves. Mrs. Pemberton tells me that the police found one Sunday night under a shrub outside the window of the bungalow, and one on the running board of the car you were driving. Also that Derwin says you told him they aren't yours and you know nothing about them. You undertook to tell me everything you know about this business, but you didn't mention gloves."

"Why should I?" Nancy demanded. "They weren't mine. I had never seen them before."

"Derwin showed them to you?"

"Yes."

"What were they like?"

"Yellow cotton with outseams, very nice, about my size, with the Hartlespoon label."

"You work at Hartlespoon's."

"What if she does?" Jeffrey sputtered. "That's no proof——"

"Mind your own business," said Nancy scornfully. "I don't need your assistance, thank you."

"Ha! You spoke to me!"

"You certainly are battering down obstacles, Jeff dear," Miranda told him. She turned to Fox. "I took a good look at the gloves when Derwin showed them to us." She smiled. "I think they would fit me as well as they would Miss Grant. The strange thing was that they were both for the right hand."

"They were?"

"Yes."

"Were they alike?"

She nodded. "Exactly alike. And both new, or almost new. Derwin seemed to think the police could trace them, but he said hundreds of pairs like that had been sold by Hartlespoon's, so I think it would be rather difficult."

"And one of them was found on the running board of Miss Grant's car?"

"So Derwin said."

"Did he tell you that, Miss Grant?"

"Yes, he did," Nancy declared, "and I don't believe it."

"You're absolutely right," Jeffrey asserted. "Who found the gloves? Some cop. If you think cops don't lie —once a motorcycle——"

"Please, Jeff dear," his sister remonstrated. "I didn't know you were hauling me over here as a witness, but now that I'm here——" She looked at Fox and smiled. "I want to say something that is hard to say without giving offense."

"Try it one way," he suggested, "and if that doesn't work, try another."

"I might not get a second chance. But I'll try. I want to ask first, does this—the fact that it wasn't my father who was killed—does that make any difference in the position of Mr. Grant and his niece?"

Fox shook his head. "I don't see how it could. Not if they thought the man in the bungalow was really Thorpe. And they did."

"Then they're still in danger?"

"I wouldn't say great danger. Unless something startling and unexpected turns up I doubt very much if either of them will be charged. Especially if Miss Grant can continue to explain suspicious circumstances as she did your father's possession of that photograph. It was given to him by a voice teacher of hers, in grateful acknowledgment of his donation towards the expenses of a recital. She had never seen him before Sunday night in the bungalow and since that wasn't him, she never has seen him."

"I knew it!" Jeffrey cried exultantly. "Didn't I tell you? Didn't I say I was perfectly certain——"

"You said that, yes," Miranda interposed crushingly, "but you were afraid to ask him and you didn't eat any dinner. Don't start your married life with misrepresentation." She returned to Fox. "But they'll still need a lawyer? And you?"

"Oh, yes. They're under bond, and that's unpleasant. They were unlucky enough to be at the bungalow without having been invited. Until the murderer is discovered——"

"Isn't that Collins man expensive?"

"He is."

"Then that . . ." Miranda sent a quick glance at Nancy and another at her uncle. "That's what I want to say. My father regrets very much that Mr. Grant and his niece have got into trouble—through no fault of theirs—on account of him. Not that it was his fault either, but that's his place, and that man was supposed to be him . . . so he feels it would be unjust to expect them to bear the expense in addition to the unpleasantness and notoriety, which can't be helped. . . ."

Nancy, flushing, opened her mouth, closed it and bit her lip. She looked at Miranda and said with restraint, "Damn it all. I took money from your father once, though I didn't know him. For the sake of my career, not to deprive the world of my gifts. Honestly, I believed it! Now that I'm working for $31.50 a week, I know more about money and I've got snobbish about it. I like my own more than anybody else's. At five dollars a week I could pay my share of the lawyer's fee in a couple of years. Don't you agree, Uncle Andy?"

Andrew Grant shook his head. "No, I can't say that I do. I'm not snobbish about anything. If Ridley Thorpe, with his millions, would feel better if I let him pay the lawyer, I'm willing to accommodate him."

"That's sensible——"

"Excuse me, Mrs. Pemberton. The trouble is, while I could easily persuade myself that it would be all right for your father to pay it, I see no reason why you should."

"I didn't say——"

"I know you didn't, but I suspect you should have. I don't think you're telling the truth. From your manner, the way you spoke, I don't think your father said a word about it. I'm sure he didn't. You were making the offer on your own hook. I'm pretty good at self-justification, I've had a lot of practice, but I'm afraid I couldn't justify my accepting that offer from you, except on the supposition that you committed the murder yourself and you don't want to see innocent people suffer on account of it."

"Really," said Miranda. "I couldn't very well confess it before witnesses, could I?"

"Not very well. I realize that. Or the alternative supposition that you know your brother did it and you feel similarly——"

"You're not funny," said Jeffrey gruffly.

"I know I'm not, Mr. Thorpe. I just threw that in. You'd never kill any one if you were sober. Tecumseh Fox taught me how to look at people." He regarded Miranda. "You might, though, if you were working on a problem and that was the only answer you got." He smiled at her. "Of course it would depend on how vital the problem was."

She smiled back. "All right, I did the murder. I want to pay your lawyer and Mr. Fox."

"No, Mrs. Pemberton, I'm sorry. I'm especially sorry because I'm out of a job right now."

"But why can't I be permitted to dislike seeing innocent people suffer even if I'm——"

He shook his head with finality. "No, please don't. I can assure you that it hurts me worse than it does you. I'll probably be paying the damn thing for years."

"You deserve to," Miranda stood up. "And you said you aren't snobbish! That's the lowest form of snobbishness, about money. Very well. Mr. Fox, when this is all over I'm going to invite you to dinner. Jiffy, come on home and get busy on your list for your bachelor dinner. Miss Grant—why don't I call you Nancy?"

"Go ahead."

"I will. Good-night, Nancy. My God, you're lovely."

Chapter 12

Twenty minutes later Tecumseh Fox had his room to himself again for the night. It was still hot, though the sun had been gone for three hours and from the darkness beyond the screens of the open windows came the amazing concert of the crickets and katydids, a disturbing bedlam to unaccustomed ears, a lullaby to those who lived with it and loved it. Barefooted, in white pajama trousers and nothing above them but his tanned skin undulating with the muscle fibres, Fox was at his desk speaking into the phone:

"Harry? This is Tec. What? Yes, I've been moving around a little. Yep, quite a show. I'm sorry to be bothering you at home—what? Thirty-two thousand? Do tell! I'm glad you did. No, that's a secret. Unload it before noon tomorrow. I know that, but get rid of it. No, not a thing, but a dollar today is worth a dozen in the sweet by and by. I want to ask you something absolutely under your hat, and be sure you keep your hat on. I know you do. Here it is: have you had any information recently, or heard any rumor, that Ridley Thorpe was running short? No, I've heard nothing myself, I'm just fishing. As far as you know, he's right

on top? Thanks. No, I tell you, I don't know a thing,
but do something for me. Ask around a little tomorrow. It won't be hard to do that without starting any
gossip yourself, with all the hullabaloo that's going on
anyhow. I want very much to know if Thorpe needed
money badly or quickly, or both. No, thanks, I'll give
you a ring after the market closes. How's the family?
Good. Good-night."

Fox hung up, went to the safe against an inner
wall, twirled the combination, swung the door open,
took an envelope from a pigeonhole and returned to
his desk. Unfolding the paper which he extracted
from the envelope, he bent the gooseneck of the lamp
still lower to get a stronger light.

The message on the paper was printed in ink:

"You have left me nothing to live for and I must
die but you must die first. I am ruined and I am
nothing to my family and friends and you did it. I
have waited, thinking to find an excuse to live,
but there is no more hope. I give you my word of
honour, you will die. It gives me deep pleasure to
tell you so, and it would be a still greater pleasure
to tell you which one of your victims I am, but I
must deny myself that, knowing only that in your
many frantic guesses I will be included. You will
meet me on the pavement or lunching at the club,
I still have enough cash for that, you will even
speak to me, and you will not know I am the one
who will kill you."

Fox read it, each word, three times, and then stud-
ied the whole under the bright light. The paper was
white, a sheet of ordinary sulphide bond torn from a
5×8 pad; the envelope was common and cheap, the
kind that may be bought anywhere 25 for a nickel. It

was addressed to Ridley Thorpe at his New York office and marked *personal*, in the same uneven hand-printing, with ink, as the message itself, and it had been postmarked in New York, Station "F," at 6:30 p.m., eight days previously.

Fox replaced it in the envelope, returning the envelope to the safe and shut the door and twirled the knob, muttered to himself, "It would stand a bet, but it may only be that he reads Galsworthy," put on the pajama top and went to bed.

The next day, Wednesday, started its series of surprises before the birds stopped saluting it. Fox was out of bed at seven o'clock, which, since it was daylight saving, meant six by standard time. Liking, as he had said, to play safe when there was a choice, he had decided to take Henry Jordan to New York with him, and since he would have to leave by 7:50 in order to reach Ridley Thorpe's office by nine, he trotted down the hall in his pajamas to knock Jordan up. Three efforts bringing no response, he turned the knob and pushed the door open, looked in, saw no Jordan on the bed, but only evidence that he had been there, entered and found the room empty. There were three bathrooms on that floor besides his private one; he trotted to each in turn and found each unoccupied. Men who live on the water are usually early risers, he knew, but still . . . He hastened downstairs to the kitchen and, silent in his bare feet, caught Mrs. Trimble in the middle of a magnificent yawn.

"Good morning, darling. Have you seen Mr. Jordan?"

"Good morning. Sleepwalking? No, I haven't."

"I have." It came from Mr. Trimble, who was seated at the table drinking black coffee with a doughnut. "Soon after I got up, going to the barn, I saw him crossing the yard to the drive."

"How long ago?"

"Coupla hours. I got up at five."

"Which way did he go?"

"He seemed to be headed for the road. I didn't ask him and he didn't volunteer."

Fox stood motionless for ten seconds, gazing at space, and then said brusquely, "May I have fruit and coffee in my room in three minutes? This will make me jump."

His first jump took him back upstairs. After a brief halt at the door of Dan's room he was in his own, dressing. In a moment Dan entered, in cerise pajamas with chartreuse piping, blinking but awake. Fox went on dressing as he told him.

"Jordan has skipped. Bill saw him leaving at five o'clock. I'll have to go on to New York. Take the old sedan and get to Port Jefferson as quick as you can. Phone Bridgeport about a ferry and if you can make better time go around by the Triborough Bridge. Jordan's boat is docked at Port Jefferson and I think that's where he went. If he's there, bring him back and sit on him. Persuade him. Make it up yourself. All right?"

"I'll get him. But the new sedan would be better——"

"No. Miss Grant wants to drive over to Westport to get the luggage she left where she was weekending. If Jordan isn't there when you arrive, phone me at Thorpe's office—Thank you, darling. No, that's all." Fox buckled his belt with one hand and ate a peach with the other. Mrs. Trimble bustled out.

Dan had questions to ask and Fox answered them as he drank his coffee, finished dressing, brushed his hair and got the envelope from the pigeonhole in the safe, more or less simultaneously. He gulped down the last of the coffee, grimacing at the heat, and left Dan at the door of his room. Outdoors, back at the garage, he found that Trimble had run the convertible out and turned it around and was wiping the windshield. He climbed in.

"Thanks, Bill. Private property, no trespassing."

"Yes, sir, I'll keep an eye out."

"Make it both eyes. Miss Grant is going to drive to Westport and I suppose her uncle will go along. They can take the new sedan. Dan will be using the old one. Ask Crocker to take Brunhilde to the veterinary in the station wagon. You'd better stick around. If a man phones from Pittsburgh about a bridge, tell him I can't come. Are you doing the cover spray on the apples?"

"Yes, sir, today. That storm yesterday——"

"Good. Look out, dogs!"

The dashboard clock said 7:22 as he swung from the drive on to the highway. That appeared to be rushing it, since his allowance for reaching Wall Street from his home was an hour and ten minutes; but he was calculating on two stopovers, a telephone call and a brief visit to the apartment of Dorothy Duke. While neither his life nor his liberty was at stake on account of the alibi he had manufactured for Ridley Thorpe—since Thorpe was not suspected of murder or any other crime—still, as a minimum consideration, he liked to have things that he arranged stay arranged, not to mention the fee involved and his aversion for apologies, except polite ones, to district attorneys. He had gone to the trouble of hauling Jordan home with him purely as a safeguard for that alibi and now that Jordan had gone on hitchhiking God knew where, he wanted the assurance of another look and a word with the only other person who could shatter it.

At a filling station on the Sawmill River Parkway he pulled up and told the attendant to fill the tank and went inside to use the phone. He knew neither the number nor the name, only the street address, so it took a few minutes to get the call through. But finally he heard the voice and recognized it from the hello.

"Hello! Is this 916 Island Avenue? No, this is the man you talked to through your window yesterday morning when I called to see Henry Jordan and he wasn't home. Remember? Thank you very much. Yes, indeed he has. Yes, I'm Tecumseh Fox. Thank you very much. I just called Mr. Jordan's number and there was no answer. Has he returned home? Oh, no, I just have a message for him. Will you do me a favor? You see, he's quite annoyed at all the publicity and he may not answer the phone. If he comes home will you give me a ring? Croton Falls 8000. That's right, easy to remember. Thank you very much. Sure, I'd love to meet your husband. We'll do that some day."

He went out and paid for the gas and was off again. At that hour the traffic was thin and he made good time—on over the Henry Hudson Bridge and down the West Side Highway. He left it at 79th Street and headed east, crawled crosstown and across the park, and parked the car on 67th Street at the identical spot where he had parked the truck the previous morning.

The day's second surprise was awaiting him in apartment 12H of the palace on the avenue. The same functionary as before greeted him, this time with no astonishment, phoned his message and waved him to the elevator. Also as before, Dorothy Duke herself opened the door of the apartment to him, and though she looked more rested and less pinched by apprehension, her voice was squeaky with an irritation so pronounced that he was startled.

"Come on in here," she said, turning for the rear.

"No, thank you, Miss Duke, this will do——"

"Come in here a minute," she squeaked peevishly and kept going. He followed her because there was nothing else to do, entered, at her heels, a large, cushioned, perfumed room with the shades drawn and the lights turned on, and saw Henry Jordan sitting there in a chair.

Fox stood and took a breath.

Miss Duke confronted her father. "Ask him," she demanded, "whether it was dumb or not."

"Good morning," Jordan said. "How did you know I was here?"

"Good morning." Fox took another breath. "I didn't. I was on my way downtown and stopped for a word with Miss Duke. Nothing important. May I ask how you got here?"

Dorothy Duke furnished the information. "He hitched a ride to Brewster and took a train. I used to invite him to come to see me and he never would. Now he comes just when——"

"I didn't come to see you," Jordan protested. "I came because it was absolutely necessary. I had let myself be bullied into joining in a deception——"

"It isn't costing you anything, is it?"

Fox shook his head at her. "Please, Miss Duke. It isn't costing him anything, but he isn't making anything either. Mr. Thorpe offered him a lot of money to help us out and he wouldn't take it. You understand how we handled it, I suppose."

"Certainly I do. It was obvious as soon as I heard it on the radio last night."

"Of course. Well, as I understand it, your father consented to help us only for the purpose of protecting you from undesirable publicity. Don't you appreciate that?"

"Sure I do." The squeak was gone. "I told him I did, I think it was swell of him. But he shouldn't have come here! What if somebody followed him, or saw him downstairs and recognized him from his picture in the paper? It's mighty damn dangerous!"

"I agree with you there. Will you tell me why you came, Mr. Jordan?"

"I will." The little man's tone was uncompromising. "I came because there had been a murder done and I had been browbeaten into furnishing an alibi for a man, and I wanted to make sure that man had been where he said he was at the time the murder was committed. The only way I could do that was come and ask my daughter."

"Do you mean you suspected that Thorpe had committed the murder himself?"

"I didn't suspect anything. But wouldn't I be a fool if I let myself in for a thing like that without making sure? A man had been killed at that bungalow that Thorpe owned. You and he came and told me that he didn't want it known that he was down at that cottage, and asked me to furnish a false alibi for him. I agreed to do it, but I made up my mind last night that I'd find out for sure whether he could have been at that bungalow himself. I'm not in the business of furnishing an alibi for a murderer, not even for the sake of—not for anything."

"Neither am I," Fox declared. "But I thought you

already knew that Thorpe spent his weekends with— at the cottage."

"He did," Miss Duke put in. "He knew all about it."

"What if I did?" Jordan demanded testily. "Did I know for certain he was there that weekend? I didn't know anything for certain. I hadn't even heard about the murder until you chaps came alongside and boarded me. I had every right to come and see my daughter and satisfy myself——"

Dorothy Duke, who had sunk into cushions on a divan, sprang up again. "That's not why you came!" she squeaked. "You didn't doubt for one second that he was at the cottage with me! You came for the pleasure of reminding me that you had warned me that my way of living would bring trouble! And to tell me that the only thing that was preventing trouble now was your coming to the rescue! And I wouldn't be surprised—I was expecting it any minute—you were going to threaten that if I didn't agree—that you would—that if I didn't . . ."

She flopped on to the divan, buried her face in cushions and wept.

Fox looked down at her with the helpless exasperation that is a man's first reaction to a woman's tears from Singapore to Seattle, going either direction. From behind him came Jordan's quiet voice:

"Now listen to that, will you? Without the slightest justification, the slightest reason—Mr. Fox, this must be embarrassing for you. It is for me too. I would like you to know that I have not plagued my daughter about her way of living. Five years ago, when I first learned of her relations with Mr. Thorpe, I disapproved and told her so. She was too old to bow to my authority and too independent to be influenced by my counsel. I regretted it certainly, but I haven't plagued her. It wouldn't have done any good. I admit I threatened her once, a long time ago. I insisted on knowing who the man was and on meeting him, and threatened to take steps to find out unless I was given that much satisfaction. I wanted at least to know that she had not become a gangster's moll. I was to some extent reconciled when I learned that the man was Ridley Thorpe, as I suppose many eighteenth-century fathers were when they discovered that it was a duke or an earl. I also acknowledge the fact that it is her life she is living. I have never tried to coerce her and she has no right to accuse me of coming here to threaten her. It is a relief to me to speak of this to another person. I agreed to do what I was asked yesterday, by you and Mr. Thorpe, because I don't care to have my friends read in a newspaper that Thorpe was weekending with his mistress, Dorothy Duke, and that her real name is May Jordan and she is my daughter."

Miss Duke sat up. "You didn't intend to threaten——"

"I did not. Did I say anything that would give you any reason to suppose I did?"

"No, but I thought——"

"You didn't think at all. You never do."

"Well," said Fox, "I don't blame you a bit for coming here to make sure you weren't shielding a murderer. I did the same thing myself yesterday. But your daughter's right that it was dangerous. If some bright newspaper reporter was hanging around my place and followed you here and learns that you got out at five o'clock in the morning to come and call on your beautiful young daughter who lives alone on Park Avenue—we'll hope he didn't. Are you convinced now that you weren't persuaded to furnish an alibi for a murderer?"

"Yes. My daughter wouldn't lie to me."

"Good. I'm due at Thorpe's office at nine o'clock and I want you to go along. You've got too much initiative to be left alone. I would have driven you here to see your daughter if you had asked me to. Stick with me for the day and we'll see if we can't develop a little mutual trust."

Jordan made the objection that he wanted to go and see about his boat. Fox spent minutes cajoling him out of that and finally succeeded. They were in the hall on their way out, with Miss Duke bestowing a filial kiss on her father's cheek, and then she looked at Fox and provided the day's third surprise.

"I'd like to give you a message to an old friend," she said, "but I don't suppose it would be wise to let him know you've been to see me, because he'd wonder why?"

Fox smiled at her. "Let me have the message and I'll furnish the wisdom. Who's it for, Mr. Thorpe?"

"Oh, no." She returned the smile. "If you think it's safe, give Andy Grant my love and tell him if he wants a character witness he can call on me."

Fox hoped that in the dim light of the hall the flicker of astonishment in his eyes was not too visible. "Oh," he said casually, "is Andy an old friend of yours?"

She nodded. "A long ways back. I haven't seen him for ages. I was his illusion once."

"I didn't know Andy had any illusions."

"Neither have I now. I said a long ways back. Will you give him my message?"

"I'll think it over. Good-bye and be a good girl."

He left the building with a frown on his forehead

and Henry Jordan at his elbow, went to where he had parked the car and headed downtown. But that part of the trip was fruitless, though at the end of it he did receive the fourth surprise. After fighting traffic, searching for space to park and walking four blocks with Jordan beside him, he entered the towering edifice on Wall Street and took an elevator to the 40th floor; and after consulting a smart young woman with red hair, arguing with a smart young man with bleary eyes, walking a carpeted corridor a hundred feet long and establishing his identity beyond question to a man with spectacles who, queried, would have reserved his opinion on the globosity of the earth, Fox was told by the last:

"Mr. Thorpe has decided to remain for the day at his country residence, Maple Hill. I am instructed to tell you that he telephoned your home at half-past seven this morning, to tell you to go there instead of here, but you had already left. He would like you to go to Maple Hill at once. The directions for reaching there——"

"Thanks," said Fox, turning, "I know where it is."

On his way out, with Jordan, he told the smart young woman with red hair that there would be a phone call for him from a Mr. Pavey and asked that Mr. Pavey be requested to proceed at once to Maple Hill.

Chapter 13

Maple Hill was on a height a little north of Tarrytown. There was nothing much to the mansion and grounds except wealth; it had not the twilight charm of antiquity, nor the bold beauty of a creative imagination disciplining nature, nor the dazzle of an impudent modernist playing with new planes and angles. But it was spacious and rich and everything was there that should be: curving drives bordered with twenty-foot rhododendrons, majestic elms and enormous rotund maples, rose and iris gardens, tennis courts, pools, manicured evergreens, luxuriant shrubbery, undulating lawns and a forty-room house.

At the entrance to the estate Fox stopped the car, for though the massive iron gates stood open, a heavy chain barred the way and a uniformed guard strolled towards him, scowling inhospitably. Again Fox established his identity, but that was not enough, in spite of the fact that he was expected; the guard entered the stone lodge to telephone up the hill that the caller was accompanied by a man named Henry Jordan, and only after he received satisfaction on that did he unfasten the chain and drag it aside. Near the top of the hill

Fox caught sight of another guard standing at the edge of a filbert thicket, this one in shirt sleeves with a gun in a belt holster. He muttered to Jordan, "Locking the door after the horse is stolen," and Jordan grunted, "That wasn't the horse, it was only one of the donkeys."

The drive leveled with the ground immediately surrounding the house. Fox stopped the car under the roof of the porte-cochere, at the lifted hand of a bald well-fed man in a butler's costume who stood there, and was told that Mr. Thorpe was at present engaged but would see him shortly. He drove on through, arrived at a large gravelled space and maneuvered the car into the shade of a maple tree. Five or six other cars were already parked there and among them he observed the Wethersill Special which Jeffrey Thorpe had been driving on Monday. He got out and invited Jordan to come on and find a cool spot, but the little man shook his head.

"I'd rather wait here."

Fox insisted. "You're an old friend of Thorpe's, you know. He was weekending on your boat. It would look better to the company. See that state police car?"

"You understand, Mr. Fox, that I'm not entirely comfortable at this place."

Fox said he appreciated that, but that he had accepted a rôle and ought to play it, and Jordan, looking neither happy nor amiable, climbed out and went with him.

Crossing the gravel to a path and following it around a corner of the house, they were led to a flagged terrace with an awning and on it Fox was faced with the fifth surprise of the day. At the outside edge of the terrace, Jeffrey Thorpe stood erect as a sentry with his back towards the house and five paces behind him, her face flushed and her jaw set, Nancy Grant sat in one of the summer chairs.

Jeffrey turned his head enough to see who was coming. "Hello," he said grumpily. "Hello, Mr. Jordan."

"Good morning." Fox included Nancy in it. "Stop in on your way to Westport, Miss Grant?"

"This is not on the way to Westport and you know it," said Nancy. "Mr. Thorpe's secretary phoned that he wanted to see Uncle Andy and we came here first."

"How did he know Andy was at my place?"

"I told him," said Jeffrey, with his back still turned. "I told Vaughn I was there last evening, and I arranged with him to tell my father that I am in love with Miss Grant and I'm going to marry her if I can, and for the first time in my life I've got something to work for and I'm going to work for it. And at it. I don't care if it takes me twenty years——"

"Will you please tell him," Nancy demanded, "how comical he is?"

"Tell him yourself." Fox dropped into a chair and motioned Jordan to one. "Have you stopped speaking to him again? That will get tiresome eventually."

Jeffrey wheeled to face them. "There's no use appealing to her," he declared. "She's as stubborn as a mule. That's all right, I knew she had a temper—it was when she flared up that time at the opera that I saw how beautiful she was. I understand what she's doing—she's going to keep me on ice until she figures she's evened up for that. I stopped talking to her just before you came. I was standing that way with my back to her because she said if I spoke to her or looked at her she'd howl for help, and since I had already followed her from the music room to the front terrace and from there here, I was afraid she might. What is it, Bellows?"

The butler had emerged from the house. "May I ask, sir, if any refreshment is desired?"

"Oh, sure. I was preoccupied. What will you have, Miss Grant?"

Nancy violated etiquette by looking directly at the butler to tell him she would like orange juice, Jordan admitted he could use a glass of water, and Fox and Jeffrey asked for highballs. As Jeffrey, with a wary glance at Nancy, moved to a chair not more than two yards from her, Fox asked him:

"Is Grant in the house with Kester now?"

Jeffrey nodded. "I think Vaughn took him into the library to see Father. Or, I don't know, there's quite a collection scattered around. Five or six directors and vice-presidents and that kind of muck have shown up, and they're in there some place, and that rooster what's-his-name is pacing up and down the front terrace muttering to himself——"

"Derwin?"

"No, the colonel with the chest. Briss something——"

"Oh, Colonel Brissenden."

"Yeah, that's him. They've kept him waiting nearly an hour and he's as sore as a boil. I beg your pardon. Miss Grant, I see by the face you made that that expression is disgusting to you and I humbly apologize. I *humbly* apologize." He gazed at her face a moment and burst out indignantly, "I tell you, when you look like that, it's inhuman not to let me look at you! Can I help it how I react? I'll tell you something, my sister has an account at Hartlespoon's, and she's going there to look at clothes and I'm going with her, and you'll model the clothes, and by God I'm going to sit there for hours and look at you and what are you going to do about that? Now, damn it, please—please don't! I'll control it!! You haven't had your orange juice! I'll talk to Fox." He turned. "I've got a request to make of you anyway. That photograph you took home with you yesterday. You don't need it any more, do you? I'd a lot rather have her give me one, but that will take time. . . ."

Fox raised the obvious objections, but Jeffrey persisted. It appeared that he really did want the photograph. The refreshments arrived and were distributed, and Jeffrey took a gulp of his highball and pursued his argument to a point where it became probable that he was merely trying to force a contribution to the discussion from Nancy. She sipped her orange juice with an air of aloof indifference that might have been thought slightly unnatural for a girl who was hearing a personable and eligible young man intimate that a picture of her was the most beautiful and desirable inanimate object on the face of the earth. She was doing a good job of it when her ordeal was mercifully ended by a voice from the doorway pronouncing Fox's name.

Vaughn Kester stood there. "Through this way, Mr. Fox?"

Fox excused himself and entered the house. He was conducted down a side hall, that not being the main entrance, through a room which contained among other things a grand piano elaborately carved and across another hall into a room somewhat larger but less formal. Two of its walls were completely lined with books; a third had French windows, standing open to invite emergence on to a shady lawn made private by a nearby screen of shrubbery; and on its fourth side an enormous fireplace was flanked to the right and left by more books. Cool-looking summer rugs were on the floor, the chairs were cool too with linen covers, and the familiar staccato click came from under the glass dome of a stock ticker, which was at one end of a large flat-topped desk. Standing, fingering the tape, frowning at it, was Ridley Thorpe, shaven, groomed, refreshed, himself. Fox told him good morning. "Good morning." Thorpe let the tape drop. "I'm sorry you had the trip to town and back. You had already left when Kester phoned your place. May I have that letter from that lunatic?"

Fox took it from his pocket and handed it over. "I doubt if it was written by a lunatic, Mr. Thorpe. I thought perhaps its style and contents had suggested someone to you."

Thorpe grunted. "Nothing very definite. We'll go into this later. I have—by the way, I said I'd pay you when your job was successfully completed. Did you make out that check, Vaughn?"

Kester got it from a drawer of a smaller desk and handed it to his employer with a fountain pen. Thorpe glanced at it, signed it, and gave it to Fox. Fox too glanced at it and said, "Thank you very much," as he put it in his pocket.

"You didn't earn it," Thorpe declared. "I should have offered you five thousand, that would have been ample, but I was close to desperate and my head wasn't working. Not that you didn't handle it well; you did. It was a perfect job. If you had taken me to White Plains, saying you had found Jordan's boat and me on it, there would have been a certain amount of suspicion and investigation. The way you did it, leaving me there and letting Luke and Kester be discovered on your boat with you, was good work. I admire it. I want to hire you to find out who killed Arnold.

I'm not making any more foolish offers, but I'll pay
you all it's worth. Unless he is found and taken care of
I'll get killed myself and I doubt very much if the
police——"

Fox interrupted. "I'm not sure I can take the job. I
understand you sent for Andrew Grant. I'm working
for Grant and I can't undertake——"

"There'll be no conflict unless Grant killed Arnold
and I don't think he did."

"What did you send for him for?"

"Because my daughter asked me to. Also because
he was there at the bungalow and I wanted to question him myself."

"All right," Fox conceded, "I'll talk it over, anyhow. I already have an idea about that letter you
got——"

"It'll have to wait," said Thorpe brusquely. He
glanced at his wristwatch. "Good gracious, it's eleven
o'clock. I only called you in now to get that letter.
Colonel Brissenden of the state police is here and he'll
want to see it. I'll get rid of him as soon as possible,
but then I must have to talk with some of my business
associates who have come up from New York. This
thing is making a lot of trouble and causing a lot of
foolish rumors. You'll have to wait till I'm through. If
you get hungry, find my daughter and tell her to give
you some lunch."

"It's only a thirty-minute drive to my place. I'll go
there and you can phone——"

"I'd rather you'd wait here. I may be through
sooner than I expect. Take a dip in the pool or something. Vaughn, bring Colonel Brissenden."

Fox returned to the outdoors by the way he had
come. Two men were standing talking in the living
room as he passed through, one large and fat and

florid, the other angular and hollow-cheeked, with a nose whose bridge took all the space between his eyes. They looked worried and ill-humored and stopped talking when Fox appeared. He continued on to the flagged terrace at the side of the house and found that its only remaining occupant was Henry Jordan, still in his chair. He got his glass from the table where he had left it and finished the drink before inquiring:

"Did they go off and leave you?"

Jordan nodded. "The young lady jumped up and went, and young Thorpe followed her."

"Which way did they go?"

"Down that path."

A glance showed that the path was deserted up to a bend where it disappeared around a rose trellis. Fox shrugged and informed Jordan, "I'm sorry, but we're held up here. Thorpe has to see a policeman and then have a business talk first. It may be a couple of hours or more. Did you have any breakfast?"

Jordan looked morose. "I'm all right. My daughter gave me a biscuit and tea. I wouldn't eat anything at this place. I'd just as soon not see Thorpe. Is there any chance of him coming out here?"

"No, I don't think so. He's in the library on the other side of the house, busy dominating. I don't like him much either. Want to walk around a little?"

Jordan said he was all right where he was, and Fox left him and strolled on to the lawn. Some scale on a limb of dogwood caught his eye and he stopped to examine it with a frown. It was a shame, he reflected, that with millions of dollars a man couldn't keep scale off his dogwood. Going on, he found himself skirting the border of an elaborate series of trellises covered with climbing roses. As he neared its farther end there was a halt in his step, as of a momentary inclination to turn towards a gap in the trellis; then he resumed his course. Another vast expanse of lawn, punctuated with trees and shrubbery, opened to his view; and there were two moving figures at a distance. Nancy Grant was strolling along the straggling edge of a planting of junipers and fifty paces behind her, now sidling forward, now pausing as if for a reinforcement of resolution, was Jeffrey Thorpe. Fox stood there watching them, then suddenly burst into laughter, turned and entered the central path between the trellises, marched down it for ten yards, stopped abruptly and said aloud:

"Hello, when did you get here?" Then he started laughing again.

The bulk of a broad-shouldered man emerged from the luxuriant thorniness of a golden climber and Dan Pavey's rumble announced aggressively, "Something is funny."

"Yes," Fox agreed.

"You saw me as you went by."

"Yes. I wondered what you were watching from ambush. I went on and saw them. It struck me as funny. It also struck me as funny when I saw you were blushing. I never saw you blush before. So that's why you volunteered that advice to Miss Grant last night; you were covering up. I didn't get it at the time."

Dan, scowling, uttered a sound that was half growl and half grunt. "What do you mean, covering up?" he demanded. "Covering what up?"

"Nothing." Fox waved a hand. "I apologize. None of my business. How long have you been here?"

"I got here at 10:47," said Dan stiffly. "Jordan wasn't around his boat. Nobody was. I phoned

Thorpe's office and got your message to come here, and I came. They told me you were in with Thorpe. The first thing I see is Jordan sitting on a terrace. I didn't know whether you knew he was here, so I——"

"You're going to tell me it was him you were watching?"

"I am."

"Don't do it. I'd have to laugh again. The first time I ever saw you blush. I have to stick around here for a talk with Thorpe. You might as well go on home."

"You mean now?"

"Yes. There are enough complications as it is. Go home and look at yourself in a mirror. If I need you I'll let you know."

Dan, with his jaw set square, with no protest or comment, without even any attempt to propose a superior alternative, tramped off down the trellis path. Fox, watching the broad back receding through the bower of roses, waited till it had disappeared at the far end before muttering to himself, "I shouldn't have laughed, I handled that wrong."

Leaving the trellis by a transverse path, he wandered across the lawn, back past the scale-infested dogwood in the direction of the east side terrace. Jordan was still there, with his chin gloomily on his chest, and Fox veered to the left. Continuing, he heard voices and, proceeding around a corner of the house, he came to a much larger and more elaborate terrace and saw two people standing at the edge of it, talking. He approached.

"Good morning, Mrs. Pemberton. Hello, Andy."

They returned his greeting. Miranda looked slim, cool and informally impeccable in a white blouse and yellow slacks. Grant asked Fox, "Have you seen my niece around anywhere?"

Fox waved a hand. "Off in that direction being stalked by young Mr. Thorpe. Mrs. Pemberton, I may have to ask you to change that dinner invitation to a lunch. I'm waiting around for a talk with your father and it may be a long wait."

"I'll be glad to feed you," she declared, "but it won't cancel the dinner. I'm trying to persuade Mr. Grant to stay."

"And I interrupted. I apologize. May I wander around a little and look at things?"

She said yes but didn't offer to accompany him, so he strolled off. Around on the third side of the home he chatted a little with a man who was removing the unsightly tops of oriental poppies and learned, among other things, that they did not use miscible oil as a dormant spray on dogwoods. Stopping to inspect various objects on the way, such as a mole trap of a construction he had not seen and a new kind of border sprinkler, he came to a drive which headed in the direction of a group of outbuildings and followed it. In front of a stone garage which would have held at least six cars, with living quarters above, a man was jacking up a wheel of a limousine. Fox passed the time of day and wandered on. On the other side of an extensive plot of grass was a large greenhouse and he gave that thirty minutes or more. He always found a greenhouse fascinating, but of course there were very few things that he did not find fascinating. There seemed to be no one around, but as he emerged at the far end he heard a voice and, circling a bed of asparagus, he saw whose it was. A little girl sat on the steps of the porch of a little stone cottage, talking to Mrs. Simmons. He saw her affected gestures with her hands and heard her affected mincing tones:

"You know, Mrs. Simmons, it's really *frightful*!

Would you believe it, they go to the movies every *day*! Oh, Mrs. Simmons, I don't know what to *do*! My children say to me and my husband, they say if *they* can go to the movies every day, why can't *they* go too and my nerves just get all out of my control—*Ooh!* Who are you?"

"Excuse me," said Fox, smiling down at her. "I apologize." He bowed politely to empty space at the left. "How do you do, Mrs. Simmons? I guess I frightened you too. I apologize." He turned to the other lady. "I'm just a man who came to see Mr. Thorpe and he told me I could walk around. My name is Fox. Do you live here?"

"Yes. You scared me."

"I'm sorry. I said excuse me. I suppose you know who Mr. Thorpe is?"

"Of course I do." She was scornful. "He owns my daddy. Anyway my mommie says he does. I heard her. Does he own you too?"

"No, he doesn't own me, he just rents me."

She shrieked in derision. "Aw, go on! You can't rent a man!"

"Well you can't own one either, or at least you shouldn't. Is your daddy the gardener?"

"No, he isn't. He's the *head* gardener. My name is Helen Gustava Flanders."

"Thank you very much. I'll call you Helen. You can call me Mr. Fox. Those are very beautiful gloves you have on, but they look as if they're too big for you."

She looked complacently at the yellow cotton gloves baggy on her little hands, with the fingers flopping. "They're streemly nice," she declared.

"Sure," Fox admitted, "they're nice enough, but they're a little too big. Besides, they're not mates. They're both for the left hand. See how that thumb's in the wrong place? Would you mind telling me where you got them?"

"Why, of course, Mr. Fox." She giggled. "I went shopping in the stores and I bought them. I paid sixty dollars."

"No, Helen, I mean really. No faking."

"Oh." Her eyes looked at his. "If you mean no faking, Miss Knudsen gave them to me."

"When did she give them to you?"

"Oh, about a year ago."

He abandoned that detail. "Do you mean Miss Knudsen the cook?"

"She's not a cook." She was scornfully derisive again. "She's Mrs. Pemberton's maid. Mrs. Pemberton is Miss Miranda. She swims naked. I saw her."

"Did Miss Knudsen give you the gloves yesterday? Or Monday?"

"Yes," said Helen firmly.

"Well," said Fox, "I think she was nice to give them to you, but I tell you what. Those are both for the left hand. You give them to me and I'll bring you another pair that will——"

"No," said Helen firmly.

"I'll bring you two pairs, one yellow and one red——"

"No."

It took time, tact, patience and guile; so much time, in fact, that Fox's wristwatch told him it was 12:35 when, having circled back around the greenhouse, he stepped behind a shrub for a strictly private inspection of his loot and satisfied himself on these details; the gloves were yellow cotton of good quality, soiled now but little worn, were exactly alike, both for the left hand, and bore the Hartlespoon label. He put them in his pocket, left the shelter of the shrub and

cut across towards the garage, thinking to follow the
drive back to the house as he had come. The limousine
was still there in front of the garage, but not the man.
He went back up the drive frowning, paying no attention to objects that had been worthy of keen interest
an hour before. Suddenly he stopped dead still, jerked
his chin up and stood motionless. From somewhere
ahead of him a car had backfired. Or someone had shot
a gun.

A car had backfired.

No, it sounded more like a shot.

He moved again, walked faster and went into a
jog, leaving the drive to make a bee-line for the house,
still at a distance beyond intervening trees. He heard
excited voices, shouts, and broke into a run. To his
right, he saw a man running, headed also for the
house, one of the guards loping like a camel with a
revolver in his hand. The guard was aiming for the
front entrance, but Fox, judging by the direction of
the voices, swerved to the left, crossed an expanse of
open lawn, crashed through some shrubbery, saw
French windows standing open and kept going right
on through them.

He was in the library. So were a dozen other people, including Ridley Thorpe, who was sprawled on
his face on the floor, and also including Colonel Brissenden, on his knee besides Thorpe, barking as Fox
entered, "He's dead!"

Helen Gustava Flanders' gloves had been the
sixth surprise of the day. This was the seventh.

Chapter 14

Two seconds of the silence of stupefaction followed the colonel's announcement. Then there were sounds, the little noises that men and women make when sudden shock has stretched their nerves too tight, primitive throat noises older by geological epochs than the articulation of words. Under cover of that, Tecumseh Fox's gliding movement as he made the door to the hall went unnoticed. Two women in maid's uniforms were in the hall clutching each other; he ignored them and proceeded swiftly to the music room. He had his hand on the lid of the grand piano when he heard steps from the other direction and Nancy Grant entered, panting. She saw him and demanded, "What is it? Where's Uncle Andy? He was yelling my name. . . ." Fox pointed and said, "On through there," and as her back passed from view he lifted the lid of the piano with one hand and took the gloves from his pocket with the other, thrust the gloves in beside the last bass string and let the lid down. Then he returned to the library and with a glance took it in.

Jeffrey Thorpe was standing with his toes almost touching the body on the floor, looking down at it, his

face white and his mouth working. His sister was at
his side, a little behind him, grasping his sleeve and
looking not at the body but at him. Andrew Grant had
his hands on his niece's shoulders and was pushing
her into a chair. Luke Wheer had his back flattened
against a wall of books, his head bent and his eyes
closed like a preacher leading a congregation in
prayer. Bellows, the butler, had his hands clasped
over his bosom, surely in unconscious imitation of a
gesture seen in the movies. Henry Jordan sat on the
edge of a chair, staring at what he could see of the
form on the floor, rubbing his chin as though to get
the lather in for a shave. Vaughn Kester's rear, his
back erect and rigid, was pressed against an edge of
the desk; Fox couldn't see his face. The two men
whose talk Fox had interrupted in the music room,
and three others whom he had not seen before, were
grouped the other side of the stock ticker, which was
still clicking away. A state trooper, bending over, was
straightening up with something blue fluttering from
his fingers. Brissenden barked at him:

"Put that down! Don't touch anything!"

"It got kicked," the trooper protested. "That man
kicked it as he went across——"

"Put it on the desk! Don't touch anything! Get everybody out of——"

"That's mine!" It was a cry from Nancy. Brissenden whirled to her:

"What is?"

"That blue thing! That's my scarf! How——" She
started up from the chair, but her uncle's hand on her
shoulder kept her there.

"Well, don't touch it! Nothing in this room is to be
touched! Hardy, take them all—what are you doing?"

A man from the group behind the stock ticker had

slid around to the desk and was extending an arm across it. Without arresting his movement he said in a thick determined voice, "I'm using this telephone."

"No! Get away from there!"

The man said, "I'm phoning my office," took the phone from the cradle and started to dial. Brissenden, beside him in two bounds, snatched the phone from him with one hand and with the other shoved him back so violently that he staggered and nearly fell.

"Break your neck," said the colonel quietly. It was too serious for barking. "Kester, will you turn off that ticker? Thank you." He surveyed the throng. "Thorpe's dead. He was murdered. He was shot in the back and the gun that shot him is there on the floor. Everybody here heard the shot and one of you fired it. I know some of you are important people; one of you is so important that it's more important for him to phone his office than for me to do my duty. You, come over here."

The uniformed guard, with his revolver still in his hand, had finally found the spot and was standing by the windows. He tramped across.

"What are you, a Corliss man?"

"No, sir, the Bascom Agency."

"Have you got any sense?"

"Yes, sir."

"Use it. Hardy, take them all into the next room, the one with the piano. There's to be no talking, no telephoning, and no leaving the room. If anyone gets tough, you will too. If anyone tries to leave, I instruct you to shoot their ankles off if you have to. This man will help you. If anyone goes to a bathroom, he will go along and no one will wash their hands. They will be examined to find out who has shot a gun. I'll stay here and use this phone myself."

Tecumseh Fox stated a fact, not aggressively, "You're violating five or six statutes, Colonel."

"Am I? Did you write them?"

"No, but I like them. You ought to be able to handle this job without declaring martial law. It gets me a little sore, that's all. If I happen to feel like talking or washing my hands and I get shot in the ankle, you're going to have some trouble with your own neck."

"Are you refusing——"

"I'm not refusing anything, yet. I'm just saying I like the law. I'll string along, within reason. You certainly have a right to clear this room, but it's hot as the devil in the music room." Fox encompassed the faces with a glance. "I suggest, ladies and gentlemen, that we go to the side terrace."

A general movement started. Brissenden snapped: "You! Butler! What's your name?"

"B-b-bellows, sir."

"Can you disconnect the phones so that this is the only one working?"

"Why, yes, sir."

"Do so. Immediately."

Bellows looked at Jeffrey and Miranda. Jeffrey took no notice; Miranda looked at Fox.

Fox shrugged. "Suit yourself, Mrs. Pemberton. The police have no legal control of any part of this house except this room in which a murder was committed. You may——"

"Damn you, Fox——"

"Take it easy, Colonel. I merely stated a fact. I was adding that Mrs. Pemberton may cooperate with you if she wants to."

Miranda said, "Do as Colonel Brissenden asks, Bellows."

"Yes, madame."

The general movement was resumed and the colonel was left alone in the room with his job. Hardy and the Bascom man went along, looking grim but not too assured, for the migration, without halting in the music room, continued to the side terrace and that left them in embarrassing uncertainty regarding the proper procedure as to ankles in case of mutiny.

No mutiny arose. There was murmured and muttered talk, first among the business associates, but no washing of hands. The angular hollow-cheeked man went over to Fox and asked who he was, and Fox told him. The questioner gave his name in return, Harlan McElroy, and didn't need to add that he was a director of the Thorpe Control Corporation as well as thirty others. Jeffrey sat scowling, lighting cigarettes and forgetting to smoke them; once his eye caught Nancy glancing at him and he started to get up, but dropped back again. Miranda and Vaughn Kester spoke together in undertones for a while, then Miranda disappeared into the house and soon after she returned maids came with luncheon trays. Fox ate his and the others did, more or less; but Luke Wheer and Henry Jordan ate nothing.

Meanwhile the law had been arriving. From the side terrace a curve of the main driveway was in plain view. Two of the cars were the familiar brown of the state police and Fox recognized most of the others. One was the old Curtis of the county medical examiner; in another District Attorney Derwin sat beside the driver. They were entering the house, apparently, from the other side; sounds of activity came from within. Soon after the luncheon trays had been served, three men, one a state trooper and the others in plain clothes, emerged on to the terrace, said nothing whatever, scattered and sat. Miranda, after pecking at her tray a while and having obvious difficulty swallowing, left it and made a tour of her guests, speaking to them. When she got to where Grant sat beside his niece, she put her hand on Nancy's and Nancy drew hers away.

"Sorry," said Miranda.

Nancy colored. "Oh! I didn't mean—it's just that I —please—I'm sorry——"

"So am I," said Miranda and passed on. She stopped in front of Tecumseh Fox:

"We can't count this in place of that dinner, Mr. Fox." A shiver went over her. "This is horrible."

He nodded. "Pretty bad."

"Have you enough to eat? There's plenty of the chicken salad."

"I have enough, thanks."

She frowned down at him and made her tone still lower. "Tell me. Should Jeffrey and I be in there with them? Should we let them do whatever they want, however they want? Like going through things, for instance?"

"That depends." Fox passed his napkin across his lips. "Legally you can do a lot of restricting and obstructing. You can't keep them from going over the library, but if there is anything anywhere else in the house that you don't want them to find, whether it would help them in their job or not, you can certainly make it difficult for them. It's your house."

She bit her lip. "The way you put it, it sounds— offensive. I don't want to obstruct them—in their job. I don't regard this as my house and I'm sure Jeffrey doesn't regard it as his—but to be put out here on the terrace with a lot of men in there——"

"Mr. Kester!" A voice was raised from the doorway. "Come in, please."

Kester got up and went. Harlan McElroy and another man started for the voice with voluble protests that they must leave for New York . . . that they should be permitted. . . .

"I understand, Mrs. Pemberton," said Fox. "I will say this, that if anything like this happened in my house, I would regard it as proper to prevent them from making it an occasion for a general inventory of my personal possessions or an inquiry into my purely private affairs. I also think you should telephone, at once, to your father's attorneys, Buchanan, Fuller, McPartland and Jones."

"Thank you. I will," said Miranda, and turned and swiftly entered the house.

Fox took the last bite of the chicken salad, saw two feet stopping in front of him, looked up and was facing the scowl of Jeffrey Thorpe.

"I heard my sister saying my name," Jeffrey growled.

Fox nodded. He was chewing.

"This is one hell of a thing. It . . . it's got me. This second time."

Fox swallowed enough to talk. "Your sister was asking me what you and she should do."

"What did you tell her?"

"I told her I wouldn't trust any investigator to set his own limits and to telephone your father's attorneys."

"That sounds—sensible." Jeffrey set his jaw and in a moment released it for speech. "Sunday night was different somehow—off up there in that bungalow— but this is right here in our own house. I was born in this house. I was . . . it was nice here when I was a kid and Mother was here——"

"Hold it, son," Fox said sharply, in an undertone. "You've taken some punches. Sunday night your father killed. Yesterday he came back to life. Today killed again. Three knockouts in a row are tough going."

"I'm all right," the boy declared. "I think I am. You say my sister is phoning my father's lawyers? You mean that Buchanan-Fuller outfit?"

"Yes."

"They're a bunch of damned stuffed shirts. I want to ask you something. Would you mind telling me why my father asked you to come here today?"

"No, I wouldn't mind. He said he mistrusted the ability of the police to discover who killed Corey Arnold and he wanted to hire me to work on it."

"Did you agree to do it?"

"We were going to discuss it later. I told him I was working for Grant."

"I want to hire you to work on this."

"You do? Why, do you mistrust the police too?"

"Well, I . . . yes. That's it. I mistrust them. I don't like the way—look at that rooster Brissenden——"

Fox pivoted out from his hips to shove away the table with his tray on it, and to reach for a chair and pull it closer. "Sit down here," he muttered, "and I won't have to talk so loud. That man has an ear cocked to listen."

Jeffrey yanked the chair another foot forward and sat. Fox went on, "I could just say no and let it go at that, but I feel kind of sorry for you, so I want to explain that you'd be wasting your money. If I discovered that a member of your family had fired that shot,

the fact that I was in your employ wouldn't prevent——"

"Don't be a goddam mucker, Fox."

"All right. Weren't you worried by the fear that
your sister killed Arnold? Sure you were. And now
you're afraid—don't glare like that. Learn to control
your face. Do you play poker? Pretend you didn't fill
and you're going to ride it. You're afraid she did this
too, and you think the police may miss it but I may
not and you want to sew me up. I'll tell you what I'll
do. I admit I would like to work on this and it would
be a big advantage——"

"Mr. Thorpe! Come in, please?"

Jeffrey shot up out of his chair and strode to the
door that was being held open for him, fifteen pairs of
eyes following him across the terrace.

Fox arose to retrieve a bunch of grapes that was
left on his tray and, pulling one off and popping it into
his mouth, wandered to the far edge of the terrace
where Henry Jordan sat gazing gloomily at a twig of
clematis hanging listless in the still heavy air.

"You ought to eat something," Fox declared.

Jordan shook his head. "I was hungry and I didn't
want to eat here and then this—my appetite went."

"Eat anyway. Keep your voice down. Where were
you when you heard the shot?"

"Sitting under a tree around the corner there.
Some men came out here and I left."

"Was anyone with you? Anybody in sight?"

"I didn't see anyone."

"That's too bad." Fox spat a seed on to the lawn
and took another grape. "You're stuck for a good one.
What I want to say, I regard our obligation to guard
Thorpe's little secret as still binding. Do you?"

"Yes."

"I thought you would, for your daughter's sake if nothing else. But they'll make it hard for you. They'll want the details of your friendship with Thorpe. Keep it simple. Don't put in any complications you don't have to."

"I'll try to." Jordan gulped. "I'm glad you came and spoke to me. I'm afraid of it. My mind doesn't work fast."

"It'll work better if you eat something. I mean it. I'll send for a tray for you. Keep it simple and don't get rattled."

For errand boy he selected the trooper named Hardy, figuring that he had established a little prestige there. Hardy having acquiesced and departed for a tray for Mr. Jordan, Fox ate another grape and continued his wandering to the two chairs behind a table near the wall of the house, where Andrew Grant and his niece were sitting and saying nothing. They looked up at him. He pushed a tray away and sat on the edge of the table. There was no warden within ten yards.

"I certainly pick good places to go calling," said Grant grimly.

"You sure do," Fox agreed. "Did you shoot Thorpe?"

"No."

Nancy began, "It's the most incredible——"

"Please, Miss Grant. I'd like to ask a couple of questions and get brief answers. One of us may be called in there at any moment." He returned to Andy. "Where were you when you heard the shot?"

"I had just left the front terrace, heading this way, starting to look for Nancy. Mrs. Pemberton had gone into the house a little before, asking me to wait there for her, but I wanted to find Nancy to tell her I had agreed to stay for lunch."

"Was there anyone in sight at the moment you heard the shot?"

"I don't think so. I didn't see anyone."

"Let's hope someone saw you." Fox shifted to Nancy. "Where were you?"

"Right here. On this terrace."

"Who else was there?"

"No one."

"What about Jeffrey Thorpe?"

Nancy's chin went up. "I don't know where he was. He had followed me down to the swimming pool and I was trying my best to tolerate him on account of what you said last night, but he—he annoyed me and I told him a few things and left him there and came back here."

"Weren't there some men here?"

"Not when I heard the shot. They were there when I came, four of them, I think, but pretty soon they went in the house."

"How long before the shot was fired?"

"Ten minutes. Maybe fifteen. What I don't——"

"One second. Were you here when Andy came by after he heard the shot?"

"I didn't come this way," Grant said. "The shot didn't startle me much because I thought it was a car, but then somebody in the house let out a yell and I ran across the front terrace and in that way."

Fox grunted. "Better and better." To Nancy: "That blue thing that was on the floor in the library. You say it's your scarf?"

"Yes, it is. That's what I was saying is incredible——"

"Why is it incredible?"

"Because I don't know how it got there. I know I didn't take it there."

"You didn't have it on when you went through the music room."

"I know very well I didn't. I hadn't had it on at all. When we got here and got out of the car I left it on the seat."

Fox frowned. "You must be mistaken."

"I am not mistaken! I left it there on the seat of the car and I haven't been back there!"

"Don't talk so loud. This begins to have points. If you were right here on this terrace, why did it take you so long to get into the house, and where were you when you heard Andy calling your name, and why were you panting when you went through the music room?"

Nancy flushed. "If that's the tone——"

"Nonsense. Never mind my tone, you'll hear worse ones when they get you in there. I'm in a hurry."

"Answer him," Grant said.

"Well, I . . ." Her color stayed. "I was panting because I had been running. The shot didn't sound like a backfire to me, it sounded like a shot. I couldn't tell what direction it came from, but I thought it came from the swimming pool. I suppose the reason I thought that was because that idiot had been talking, trying to be funny, talking about committing suicide if I didn't——"

"What idiot? Jeffrey Thorpe?"

"Yes. Like a perfect fool, threatening to kill himself unless I—but the shot wouldn't have made me think of that if it hadn't been that he had had a revolver in his pocket and naturally——"

"Did he show you the revolver?"

"No, he didn't show it to me, but I saw it. So did Uncle Andy."

"Did you?"

"Yes," said Grant. "When we drove up here he came out to welcome us, and a corner of his jacket caught on something and there was a gun in his hip pocket. A big one. Nancy and I both saw it."

To Nancy again: "Was it still in his pocket at the swimming pool?"

"I don't know. I didn't see it, but I had seen it, and then his talking like an idiot about killing himself— when I heard the shot I thought it came from the direction of the pool and I jumped and ran. I ran all the way to the pool and it's quite a distance. There was no one there. The water is clear and he wasn't— there was nothing in it. Then I heard Uncle Andy calling, yelling my name, and I ran back to the house."

Fox looked at Andy. "You were in the library with the rest of them when I got there."

He nodded. "I entered by the front terrace and the voices guided me to the library. There was already a lot of commotion in there, half a dozen people. Pretty soon everyone else was there, but not Nancy, and I guess I got panicky. I ran through the house out to this terrace and yelled for her. I couldn't hear any answer and I ran around the house to where the cars were parked, and then on around to the other side, but there wasn't any sign of her. From there I could hear the voices in the library and I thought I recognized hers, so I went through some shrubbery and entered by the French windows, but she wasn't there. Then you came in and then you went out. I was just going after you to ask if you had seen Nancy when she came."

"How did you know you could get into the library —hold it."

Fox slipped off the table and stood. The door from the house had opened for the exit of District Attorney

Derwin. He was in his shirt sleeves and his face was covered with perspiration. He took four paces on the flags, stopped, looked the party over and spoke:

"If you please, everybody! I won't insult you by apologizing for the inconvenience you are enduring. To talk of such inconvenience in the presence of such a tragedy, such a crime, would be—uh—insulting. We are doing all we can. Two of my assistants are talking with Mrs. Pemberton. Colonel Brissenden is talking with Mr. Jeffrey Thorpe. I am talking with Mr. Kester."

A man blurted, "Is there any reason——"

"Please! We are doing all we can to expedite matters. We would like first to have from each of you a brief statement as to where you were and what you were doing when the shot was fired. You will be asked to sign it. Sergeant Saunders of the state police is in the breakfast room and you will be taken there one at a time to give him the statement, which he will take down. Also in that room is the equipment for examining a person's hands to ascertain if that person has recently fired a revolver. You will be asked to permit the examination. You have the right to refuse to permit it, but we hope that none of you will. Mrs. Pemberton, Mr. Thorpe and Mr. Kester have already permitted it. When that is concluded we shall proceed to further steps with all possible expedition."

He turned. A man darted forward expostulating. Derwin snapped at him:

"We're doing the best we can!"

He disappeared inside. A man who had come out with him looked around and said, "Miss Grant? Come with me, please."

Chapter 15

Two hours later, Fox, ushered into the library by a trooper and guided to a chair which was turned to face directly the light from the expanse of windows, glanced around before he sat. To his accustomed eye the room, though its contents were in order, displayed numerous signs of having been subjected to a rigorous police examination. The place on the rug where Ridley Thorpe's body had sprawled was vacant. Four men were looking at him. District Attorney Derwin, sweating more generously than ever, was seated at Ridley Thorpe's desk, and off at his right was a pimply young man with a stenographer's notebook and fountain pen. At the far end of the large desk was a slightly older young man with horn-rimmed glasses, whom Fox recognized as an assistant district attorney, and standing near the door was the trooper who had brought Fox in.

Derwin said, not belligerently, "Well, Fox, this time apparently it was really Ridley Thorpe. What do you think?"

Fox smiled at him. "Reserving decision, Mr. Derwin. I only saw him when he was lying face down."

Derwin nodded without attempting to return the

smile. "I like to be prudent too, but we're going on the assumption that it was Thorpe." He picked up the top paper from a pile. "You seem to have been further away than anyone else when it happened. A third of a mile or more. Down the other side of the greenhouse. Are you interested in greenhouses?"

"Sure, among other things." Fox threw one knee over the other and folded his arms. "If you want to make it a sparring match I don't mind, but it would be a waste of time. I was waiting to have a talk with Thorpe and was out strolling around."

"You had already had a talk with Thorpe, hadn't you?"

"A very brief one. Kester, his secretary, was present. Thorpe asked me to wait until he had seen Colonel Brissenden and some business associates."

"What did he want to talk to you about?"

"He said he mistrusted the ability of the police to discover who killed Arnold and he wanted to hire me to do it."

"You agreed with him about the ability of the police, of course."

"I neither agreed nor disagreed. It promised to be an interesting job."

"And a lucrative one?"

"Sure. Thorpe could afford to pay."

Derwin glanced at the paper in his hand. "You say here that you were on the service drive about 300 yards from the house when you heard the shot, that you thought it might be a car backfiring but walked faster, then you heard excited voices and began to run. When you were about 150 yards from the house you saw a man running towards it from another direction, one of the guards with his revolver in his hand."

"That's right."

"Did you see anyone besides the guard?"

"No. From the time I left the greenhouse until I entered the library, I saw no one but the guard."

"Had you seen someone in the greenhouse?"

"No. I merely used that as a starting point. Let me put it this way: I saw or heard no one and nothing, at any time, that would help you or me to find the murderer."

"That ought to cover it," said Derwin dryly. He glanced aside at the gliding pen of the stenographer and in the other direction at the face of his assistant, a solemn owl with the horn-rimmed glasses, and then looked at Fox again and asked abruptly:

"How long have you known Ridley Thorpe?"

"I met him in your office yesterday evening."

"Was that the first time you ever saw him?"

"Yes."

"Did you ever do any work for him?"

"No."

"Did you ever sell him anything?"

"No."

"Was he ever indebted to you for any services performed for anyone, or for anything else?"

"No."

"Did he ever pay you any money, cash or check, for anything whatever?"

"No."

"Will you swear to that?"

"Certainly not," said Fox impatiently. "Not since you've made it so plain that you've found the stub of the check for fifty thousand dollars that he gave me this morning."

Derwin stared. The trooper shifted to his other foot. The owl emitted a little grunt.

"You admit it?" Derwin demanded, his voice raised.

"Of course I do. How can I help it?"

"You admit you just lied about it!" Derwin had a fist on the desk. "You admit you had reason to attempt to conceal the fact that Thorpe paid you a large sum of money shortly before he was murdered! There's one question I didn't ask you! Were you blackmailing Ridley Thorpe?"

"No. I haven't——"

"Then what did he pay you for? What did he pay you fifty thousand dollars for?"

Fox was looking disgusted. "This is a dirty shame," he declared. "Send for Luke Wheer and Vaughn Kester."

"I'll send for nobody! I've got it on you, Fox! I've got you! Unless you tell me——"

"You've got nothing," Fox snapped. "Specifically you've got nothing that has any connection with the murder you're investigating. I don't intend to tell you very much about that check, and I'll tell you nothing whatever unless you get Wheer and Kester in here. Make a fool of yourself and put a detention on me. That's that."

"What have Wheer and Kester got to do with it?"

"You'll hear that in their presence. Otherwise, from me, nothing. Nor from them, either, on a bet. Send for them."

Derwin, with the sweat trickling down the side of his neck, gazed at him truculently. But he gave in. He finally looked at the trooper and ordered, "Get Wheer and Kester."

The trooper went. Fox said, "You'll waste time if you start in on them. That's straight. Let me do it, if you really want to get this out of the way. You can always stop me."

"You're damned right I can," Derwin growled.

When the valet and secretary entered, after a short wait, Fox gave them a sharp glance to see what he had to deal with. He was moderately satisfied. Kester's pale cold eyes showed no signs of panic or surrender as their focus crossed his own and Luke's firm jaw promised all the stubbornness required. Fox started speaking as they crossed the room, the trooper behind them:

"I asked Mr. Derwin to send for you fellows and he kindly consented. A matter has come up that you know about. He has found the stub of a check which Mr. Thorpe gave me this morning."

"I know he has," Kester said. His voice was squeaky with strain. "He showed me the stub, in my writing, and I told him I made the check out as ordered by Mr. Thorpe and gave it to him. Beyond that I know nothing about it."

Fox shook his head. "I'm afraid that won't do, Mr. Kester. The trouble is that Derwin insists that I tell him what the check was in payment of, which is understandable when you consider that Thorpe was murdered within two hours after he gave it to me and that I had just got through denying that Thorpe had ever paid me anything. He suspects that there is some connection between the check and the murder, and you can't blame him. We'll have to clear it up, for two reasons. First, if we don't, he'll fuss around with us on that and won't get his job done, which is finding a murderer; and second, he'll do things to me that I'll regret immediately and he'll regret later."

Kester's eyes on Fox were hostile and menacing. "If you mean you're going to clear it up by——"

"Come to the point!" Derwin blurted.

"I'm there now." Fox turned to him. "Thorpe gave me that check to pay for a job I did for him. The job was legal, proper, involved no moral turpitude and had no bearing whatever on either of the two murders you're investigating. I asked you to send for Wheer and Kester because I know you wouldn't accept that statement from me without corroboration. They both know the statement is true. They know what the job was, they know that Thorpe agreed to pay me fifty thousand dollars if I performed it satisfactorily, and they know that I did so perform it."

"Come to the point! What was it?"

Fox shook his head. "No, Mr. Derwin. I'm pretty sure that neither Wheer nor Kester will tell you that and I'm darned sure I won't. And with them to confirm me that I did nothing actionable and nothing that would help you solve a crime, I don't see what you can do about it."

"I can have you committed——"

"Sure, I know, you can fiddle around and make me pay for a bond and all that gets you is the assurance that I probably won't skip the jurisdiction, and what good will that do when you couldn't drag me away from Westchester County right now with a five-ton truck? Let me make a suggestion: if you think there is any chance of prying out of Wheer or Kester or me any information about the job Thorpe paid me for, which there isn't, turn us over to three of your subordinates and you go on with your business."

Luke Wheer said with explosive approval, "That's telling him, Mr. Fox!"

Vaughn Kester observed, his eyes merely frosty again, "You had me worried. If Mr. Thorpe were alive, he would feel that his judgment of men had once more been confirmed——"

"Get them out of here!" Derwin barked at the trooper. The trooper opened the door, and they about-faced and tramped out.

Fox unfolded his arms and stretched. "I apologize," he said courteously. "I've been sitting too long. I have another suggestion to offer: I'll swap a couple of ideas for a little information. Such as whether the shot was fired from outdoors, through those open windows, or from inside the house. I suspect the former. I couldn't detect any smell in here. Also, the fact that Miss Grant, sitting on the side terrace, guessed that the shot came from the direction of the swimming pool, is quite understandable if the shot was fired outdoors, otherwise less so. Of course anyone who was in the house could have slipped out by the hall entrance, fired through the windows and slipped back in again. But if the shot was fired outdoors, how did the gun get in here on the floor? Thrown in, do you think? Pretty slick. It's an extraordinarily fine problem, if it's still open, and I suppose it is or you wouldn't be fooling with me. How did Miss Grant's scarf get in here? Did the murderer use it to cover his hand? I suspect so, since the examination we let you make apparently didn't get any results. In that case, it was someone who had an opportunity to get it from the seat of the car where she left it. Does that eliminate anybody? I suppose not. And who has an alibi and who hasn't? With the authority you have to drag them in——"

"Shut up!" said Derwin savagely. "You're making a mistake not telling me about that check."

"No. I'm not. Even if it were a mistake I'd have to make it, because a part of the job was the pledge of secrecy that went with it. What about the swap I suggested?"

"Swap? If you have any information regarding——"

"I didn't say information, I said ideas. For export, to be balanced by imports. I'd like very much to examine Miss Grant's scarf. Also to know whether it was the same gun as the one that fired the bullet that killed Arnold Sunday night. You must have sent it to a microscope. Information is what I want."

"You won't get it from me."

"I'm sorry." Fox stood up. "Are we through?"

"We are for now."

"I suppose I'm to stick around?"

"No. I can get you if I want you. I don't want you around this house. You talk too much."

"The devil you say." Fox frowned. "You can't put a guest out, you know. I was invited here by the owner."

"The owner is dead."

"The previous owner is dead. The present one is alive. Property rights hate a vacuum as much as nature does. You say I talk too much. I hereby inform you that I am now going to have a private talk with Mrs. Pemberton."

Derwin looked him in the eye. "You will leave this place within an hour. If it's necessary to escort you, I'll provide the escort." He turned to the trooper. "Bring in Henry Jordan and ask Colonel Brissenden to step in here a moment."

Chapter 16

In the side hall between the library and the music room, two men in unpressed summer-weight suits with straw hats on the back of their heads were having a muttered conversation. Fox pushed past them to get at the door which was an exit to the side of the house which had the French windows, but all he saw out there was two state troopers and a bareheaded man in shirt sleeves going over the lawn and shrubbery inch by inch. Fox re-entered the house, approached a man standing on guard at the door of the music room and said, "If you please. Is Andrew Grant still in there with Colonel Brissenden?" The man nodded without speaking.

Fox detoured through another room to reach the hall which led to the terrace at the other side of the house, but found no one visible except a trooper seated in the hall, and on the terrace a Bascom uniformed guard trying to take something out of the eye of a muscular giant whom Fox recognized as Lem Corbett, a county detective. Fox went on by and took to the lawn. As he rounded the far corner of the house he heard voices and found their source when he reached the front terrace. It was a sufficiently curiously assorted quartet to cause him to send them a second glance, but he was going on without halting when one of them called:

"Fox! Come here a minute!"

He altered his course. The same voice, which was that of Harlan McElroy, the hollow-cheeked multiple director, resumed:

"This is Mr. Fuller, of Mr. Thorpe's counsel. Tilden, this is Tecumseh Fox."

Fox shook hands with the lawyer, who looked nondescript except for his bitter sensitive mouth and hard noncommittal eyes. Then he glanced at Nancy Grant and Jeffrey Thorpe and asked casually, "Having a conference?"

"Oh, no," Fuller said, "I'm just getting a picture of what happened before I see the district attorney. This is a frightful business. Frightful. Miss Grant informs me that you are acting in her interest."

"I'm not doing much in anyone's interest, I'm afraid," Fox admitted. "I was engaged by her for her uncle in connection with the murder of Arnold, Sunday night." He looked at Jeffrey. "How did you get along with the colonel? No blows struck?"

Jeffrey grunted. "I behaved myself pretty well. He was sore at me to start with because I told him to go to hell the other day. He kept going over and over where I was, and why and why not, when I heard the shot fired that killed my father."

"Where were you, by the way?"

"I was out behind the rose trellis, going over my past. I could see Miss Grant sitting on the terrace, but she couldn't see me. When she darted off towards the swimming pool I started to run after her, but then someone in the house let out a yell and I turned and headed for that."

Fox nodded. "I've heard a lot about that yell, but I don't know yet who yelled it."

"Vaughn did. Kester. He was the first one in there. The other thing the colonel kept harping on, they've learned from some kind friend that I had been trying to get a stake from my father and hadn't been able——"

Fuller interposed, "I don't think it's necessary to go into that, Jeffrey——"

"Nuts. You mean in front of Fox? They took it down in shorthand, didn't they?" He returned to Fox. "Mr. Fuller is a lawyer. He sends for Miss Grant to speak to her, and what he wants is to ask her to lie and say she saw me standing behind the rose trellis at the time the shot was fired, so I can't be charged with murdering my father! That's the kind of——"

Fuller started to sputter. McElroy put a restraining hand on him. "Take it easy, Clint, the boy's upset."

"Yes," said Jeffrey truculently, "I'll tell the world I'm upset!"

Nancy put in, in a thin voice, "He didn't ask me to lie, Mr. Thorpe."

"Of course I didn't!" Fuller declared. "I merely wanted to establish definitely whether you had seen him or not."

"Well, she didn't," said Jeffrey. "Are you my lawyer? That's fine. I've got no alibi and the cops know I didn't like my father, and I'll inherit a pile from him, and I wanted money and he wouldn't give it to me. Work on that." He turned precipitately and tramped off across the terrace, unheeding Fuller's call:

"Jeffrey! I want to ask——"

"Let him alone," McElroy said. "He's upset. We

can find him when we're through with Miss Grant and Fox."

"I'm afraid you'll have to postpone me too," said Fox. "I have to find Mrs. Pemberton and arrange not to get thrown off the place. Do you know where she is?"

Nancy nodded. "Over there on the lawn. I saw her when I passed about ten minutes ago."

"Thank you very much. I'll see you later," Fox promised and deserted them.

He found her, seated on the grass in the shade of trees which had prevented his seeing her when he had looked out from the side hall entrance. He frowned when he saw that Vaughn Kester was with her, but had it erased by the time he came up to them. Kester arose as he approached and Miranda said:

"Stow the etiquette, Vaughn. Only the British dress for dinner when the ship's sinking."

"Then I won't apologize for interrupting," said Fox. "Are you British, Mr. Kester?"

"No," Kester replied curtly, without vouchsafing any vital statistics. "Did you want to ask me something?"

"Nothing in particular. I just wandered down to tell Mrs. Pemberton that when she is disengaged I'd like to have a few words with her in private."

"If it's urgent," said Miranda, "I'm sure Vaughn will disengage me immediately."

"Certainly," Kester declared stiffly.

"Well," said Fox, "I'm afraid it's urgent. If I don't say it now, I'm afraid I won't get to say it at all. Derwin says I talk too much and I have to get out of here."

Kester bowed, said, "I'll see that it's done the way

you want it, Miranda," turned on his heel and marched off across the turf.

Fox sat down on the grass, cross-legged, three feet from Miranda, facing her. Her handsome features were not now impeccably arranged; the corners of her mouth were down, her sleepy lids looked flabby and there was grey in her skin.

"Well?" she asked.

"Well," said Fox with his eyes on her, "there are several things I want to say, but first I have to ask a question. What time did you go to the bungalow Sunday night, how long did you stay, and what did you see and do while you were there? I mean your father's bungalow where Corey Arnold was killed."

"Oh." Miranda had blinked and blinked again, but had done nothing else. "You mean that bungalow."

"Yes. You have admirable control of your nerves. Under the circumstances, extraordinary. You may stall for a couple of minutes if you want to, to get your head working, but it won't do you any good. I have the gloves. The ones for the left hand."

"You have?"

"Yes. Your maid, Miss Knudsen, gave them to a little girl named Helen Gustava Flanders and I got them from her. I was starting for the house to ask you about it when the shot was fired that killed your father."

"Do you mean you have them or Mr. Derwin has them?"

"Neither one. I was afraid the colonel might overdo it and search us, and I hid them in the piano."

Miranda took a breath. It was her first since he had asked his question and it was half gasp and half sigh.

"I'm disinclined to think that you killed either Arnold or your father," said Fox. "If you did, I get a black mark, because I sized you up wrong. But you'd better go ahead and tell me about it."

Miranda suddenly moved. He thought she was arising, but she only got up to her knees, went close to him on them and said, "Lift your head up, I want to kiss you."

He raised his face to her, and she bent to it and kissed him competently and thoroughly on the lips. Then she dropped to her former position.

"That," she said, "was a feeble expression of gratitude for your not telling the police," she shivered. "Lord, that would have been awful! Now I'll tell you about it. It was around half-past eleven when I got there Sunday night. A car was parked on the road near the gate——"

"Excuse me. I want the whole works. There must have been quite a build-up. Just the essentials, because we may be interrupted and if I'm to rescue those gloves from the piano——"

"All right." Miranda was crisp. "You already know that Jeff and I had dinner at the Green Meadow Club with Vaughn, Sunday evening."

"Yes."

"Well. Five months ago Jeff decided that he wanted a quarter of a million dollars to start a publishing business. He had determined he wanted to make a man of himself. Why he thought being a publisher would do that, I don't know. I didn't know then even why he wanted to be a man, but of course it was Nancy Grant. When he found her he wanted to be able to stick his chest out. Father was displeased with him, because he hadn't stayed in the office when he was started there, and he wouldn't even discuss it with him. I tried a couple of times to talk Father into it, but it was next to impossible——"

"Just the essentials. By the way, while you were kissing me I thought I heard you murmur that you would like me to stay to dinner and spend the night, and also that you wish to hire me to stay here and investigate. At a dollar a year. I annoy Derwin, but he can't kick me out if you've hired me. Did I hear right?"

"Certainly." Miranda nearly smiled. "But to avoid misunderstanding, that kiss was pure gratitude. I think I am going to marry Andrew Grant, but don't tell him."

"I won't. Thank you very much. Go ahead."

"I was saying it was next to impossible for me to get Father to discuss anything with me seriously. I didn't like him on account of the way he had treated Mother and he knew it. Some day I'll tell you about him; he was inhuman and fascinating. Jeffrey began to get sort of wild. I got a letter from him last Saturday that scared me a little and Sunday I flew down from the Adirondacks and found him, and arranged for us to meet Vaughn that evening and see what we could do about the quarter million. Vaughn was far from encouraging about the prospects. We left him around nine-thirty. Jeff went off to Long Island and I came on home, here, because I was tired. But I kept thinking about it and got pretty mad. I got in a car and drove to the bungalow. I had never been in it, but I knew exactly where it was, because Jeff and I drove around and found it one day a long time ago, out of curiosity. What I intended to do was blackmail my father. I fully expected to find that some woman was there with him and I thought under those circumstances I could make him talk sense. You would understand that if you knew how fearful he was that his reputation——"

"Let's save that. Just what happened that night."

"I'm paying you to listen. A dollar a year. When I got there I saw that car parked and the gate standing open, but I wasn't stopping then for little things like that. I drove right in and on to the bungalow, easing along in high to keep my engine silent. When I got out and stood there I could hear a man's voice that didn't sound like either my father's or Luke's. That stumped me and instead of going to the door I sneaked around to the side where there was light shining from a window, and got behind a bush and looked in. A girl was sitting in a chair with her hands covering her face and a man I had never seen was talking on the telephone and I heard him saying that Ridley Thorpe had been killed. I stood there a minute pulling myself together enough to be able to move. I didn't really decide not to go in or decide what to do, but the first thing I knew I was back in the car and on my way out. Then before I got to the road I stopped the car to think a minute and automatically, because I always wear them when I drive, I started to put on my gloves. I had one on and was looking for the other one before I remembered that I had come away with two right-hand ones. I thought I'd better find the other one, but I couldn't; it wasn't there. It had been tucked in a pocket of my jacket and it was obvious that if it wasn't in the car it must have dropped out of my pocket at the bungalow. And like a perfect nitwit, I got panicky. Plain unadulterated funk. I sent the car down the driveway in second gear, roaring. At the gate I had a crazy impulse which seemed brilliant at the moment and I stopped alongside the parked car and threw the other glove in it through the window, only I couldn't even do that properly. It dropped on to the running board instead of going in. I started to open my door to get out and do it right, but my hand was trembling so I actually——"

"Fox! Mis—ter Fo-o-ox! Fox!"

Fox bellowed, "Here!" and stood up.

A trooper came on the trot. "Mr. Derwin wants to see you at once!"

Fox made a disrespectful face and the noise that goes with it. "Excuse me, Mrs. Pemberton. I'm taking the whole dose, at least on trial. Don't go monkeying around that piano. I'll attend to it. Thank you for hiring me. If I feel like resigning, I'll let you know."

"Mr. Fox!"

"Coming!"

He went up the grassy slope, nodded to the trooper's information that Derwin was in the library, and when he got to the house, entered by the French windows. In addition to the four who had been there previously, Colonel Brissenden and another trooper were standing beside the desk. Fox had guessed that he was being summoned for the purpose of ejection, but he abandoned that notion with his first glance at Derwin's face. It bore the expression of a novice gambler who has been dealt a full house pat, and Fox's nerves tightened into wariness all over his body as he dropped into the chair that was indicated for him.

Derwin's eyes met his. "I'm sorry to interrupt your talk with Mrs. Pemberton."

"That's all right. We were through."

"That's good. A while ago you advised me not to waste time in a sparring match. So I won't. I've found out what the job was that Thorpe paid you for. I've found what you got for him."

"Have you?" Fox looked interested. "Where did you find it?"

"Here in a drawer in the safe. It was found hours ago, before I got here, but we've just learned the part it played. Would you like to look at it again?" Derwin opened the flap of a canvas case that was before him on the desk, took from it an object and extended his hand.

Fox took it and inspected it. It was a revolver, old but in good condition, of a make he had seen only once before in all his experience, a German Zimmerman. He frowned. "You found this in a drawer of Thorpe's safe?" He held the muzzle to his nostril and sniffed. "It's been fired quite recently."

"Yes. We did that in our tests."

"What did you test it for? If it was found in the safe it can't be the gun that killed Thorpe."

Colonel Brissenden made a noise of impatience. Derwin snapped, "It isn't. As you damn well know, it's the gun that killed Corey Arnold at the bungalow Sunday night."

Chapter 17

Fox gazed at the district attorney through an extended silence. Without saying anything, he inspected the revolver again, carefully on both sides, and then leaned forward to place it gently on the desk so as not to mar the polished surface.

He leaned back and folded his arms. "This is beautiful," he declared. "Perfectly magnificent. The gun that killed Arnold found in Thorpe's safe! I appreciate your telling me this. I take it that the tests were conclusive?"

Brissenden said succinctly, "Yes." Derwin merely nodded.

Fox glanced around at the faces. They had their eyes on him like a circle of hungry cats surrounding a robin. "It's an amazing find," he declared. "Simply amazing. I congratulate you. What are we going to say next?"

"We're waiting," said Derwin, "for you to tell us where and how and when you got the gun and delivered it to Thorpe. If you want to gab a little to work yourself up to it, go ahead, we're in no great hurry." He clamped his jaw. "But you're going to tell us."

"Let's see." Fox pursed his lips. "How would you

figure it? You wouldn't figure it was Kester who killed Arnold, because Kester probably had access to the safe, and so Thorpe wouldn't have put the gun there after I got it and delivered it to him. You wouldn't figure it was Thorpe himself who killed Arnold, since in that case he would have been in possession of the gun already without hiring me to dig it up for him. We'll count Luke out on sentimental grounds. Of course there are Thorpe's business associates, but I doubt if you figured it was one of them, for it isn't likely that I would have been able to work so fast in that quarter. Also it must have been someone whom Thorpe didn't want to denounce to the police, for he had a chance to do so with the colonel this morning and didn't do it. That not only narrows it down, it makes it obvious. It was the son or daughter. Jeffrey or Miranda. So the only question is which? What do you think, Colonel?"

"I think," said Brissenden curtly, "that it isn't necessary to let you go on shooting off your mouth. You must have known that we would find that gun and that, as a matter of routine, we would fire bullets from it and compare them with the bullet that killed Arnold. Therefore you must have invented an explanation for it, to be ready for us. We're going to get the right one before we're through, but if you want to give us the phoney one first, go ahead and get it over with."

Fox shook his head. "I don't get it, I swear I don't. You find a gun in Thorpe's safe that was used for a murder. Granted that he didn't just find it under a stone or receive it in the mail, why pick on me among all the possibilities? Let's get down to cases. I hereby state that I never saw or heard of that gun before, didn't know it was in existence, didn't know it was in

Thorpe's possession, didn't know it was in his safe. Now what?"

"You're lying," Brissenden snapped.

"No, I'm not lying. My unqualified denial gives you the ball. Put up or shut up."

"We're giving you a chance——"

"I'm done. Put up or shut up."

"Let me put it this way," Derwin suggested. "We find this gun here in the safe and learn that it's the one that killed Arnold. We consider all the various suppositions that might conceivably explain its presence here. We know that you met Thorpe yesterday evening for the first time and that since then you have done something for which he paid you fifty thousand dollars. It must have been something important, because that's a lot of money. We know that you lied to me about getting money from Thorpe and that you refuse to tell what you did to earn it. We look at our facts and we draw an inference. On the strength of that inference we demand an explanation from you." Derwin laid a fist on the desk but his voice stayed calm. "You are not a member of the bar and you can't plead privileged communication. You say Thorpe pledged you to secrecy, but he's dead now himself and you don't need me to tell you that a pledge of secrecy to a murdered man is no valid excuse for shielding his murderer, no matter who it is. Even, for instance, if it should be the man's own son. As Colonel Brissenden said, we're giving you a chance——"

"Returned with thanks," Fox broke in. "I simply haven't got it in stock. You might as well give me a chance to tell you how long is a piece of string."

"You refuse to tell us where and how and from whom you got this gun?"

"I deny that I know anything about it."

"You stick to that?"

"I do. And I warn you that you're wasting your time again. By the way, I should inform you that I won't be able to leave this place within an hour as you requested. Mrs. Pemberton has engaged me to carry on an investigation——"

"That's all right," Derwin said quietly. "Developments have made it desirable for you to stay, anyhow."

Fox didn't like it. By their character as he knew them, they should have been furious. Brissenden should have been barking and Derwin should have been pounding the desk. Instead of which, he was calmly replacing the revolver in the canvas case, closing the flap and pushing the case aside, and reaching across the desk for a similar case that was lying there.

Fox didn't like it at all. He said, "You spoke of an inference, Mr. Derwin, and on the strength of it you demanded an explanation. I want to say, meaning no offence, that it's neither good logic nor good tactics——"

"Forget it," said Derwin brusquely. He had opened the flap of the second case, but without taking anything from it he leaned back and met Fox's eyes. "I didn't pretend that I had any proof that you knew about that gun or had anything to do with it. If you did have, we'll find it out before we're through and I'm warning you now that if it leaves you open to any charge it will be made and prosecuted. So much for that. We'll go on to a matter in which I do have proof."

"That's different. I do promise not to deny anything you can prove."

"Thank you. You know, of course, that guns have a number stamped on them, and that all sales are recorded and can be traced."

"Yes, I know that."

"Of course. What would you say if I told you that the gun that killed Thorpe in this room today was sold to you on October 11th, 1936, by B. L. Holmes and Company of 416 Madison Avenue, New York City?"

"I wouldn't say anything. I wouldn't believe it."

"Well." The cat had its paw on the robin. Derwin took something from the second case and extended it in his hand. "Is that your property?"

Fox took it. It was a Dowsey automatic .38, clean and new. On the metal binding of the grip "TF" was deeply engraved in block letters.

Fox nodded. "It's mine. If you're going to tell me that this is the gun that killed Thorpe——"

"I do tell you that."

"Call that beautiful?" Brissenden sneered. "Call that perfectly magnificent?"

Fox was frowning at the pistol in his hand. He slowly shook his head. "No, I don't. Colonel. I call it highly confusing and momentarily embarrassing."

"Well?" Derwin snapped. "Are you out of stock on this one too?"

Fox looked at him. "Don't kick me when I'm down, Mr. Derwin. Please. And please answer two questions for the record. Is this the pistol that was found here on the floor when Thorpe was killed?"

"It is."

"Have you proven by test that this pistol fired the bullet that killed Thorpe?"

"We have."

"All right. You've got me. Put a detention on me. Throw me in a dungeon. Do whatever seems appropriate, but don't expect me to furnish one ray of light on how that pistol got here."

Brissenden sprang up and roared, "By God, if you think you can get away with this one!"

Derwin inquired sarcastically, "Another pledge of secrecy, huh?"

"No, sir. I just don't know anything about it."

"Is that your pistol?"

"It is."

"Did you have it when you came here today?"

"No. I wasn't armed."

"When did you see it last?"

"I don't know—now wait a minute, give me a chance! This hurts me worse than it does you! I own six revolvers and nine pistols. Two or three of them are souvenirs, but most of them I bought. Three of them are Dowsey thirty-eights, like this. I keep all my guns in a drawer in my room at my home, except an old Vawter that I let Bill Trimble, the farmer at my place, have to pop at woodchucks. Dan Pavey, my vice-president, often goes armed, usually with a Dowsey. Yesterday I carried a Howell thirty-two and a little toy Sprague, but today I carried nothing. I didn't even open that drawer this morning, and I have no idea what's there and what isn't." Fox spread out his hands. "That's all I can tell you."

The district attorney looked at the colonel. Brissenden growled, "Go ahead," and Derwin turned to Fox.

"Where's Pavey?"

"At my home. At least I told him to go there when he reported to me here several hours ago——"

"Ah! He was here, was he?"

"Not at the time Thorpe was shot. Around eleven o'clock."

"He didn't come here with you?"

"No. I left home early this morning."

"What time?"

"Twenty-two minutes past seven."

"Where did you go?"

"Here."

"Straight here?"

"No. I had an errand to do."

"What was the errand?"

Fox shook his head. "I'm sorry. Private business."

"Was it the job that Thorpe paid you for when you got here?"

"That's out and you know it is. You're asking me about my pistols and God knows you have a right to."

"Thanks." Derwin was sarcastic. "Will you tell me where you went on your errand?"

"No. No connection with the pistols. I didn't have one with me."

"Was any one with you on your errand?"

"Yes. Henry Jordan. He came along because we were coming here later."

"Did Jordan have a pistol with him?"

"No—Wait a minute, let's sew it up as we go along. I didn't search Jordan, but it is my belief that he carried no gun. He couldn't have had one of mine unless he sneaked into my room while I was absent or asleep and took one. I'd give big odds on it."

"Have you given or lent a pistol to any one?"

"No. Never."

"Who else could have sneaked into your room and got one?"

"Lots of people. Any of my guests. People who work for me——"

"What about those who were here today? Has any of them besides Jordan had an opportunity to do that?"

"Yes. Andrew Grant and his niece are staying at

my house. Jeffrey Thorpe and Mrs. Pemberton were there a little while last evening, but not alone in that room and they couldn't have been."

"Has Kester been there? Or Luke Wheer?"

"Not to my knowledge." Fox tightened his lips. "I'd like to say something. This surprise you've sprung on me is just sifting through, and I'm getting good and sore. I'm not in the practice of covering up for murderers, which you may believe or not according to your inclination, but even if it were a lifelong habit of mine I'd abandon it now. I hope you don't get him, because I want to get him myself. Any one who takes one of my guns, one of my own Dowseys, and commits murder with it——" Fox tightened his lips again.

"That's enough!" Brissenden snapped savagely. "Your goddam cocky insolence! So you're indignant because one of your guns was used to commit a murder! Are you?" Exercising great control, he was barely shouting. "Good God, do you take us for a bunch of ninnies? Look here! Monday night, by your own admission before you had any communication from Kester, you told Derwin to buy Thorpe Control on the drop! You knew then it wasn't Thorpe who had been killed, you knew he was alive! You deliberately let Wheer and Kester be taken in that boat, and yourself with them! You do an undercover job for Thorpe for which he pays you fifty thousand dollars and you refuse to tell what it was! We find the gun that killed Arnold here in Thorpe's safe and though you have been in Thorpe's confidence, either that or you've been blackmailing him, you claim you didn't know it existed! And now we find that Thorpe was murdered with your pistol and you know nothing about that, and by God, all you can do is sit there with a smirk on your face telling us how sore you are! You ought to have your tongue pushed all the way down your throat and there are men here who can do it!"

Fox nodded at the glare. "I admit it, Colonel, it sounds terrible. But I don't admit that I smirk——"

"Oh, you don't?" Brissenden sprang up and advanced. "If you think smart gags are going to make——"

Fox was on his feet and they were chest to chest. The colonel's fists were clenched. The owl nervously removed the horn-rimmed glasses. Two troopers moved forward uncertainly. The tense silence was broken when Derwin cleared his throat and said:

"That won't do it, Colonel. It will complicate matters. He's tough enough, I know that and so do you— Fox, I want to send a man to your house to take a look at the drawer where you keep your guns and to ask some questions."

Fox shook his head. "Not unless I go along."

"You'll be staying here a while."

"Then there'll be no searching at my house without a warrant. I can't prevent your talking with the occupants. There are plenty there to talk with."

"Very well." Derwin was crisp. "You spoke of being sore. So am I. Colonel Brissenden didn't exhaust the list of your contributions to this case. I hope you won't mistrust the police so thoroughly when we're through with it. Men will be stationed immediately on all sides of this house. You will not attempt to leave the house or to communicate with any one outside of it; otherwise, you will be arrested and held as a material witness. If and when you change your mind and decide to come clean, I'll be here ready for you—Take him out."

Chapter 18

Fox, standing in the side hall, glanced at his wrist and saw it was half-past six. The expression in his eyes was a rare one, that of irresolution. For immediate exploration he had to choose between two trails and which should it be, a gun or a murderer? Resentment and wrath impelled him to the first, but sharp sense spoke for the second, since that inquiry had been already too long delayed by the jostle of events. A third desire was struggling for the field of his attention, but that he ignored, knowing as he did that his violent inclination to go outdoors was a childish reaction to the circumstance that he had been commanded to stay in the house.

Sense won; and since his own roaming was now restricted, he decided to find a button somewhere and ring for a servant. In the first room to the right of the hall, a small bare one which apparently functioned in the winter as a conservatory, there seemed to be no button; and in the adjoining one the need for a button disappeared. It was enormous and high-ceilinged, and still, judging by its furnishings, clung to its pretensions to the old-fashioned appellation of drawing room. In a corner of it, four people were seated talking in subdued tones. Fox had no desire for conversation with Fuller the lawyer or McElroy the multiple director, but the other two were Miranda and Vaughn Kester, so he approached.

"Excuse me," he said abruptly, "but things are happening. I know of no reason why I shouldn't tell you. They found an old Zimmerman revolver in Thorpe's safe, fired bullets with it and learned that it was used to kill Corey Arnold Sunday night. Did your father own a Zimmerman revolver, Mrs. Pemberton?"

She was looking up at him with a frown. "Heavens, I don't know. But I know he didn't kill that Arnold man. I knew my father better than——"

"Excuse me. Did he, Kester?"

"Own a Zimmerman revolver? No. Mr. Thorpe hated guns and would have nothing to do with them." Kester's eyes were incredulous. "What you say is absolutely impossible, that they found the gun that killed Arnold——"

"Then you didn't know it was in the safe?"

"Certainly not! And I wouldn't believe it——"

"Excuse me. Here's another one. The Zimmerman is an old German revolver and can't be traced by sales records. But the one they found on the library floor today is an American pistol, a Dowsey, and can be so traced, and has been. I bought it in 1936 and have had it ever since. It's mine. It's the gun that shot Ridley Thorpe. I have no idea—what's the matter, Mrs. Pemberton?"

Miranda had done more than blink; she had kept her eyes closed to Fox's darting gaze for a full three seconds. Now his eyes were boring into hers and she was meeting them. "What's the matter?" he repeated.

"Nothing," she declared, in a voice perfectly composed. "Why?"

Fox did not blink. "As I observed a while ago, you have extraordinary control of your nerves. That private talk we were having got interrupted. I'd like to go on with it at your convenience. All right?"

"Certainly." Miranda made a movement. "I have no doubt Mr. Fuller and Mr. McElroy——"

"Oh, no, it can wait until you've finished with them. I was looking for Mr. Kester. If the rest of you can spare him——"

Fuller put in caustically, "It seems to me, Mr. Fox, that you have your hands full right now, in view of your admission regarding the weapon found in the library."

"It wasn't an admission, Mr. Fuller. They proved it and confronted me with it. I am confined to this house and will be arrested as a material witness if I try to leave it. Sure my hands are full. Among other things, Mrs. Pemberton has engaged me to investigate the two murders. Is that correct, Mrs. Pemberton?"

Miranda, looking at him, allowed her head to move barely perceptibly, down and up.

"That's correct, isn't it?" he insisted.

"Yes," she said, loud enough to carry six feet.

Fuller demanded, "You're acting for Grant, aren't you?"

"I am. That's all right, I'm licensed. If I betray the interest of one employer to the advantage of another, they can take my license away and put me in jail—Mr. Kester, will you take me somewhere for a talk? I need to ask you some things that I would have asked long ago if someone hadn't shot Mr. Thorpe with my gun."

Kester looked at Miranda. She nodded. Kester said, "All right, as soon as I'm through here."

Fox shook his head. "I'm sorry, but it's urgent. It gets more urgent every minute."

Fuller said emphatically, "I strongly advise you, Mrs. Pemberton, and you too, Kester, to use the utmost discretion in choosing——"

"Excuse me." Fox's eyes were into Miranda's again. "I say it's urgent. More so even than finishing my talk with you. If a bomb's going to explode, don't you think it would be better to light the fuse ourselves?"

She said, "Will you, Vaughn? Please?"

"Now?"

"Please."

Kester got up, told Fox, "We'll go up to my room," and led him off.

If was Fox's first trip upstairs. The upper corridor was broad and softly carpeted, and paneled in wood. The room into which Kester ushered him, a spacious chamber trying to look cool in white rugs and chair covers and counterpanes, was like an oven, with the late afternoon sun mercilessly glaring in. Evidently the household routine, which must have included drawn shades on the west side after lunch, had been disrupted by events. Kester lowered awnings, removed his coat and tossed it on a bed, and pulled a chair around to face the one Fox had taken.

"When," he demanded, "did Mrs. Pemberton engage you to investigate this?"

"Outdoors a while ago." Fox got up to remove his coat too, and sat again. "We have a lot of ground to cover, Mr. Kester, and we'll have to cut corners and move fast. Are you on their list of suspects, or have you an alibi?"

"I have no alibi." It was astonishing how chilly the secretary's eyes could look in that furnace of a room.

"Colonel Brissenden's interview with Mr. Thorpe had just ended, and I had escorted him from the library and turned him over to Bellows to let him out the back way, the shortest way to his car. At the moment I heard the shot I was in the conservatory, on my way to get Mr. McElroy and the others, thinking they were on the front terrace. The sound of the shot paralyzed me. I am not a man of action. Then I started to run back to the library, and caught my foot in the rug in the hall and fell. I scrambled up and went on. Mr. Thorpe was there on the floor, on his face, and as I stood there staring at him a second, unable to move, there was a convulsive twitch to his legs and then he was still. My next action was to pay you a compliment."

"Thank you very much. What was it?"

"I yelled for you. I yelled your name several times." The twist on the secretary's lips was presumably a smile. "I suppose I had been impressed by your handling of the job you had done for Mr. Thorpe."

"We were pretty lucky on that. What direction did the sound come from? I mean the shot."

"I don't know. Of course I've reflected on it and have been questioned. I can't say."

"Did it sound as if it were fired in the open or in a confined space? Outdoors or in the house?"

"I can't say that either. I've never heard a shot fired in a house. It sounded loud and close by."

"Was there any smoke in the side hall? Or a sour smell? You know the smell."

"I didn't notice any. Colonel Brissenden says that the position of the body indicates that the shot was fired from the direction of the French windows."

"Maybe and maybe not. He might have done a spin after it hit him. Who got there first after you?"

"Grant did. Then Bellows, and after him Brissenden. Then one of the gardeners came in through the French windows and Henry Jordan was right behind him. After that I don't know, they came in a rush from all directions."

"Was that blue scarf there on the floor when you first entered?"

"I don't know when I saw it first. I didn't even see the gun until I saw Grant looking at it and Brissenden telling him not to touch it—Speaking of guns, I'd like to ask a question."

Fox nodded at the colorless eyes that looked as if nothing would ever make them blink. "Go ahead."

"Who told you that the gun that killed Arnold was found in the library safe?"

"Derwin."

"It's incredible. Absolutely incredible. Do you suppose there's any chance that he planted it there?"

"No. None of them. They found it there all right. Who has the combination of the safe?"

"Mr. Thorpe and I, and that's all. That's why I say it's incredible. I haven't opened it for over a week until this morning, to get the checkbook. I know I didn't put that gun in there and to suppose that Mr. Thorpe did. . . ."

"He must have."

"He couldn't have. Where did he get it?"

"I don't know. According to Derwin and Brissenden, I got it and gave it to him, and that's what he paid me that check for. They call it a strong inference, which shows how careful you have to be with inferences. Nothing would be easier, for instance, than to build up a strong inference that it was you who killed both Thorpe and Arnold. Sunday night you sneaked out of the Green Meadow Club, drove to the bunga-

low, fired through the window and were back at the
clubhouse in bed by the time the police phoned to
notify you. Your motive was obvious. You knew that
Thorpe Control would drop forty points or more at
the news of Thorpe's death and jump back up again at
the news he was alive. If you could swing a buy of, say
ten thousand shares, that would make a profit of four
hundred thousand dollars. Not bad at all. That's why
you didn't make an effective search for Thorpe on Jordan's boat Monday morning, to allow time for the
market——"

Kester's expression had exhibited no change
whatever, but he interrupted indignantly: "He wasn't
on Jordan's boat! I went straight to the cottage where
he was!"

"Sure." Fox nodded. "I know that, but the police
don't. I'm building up an inference for them. But even
for me that doesn't weaken it any. You went straight
to Thorpe and stayed right with him, to make sure he
wouldn't disclose himself too soon. You were sure he
wouldn't anyway, knowing as you did how devoted
he was to his reputation."

Kester's lips were twisted again for their substi-
tute for a smile. "And then," he said sarcastically, "I
carried the gun around in my pocket for two days and
put it away in Mr. Thorpe's safe."

"Oh, no. That would have been dumb. Somehow—
this is a detail to be cleared up—Thorpe got hold of
the gun and knew it was yours, and threatened to
turn you over to the police. We have to have it that
way to give you a motive for killing Thorpe. When
you returned to the library after turning Brissenden
over to Bellows, you stepped outside the French windows, fired from there, entered the house by the side
hall, fell down to pretend you had tripped on the rug if

any one appeared at that moment, got up and re-entered the library, and yelled for me. As it happened, you see, your yelling for me wasn't a compliment at all, it was an insult. I resent it!"

"You can't possibly——" Kester's blue eyes were staring wide. "You can't—why—it was your gun that shot him! Where did I get your gun?"

"Just a detail." Fox waved it aside. "That and Miss Grant's scarf, which you used to protect your hand from powder marks. If this were anything but an idle inference, little things like that wouldn't trouble us much."

"I thought," Kester observed stiffly, "that you said we had a lot of ground to cover. You told Mrs. Pemberton it was urgent. If you wish from me a categorical denial that I am guilty of murder, you may have it. I am not. I am here to answer your questions at the request of Mrs. Pemberton——"

"All right," Fox conceded. "No more idle inferences. Let's have some facts. What about that bunch of directors and vice-presidents? Do they alibi each other? Were they in a huddle somewhere when they heard the shot?"

"I don't know, except McElroy. He told me he was in the bathroom on the other side of the music room. I don't know where the others were, but I suppose they were together, since Derwin let them go back to town."

"Probably, but we won't forget they were here." Fox pulled at his ear. "There was something—Oh, yes. That threatening letter Thorpe received, which I returned to him this morning. Had you seen it before?"

"Certainly. I open his personal mail."

"You read that even before he did, then?"

"Yes."

"Did anything about it strike you as odd?"

"Odd? Certainly. The whole thing—I would certainly call it odd."

"No, I mean something special. Some particular detail."

Kester shook his head. "No. No particular detail. What do you mean?"

"We'll pass it for the moment. Where were you born?"

"I fail to see," said Kester dryly, "any connection between an oddity in a threatening anonymous letter received by Mr. Thorpe and the place of my birth. I was born in Salisbury, Vermont."

"Where did you go to school?"

Kester stood up. "This is absurd. I am perfectly willing to furnish any information that may be helpful, since Mrs. Pemberton asked me to, but these inane and irrelevant——"

"You're wrong," said Fox curtly. "Please sit down. These are the questions I wanted to ask Thorpe as soon as I read that letter yesterday. Now he's dead and I have to ask you. I'm not going to tell you why they're relevant, but you can take it from me they are. Where did you go to school?"

Kester was frowning. "Do you mean this?"

"I do."

He sat down. "I attended public school at Salisbury to the tenth year. My family moved to Springfield, Massachusetts, and I got the last two years of high school there. I then went to Dartmouth and graduated in four years."

"Have you spent any time in Canada?"

"None."

"Been abroad?"

"Once, in the summer of 1929, for two months."

"Thank you very much. Do you happen to know where Luke Wheer was born?"

"Yes. Macon, Georgia. His people still live there. Mr. Thorpe sent them a gift every Christmas."

"He was a remarkable man. Since Luke was with Thorpe for over twenty years, he couldn't have spent much time in—the British Isles, for instance. Could he?"

"Very little. He has been there a few times with Mr. Thorpe on short trips."

"But not every year for the shooting or anything like that."

"Oh, no."

"Well, that's two of you. Now for the son and daughter. Or rather, their mother first. Was she an American, do you know?"

"Yes. You understand, Fox, this is simply ridiculous. By no stretch of the imagination——"

"Don't try it. Take my word for it, I'm being practical and sticking to the point. Mrs. Thorpe was born in this country?"

"Yes. I prepared a biographical sketch of her. You seem to be interested in Great Britain. She was there only once or twice. She didn't go abroad much, and when she did she spent her time in France or Italy."

"How about the children's governess—Jandorf who took Jeffrey to the zoo, and Lefcourt who took him to the aquarium? Do you know anything about them?"

"Not a thing. That was before my time."

"Where did they go to school?"

"Private schools here in the east and preps. Miranda graduated from Sarah Lawrence and Jeffrey went to Harvard for three years but didn't graduate."

"Have they been to England much?"

"Miranda never, I'm sure, and Jeffrey, I think, twice."

"Thank you very much." Fox leaned forward and grimaced as he felt his shirt sticking to his back. "Now here's something I can't do because I'm incommunicado. I could bust loose by getting arrested and arranging bond, but that takes time. About these business associates that were here today, we need to know whether any of them is or was English, or was educated in England or Canada or Australia, or has spent a considerable amount of time there."

"Maybe you need to know that. I don't."

"I do. Will you get on the phone and find out? You shouldn't have much trouble; they're all prominent men. There's no concealment about it; it doesn't matter if Derwin's sitting at your elbow." Fox stood up. "Will you do it?"

"The whole thing sounds preposterous."

"Sure it does. Will you do it?"

"Yes."

"Good. One other thing, have you had, or do you have, any definite suspicion about the writer of that letter?"

"No. Mr. Thorpe was an able and realistic businessman and financier. I suppose there are thousands of men who could persuade themselves that they are his victims."

"You put that very nicely." Fox picked up his coat. "That inference I built up, don't start worrying about it until I find out how you got hold of Miss Grant's scarf and my gun."

Chapter 19

Bellows, still trying heroically to look like a bald well-fed butler in spite of the appalling combination of heat and sudden death, stood erect before the employer who would pay the current month's wages and nodded to her questions.

"Yes, madame, I agree. An alfresco meal always has an air of festivity, or should have. I can put fans in the dining room."

"I think that will be better," Miranda said. "I have spoken with Mr. Derwin. There will be four to serve in the library: Mr. Derwin and his assistant, Colonel Brissenden and someone, I think a police inspector, who just arrived from New York. There will be ten or more who will eat in your quarters; you can learn the exact number from Colonel Brissenden. Since Mr. McElroy is staying, nine will be at table. My father's chair will be placed as always and will be left vacant; my brother will sit at his usual place."

"Yes, madame. Shall I serve at eight o'clock?"

"You might as well." Miranda glanced at her wrist. "That will be in forty minutes. It must be a comfort to you to know that there will be no late arrivals; the guests are already here."

"Yes, madame. If you will please allow me to request you in advance to make allowances for any
irregularities. I just overheard Redmond telling Fol-
som that she was sure she would drop something on
account of one of the persons at table being a murderer."

"I promise in advance to overlook it. I may even
drop something myself."

"Yes, madame."

Miranda left him. Her passage through the dining
room interrupted a conversation through an open
window between Redmond on the inside and a gardener without. In the west hall a muscular giant
seated on a newspaper which he had spread on a Per-
sian musnud hastily covered a yawn with a gigantic
paw at the sight of her. Through the screened entrance she could see a trooper standing at the edge of
the terrace in the shade of a trellis, talking with
Henry Jordan, her father's boating friend whom she
had never heard of before. She went on to the drawing room, saw Andrew Grant and Tecumseh Fox
there in a corner, stood hesitant a moment with her
lips compressed and went over to them.

She addressed Fox: "We can finish that talk now if
you want to."

He regarded her a moment and shook his head.
"No, thank you. With that expression of hardihood in
your eyes it wouldn't do any good. Anyhow, I'm starting for that gun from the other end."

"You were mistaken when——"

"No, I wasn't. Excuse me. I have a little errand——"

He started off, but turned to her voice behind him:
"You are invited to dinner. We'll eat at eight

o'clock in the dining room. Bellows will show you to a room upstairs if you want to comb your hair."

"Thank you very much."

Fox went. Miranda slanted her eyes up at Grant and said, "If he ever gets married I pity his wife. One look at her eyes and he'll know to a cent how much she's chiseling on the household allowance. You're an old friend of his, aren't you?"

Grant nodded. "Using friend as a euphemism, yes. I lived at his place for several months about three years ago. A sort of charity guest. I was intending to get started on the beginning of a tentative synopsis for a book."

"Oh. Are you a writer?"

"I am a delitescent writer."

"What does that mean?"

"It means that I didn't start the book. I have made a living writing advertising for the past three years, but as some forty million people are now aware, I lost my job."

"I'm trying to talk about something else for five minutes. At least you aren't wandering around your own house, seeing district attorneys and policemen and detectives wherever you look. It's impossible for me to know what it means to lose a job, to have any idea what the feeling is like, because I never had a job. What are you going to do now? When this is over?"

He shrugged. "Look for another one. This time, if I can get it, in a publisher's office. I ought to be a publisher."

She stared. "What for? To make a man of yourself?"

"Lord no. Where did you get that idea?"

"From my brother. Why should you be a publisher?"

"To make money. To mount the ladder of success. The best and most successful publishers are writers who are too lazy to write. That's me."

"Would you be a good publisher?"

"Marvelous. If I ever got started at it—and if I got out of this beastly mess—I beg your pardon. . . ."

"For what? I would call it worse than beastly. I have done something fairly beastly myself. When I came up just now was your friend Mr. Fox telling you about the gloves?"

"Gloves? No." Grant frowned down at her. "What gloves?"

"I supposed he was." Miranda frowned back. "I have a confession to make to you and your niece, but not right now. I played a dirty trick on her, only at the time I didn't know it was her. I'm hoping for forgiveness and that's why I'm trying to make a good impression on you, which under the circumstances is darned difficult. I'm not a glamour girl, but I can fry eggs, and once when I was in a bathing suit at Palm Beach a man looked at me twice."

"I don't like eggs much."

"Then I can fry potatoes. If you'd like a room and a shower, come along upstairs."

As they disappeared through the door to the main hall, Nancy Grant entered at the other end of the room from the front terrace. She looked comparatively cool, but not very fresh, since she was wearing the same skirt and blouse she had had on when escaping from the window of the courthouse Monday morning. She looked around and saw no one, stood undecided, and finally went and stretched herself out on an upholstered bench in front of an open window, with her eyes closed. A few minutes later she opened them, hearing steps, and saw Jeffrey Thorpe approaching. He looked fresh but not cool and certainly not festive.

"I was looking for you," he said.

She said nothing.

"My sister asked me to find you. We'll eat in the dining room in a quarter of an hour. Your uncle's upstairs taking a shower. If you'd like to have one I'll show you a room."

Nancy shook her head. "No, thank you. I just had a shower."

"May I ask where?"

"In a dressing room at the swimming pool."

"What did you go down there for?"

"To take a shower."

"And then walked all the way back?"

"I saw no other way of getting back. I came by degrees."

"You should have——" Jeffrey stopped. "No. There's no should about it. You're here only because you can't help it." He was scowling. "Damn it, you're talking to me."

"Not with any great enthusiasm." Nancy sat up, removed her legs from the bench and adjusted her skirt. "Since I'm talking to you, I might as well say something. I've heard you say twice that I hate you. That isn't true. That time at the opera you were arrogant and offensive, you acted like a brainless imbecile, and you helped to place me in a humiliating and embarrassing situation. I don't hate you at all. I simply have no use for you."

"I don't believe it."

She looked up at him indignantly. "May I ask why you don't believe it?"

"Because I don't want to and because I've been thinking about it." His scowl deepened. "The kind of collisions here have been between you and me and aren't the kind that produce that state of mind. They have thrown out sparks. I have never seen so many sparks in so short a space of time as you produced that night last winter."

He straddled the bench facing her. "You might suppose that the decent thing to do, with my father killed only six hours ago and me suspected by some people of killing him, would be to keep my mouth shut. But how do I know what's going to happen? How do I know but what before the night's out I'll actually be charged with murder and put in jail? I wish I could tell you what's been going on in my head this afternoon. I've been remembering days when my mother was still here and the way my father treated her, and working up a hatred for him that I never felt when he was alive, and then the realization would come that he's dead now too, and I would remember the things he did for me. He did do things for me, no doubt of that, and I tried to go over it all and decide whether I was as bum an excuse for a son as he was for a father. I decided that I probably was. But in the middle of thoughts like that would come thoughts about you."

He put out a hand, but she drew away and he let it fall to the bench. "Another reason why I don't believe that you simply have no use for me. If that's the way you really feel, you would have told what's-his-name about seeing a gun in my pocket this morning. I know you didn't tell him, because if you had——"

"How did you——" Nancy was looking at him. She looked away again. "How did you know I saw the gun?"

"I heard what your uncle said to you. That's another thing. He didn't tell either, so you must have asked him not to."

"I didn't! He suggested it himself, that we should mind our own business. And I did tell Mr. Fox. I—I didn't mean to, but it was out before I knew it."

"When did you tell him?"

"When we were all sitting out on the terrace. Soon after they called you into the house."

"That doesn't matter anyway. Your profile is the most beautiful . . . absolutely the most beautiful . . ." His voice began to tremble and he gave it up. "Fox knows that there isn't a chance in the world that I killed my father."

"How does he know that?"

"Because he knows people and he knows how much I'm in love with you, and he knows that in the condition I'm in I'm about as murderous as a butterfly, unless it was someone between you and me—Yes, Bellows?"

"Mrs. Pemberton sent me, sir. The gong sounded some minutes ago."

"I didn't hear it." Jeffrey got off the bench and faced Nancy. "If you'd rather not go in with me, follow Bellows. I'll be in in a minute."

Before the cold consommé had been finished, Miranda was feeling that it had been a mistake to tell Bellows that her father's chair should be left in its accustomed place, vacant. Not that she had any idea that without it the occasion might have been one of merriment, but after all people eating at one's table are one's guests, no matter what circumstances collected them, and the ostentatious broad back of that empty chair seemed a calculated reproach to them and a deliberate solicitation of gloom. As the cold meats were being served, she murmured something of that sort to Andrew Grant on her right and to her astonishment he replied that he hadn't noticed it.

The meal dragged along under the buzz of the electric fans. Certainly no one was endeavoring to prolong it for the sake of conviviality, but then no one was in a hurry to finish in order to do something else. There was nothing to do. The continued presence of the authorities made it probable that another campaign of questioning was in preparation; they all knew that the famous Inspector Damon of the New York police had arrived and was in the library. Dusk deepened in the room and, as the sherbet and raspberries were served, Bellows switched on the lights. The desultory and intermittent mutterings of conversation continued; there was nothing to talk about, since no one tried to talk of the only thing in their minds. The state of their nerves, their readiness to be startled by any incident whatever, was displayed when Tecumseh Fox addressed Miranda across the table, necessarily raising his voice above the fans:

"May I say something, Mrs. Pemberton? I'd like to play a game."

Eight pairs of eyes jerked to him. Miranda raised her brows: "A game?"

"Yes. Call it that." Fox signaled to Bellows, and the butler got something from a buffet and approached with it. "I'm going to ask you all to join in, if you don't mind." He took the tray from Bellows and nodded thanks and sent a swift glance around the table: Miranda and Grant, Jeffrey and McElroy, Kester and Fuller, Nancy and Henry Jordan. "This may seem frivolous to you, but it won't hurt you any. I have here eight pads of paper and eight pencils. I'm going to pass them around and ask each of you to write something, all of you the same thing, which I'll dictate, and sign your names for identification. I hope you'll have no objection, Mrs. Pemberton, since——"

"Whether I sign my name or not," put in Fuller dryly, "depends on what you ask me to write."

"Perfectly harmless." Fox smiled at him. "Just a pledge of our forefathers, a sentence of the Declaration of Independence of the United States of America. Bellows, if you will please hand the pads and pencils around——"

The butler took them, but instead of distributing them, he suddenly stiffened and stood rigid as the sound of peremptory shouts came in at the windows, apparently at some distance, and then jerked around as the explosion of a gunshot shattered the air. Everybody else jerked with him; and Redmond, crossing with a tray of iced tea, let it drop to the floor without even making a grab, and pierced the already offended air with a bloodcurdling scream.

Chapter 20

W hen, two seconds later, men came running in from the west hall, Redmond was sitting on the floor in a puddle of iced tea and broken glass, still screaming, every one had got to their feet, Jeffrey overturning his chair, Henry Jordan was white and trembling all over, Miranda was clutching Andrew Grant's arm, McElroy the multiple director was backing to the wall. . . .

"What—who——" Colonel Brissenden was yelling.

Fox yelled back, to top the screams, "Outdoors! Nobody's hurt in here! Outdoors!"

Brissenden barked an order and two troopers whirled and disappeared. He barked again and the muscular giant from the hall picked up Redmond, still screaming hysterically, like a bag of cotton, and carried her out. Derwin was gesticulating and trying to say something to a man with a prize-fighter's jaw and the morose eyes of a pessimistic poet, who, instead of listening, was looking. He strode across:

"Hello, Fox. Shot fired outdoors?"

"Hello, Inspector. Yes."

"Bullet didn't come in here?"

"Nobody saw it or felt it."

Inspector Damon nodded. "We were in the library, the other side of the house, and couldn't tell." He turned. "Here's something coming——"

The something was bellicose voices, upraised, from the darkness outdoors. They became fainter rounding the corner of the house. Brissenden trotted out. The voices, mingling with others, were heard again from the hall and at the sound of one of them Tecumseh Fox started for the door. But before he reached it the influx arrived. Two troopers entered, one on each side of a broad-shouldered square-faced man who was holding his left arm tight against his side and with his right hand grasping it above the elbow. He saw Fox, faced him and announced in a bass rumble that quivered without raged indignation:

"The double-breasted bastard shot me!"

Fox was by him. "Where, Dan? Let's see. Better sit down. Thanks, Inspector. Take your hand away so I can slit the sleeve——"

"Wouldn't it be better to——"

"No. Hold still. There. You're nice and bloody. Hold still, you don't have to look at it! No, thank you, Mrs. Pemberton. I won't need a tourniquet. Please stand back, Miss Grant." Fox glanced sharply at Nancy's white face. "You'd better sit down—put her in a chair, Andy. It's only flesh and skin . . . we ought to move into a bathroom——"

"I want to get you something first."

"Go ahead. Hold still."

"I've been trying to reach you all afternoon. They wouldn't let me in. They wouldn't call you on the phone. I had to get to you because I know who murdered Thorpe."

"You do?"

"Yes. As soon as it got dark enough, or I thought it

was, I climbed the wall and started for the house. Who would have thought one of those apes would actually shoot? And not only that, he hit me."

"It's not bad. Thank you, Inspector. Go on and tell us who killed Thorpe."

"His son did. Jeffrey."

"Did he?" Fox disregarded movements and ejaculations. "How could you see him from that distance?"

"I didn't see him. But I know the double-breasted——"

"Save that one till we get to the bathroom. I don't think I ever saw you this mad before—Don't push, Colonel, you'll get it. Two double-breasted's in three minutes. What is it you know?"

"I know he had my gun, because I gave it to him last night and if it's the one that shot Thorpe——"

"You mean *my* gun? One of my Dowseys?"

"All right, your gun. The one I was carrying."

Fox's eyes blazed. "You gave that gun to Jeffrey Thorpe?"

"I lent it to him. When he was there last night—when he came downstairs to go home. I was sitting on the porch aiming with it——"

"What were you aiming at?"

"At the bug lamp."

"Do you mean the insect trap?"

"Yes. I was showing Wallenstein how to pull it down and allow for the jump. The young ape came out and saw me and said he was going to buy a gun and wished he had one, but he couldn't buy one until morning. I asked him what for and he said for protection. Pokorny overheard it and suggested I should lend him mine——"

"I've told you a thousand times to ignore Pokorny's suggestions."

"Right. So Thorpe asked to borrow it until he could buy one, and since he had been riding around chinning with you and Miss Grant——"

"And you let him have it."

"Right. Hey, that hurts!"

"I'm squeezing out the juice. I won't mention what I'd like to do." Fox turned to Derwin at his elbow. "Do you want to ask him anything before I take him somewhere and clean him up?"

"I do." Derwin was grim. "I want him to identify that gun and to sign a statement——"

"You can have that when I get through with him. It's the gun, all right. I mean any detail as——"

"Yes." Derwin faced Dan. "Was the gun loaded when you gave it to Thorpe?"

"Certainly it was loaded!" The answer came not from Dan, but from Jeffrey Thorpe, who was there confronting Derwin. "I borrowed it from him and it was loaded, and I put it in my pocket and brought it home with me!"

"You admit that?"

"Yes!"

"Come on, let's get it bandaged," Fox said to Dan and, as they left the room, no one offered to interfere, or even paid any attention to them, for all eyes were focused on Jeffrey. Miranda had moved and was beside him, her face pale and her jaw set. A trooper had sidled over and was directly behind him.

Brissenden snapped, "Get him out of here. Bring him to the library, Hardy."

The trooper put a hand on Jeffrey's arm, but he, ignoring that, spoke to Derwin:

"You want to run me through the wringer and that's all right, but I want to ask a question. My sister told me that the gun that killed my father has been identified as one belonging to Tecumseh Fox. Is that correct?"

"It is. And therefore it's the gun——"

"Yes. I can count that far myself. It's the gun I brought here and that makes it my turn to talk. But you're not taking me to the library or anywhere else. I'll talk right here. The people who have heard this much will hear the rest. Tell your stenographer to go get his notebook. When I got home last night——"

"Wait a minute, Jeffrey!" It was Fuller, of the law firm of Buchanan, Fuller, McPartland and Jones, stepping forward. His hard non-committal eyes were aimed at the district attorney. "It is advisable, I think, that I should have a talk with Mr. Thorpe first."

"Tchah!" snorted Brissenden.

"I think not," said Derwin curtly.

"I think yes." Fuller's tone was acid. "Otherwise it will be my duty to advise him to answer no questions and give no information——"

"You can keep your advice," Jeffrey blurted. "I've been afraid all the time——"

"Jeffrey! I order you, as your attorney, to keep silent! You flouted your father's authority when he was alive; now——"

"He did not," Miranda denied quietly. She was on the other side of her brother from the trooper, her hand on his sleeve. "But, Jeff, I think Mr. Fuller's right. I think you ought to speak with him before you let them try to . . . to . . ." She faltered.

He looked down at her. "Much obliged, Sis," he said bitterly. "You think I shot him. Don't you?"

"No, I don't."

"You think maybe I did. She doesn't, but you do. I've been thinking you did all afternoon and when you couldn't look at me when you were telling me about them identifying the gun—and you knowing I had borrowed it myself last night——"

Brissenden barked, "I say get him out of here!"

Inspector Damon shook his head and muttered, "Let 'em talk."

Fuller tried to get in: "I must insist——"

"I want to get a refusal for the record," said Derwin. "I'm going to question him and if he refuses to answer on the advice of counsel, he has that right. Previously questioned, he has said nothing about having a gun. I also wish to question Mrs. Pemberton. I presume it was Mr. Fox who informed her that the gun that shot her father had been identified as his property. Anyway, she has admitted that she knew that and she also knew that her brother had borrowed one of Fox's guns, and has concealed that fact."

He glanced aside, saw that the pimply young man had got his notebook and was on a chair busy with it, and turned to Jeffrey. "Mr. Thorpe," he demanded, "what did you do with that gun which you had borrowed when you brought it home with you, to this house, last night?"

Fuller commanded, "Don't answer!"

Jeffrey had opened his mouth but closed it again. He looked at the lawyer. "You mean well, Mr. Fuller," he conceded. "It doesn't seem to me that this was the time or place to charge me with flouting my father's authority, but you have sons of your own and I suppose you had to get that dig in." He looked at Derwin. "I'm willing to grant that you mean well too, since you're the district attorney." He looked at Brissenden. "You're a pugnacious jackass, and if I get out of this alive I'm going to meet you unofficially and sock you one. Now if you'll all stop yapping I'll tell you about that gun."

"Jiffy, I order you——"

"Let me alone. If the truth won't do it, to hell with it. When I got home and went up to my room last night—oh, I'm glad you're in time to hear it, Fox, since it was your gun. How's the vice-president?"

"He'll keep for a while." Fox smiled at him. "I'm glad I'm in time to hear it."

"So am I. When I got home and went up to my room last night I took the gun out of my pocket and put it on the bed table. When I dressed this morning I put it in my pocket again. It was still there when Miss Grant and her uncle arrived around nine o'clock this morning. I tried to get Miss Grant to talk to me and she wouldn't. I got peeved, not with her, with myself, and decided that I was acting like a half-wit and that I would drive off somewhere and not come back until she was gone."

He looked at Brissenden. "That was the mysterious errand in my car which I refused to tell you about because it was none of your damn business. A few miles down the road I nearly collided with a truck and realized that in the condition I was in I was a highway menace, but the real reason I came back was that I knew Miss Grant was here and I couldn't stay away."

He looked at Nancy. "I apologize for bringing your name in so often but if I'm telling it I might as well tell it. When I sat down in the car the gun in my hip pocket dug into my behind, and I had taken it out and laid it on the seat. I felt silly with it anyhow in broad daylight and besides——" He stopped. "No, I might as well tell that too. I knew Miss Grant and her uncle had seen it in my pocket, because I had overheard a remark he made to her. Of course they'll now be asked to explain why they didn't mention that I was carrying a gun, but you can't put them in jail for that.

The fact that I knew they had seen it made me feel sillier. Anyhow, when I got back here and left the car out in the circle, I forgot all about the gun. I didn't even see it on the seat when I got out of the car, because my mind was on something else, but it must have been there, since I had put it there only fifteen minutes before, when I started out. That was the last time that I actually remember seeing it, when I put it on the seat. I haven't seen it since."

As he stopped, Fuller was at Nancy like a hawk after a chicken: "Miss Grant, you saw the gun in Jeffrey's pocket before he left you to go for a ride?"

"Yes," she said clearly and firmly. "Just a minute or two after we got here."

"You the same, Mr. Grant?"

"Yes."

"Did you see it in his pocket, or in his possession— did you see it at all—after he returned from his ride?"

"No. I didn't know he had gone for a ride, but when he returned around ten o'clock after an absence of perhaps a quarter of an hour, I didn't see the gun. Nor at any subsequent time."

"Did you, Miss Grant?"

"No."

The lawyer's eyes swept that half of the room where the guests were scattered. "Did any of you see a gun in Jeffrey Thorpe's possession after ten o'clock this morning?"

He had pushed the question through, raising his voice, in spite of an attempted interruption by Derwin, and, though the interruption forestalled vocal replies, apparently he was satisfied by the negative expression of the faces, for he turned to the district attorney and told him:

"Go ahead and ask him anything you want to."

"Thanks," said Derwin sarcastically. He glanced at the stenographer. "You have it that those questions were asked of Grant and his niece by Mr. Fuller?"

"Yes, sir."

"With no attempt at interference by me."

"Yes, sir."

Derwin confronted Jeffrey. He looked sufficiently grim and determined, though not at all happy. "Mr. Thorpe," he said gruffly, "you have a legal representative present. I think it would be proper for you to accept any advice he may give you. It is also proper for me to tell you that in my opinion, with the evidence now in my possession and the admissions you have yourself made, your indictment on a charge of first-degree murder would be procurable, but I am not at the moment making that charge. I don't intend to be precipitate, but I do intend——"

"Don't lecture him," Fuller snapped. "And don't threaten him. If you want to question him, do so."

Derwin ignored it, kept his eyes at Jeffrey and finished his sentence. "I do intend to see that guilt is punished. Your statement is that you left the gun— the gun which was subsequently used for the commission of murder——"

"That was not his statement," Fuller contradicted. "The identity of the weapon used."

"Very well. Your statement is that you left the gun which you had borrowed from Tecumseh Fox—at his home from his employee—on the seat of your car when you returned from a ride about ten o'clock this morning?"

"That's right," said Jeffrey.

"And you haven't seen it since?"

"That's right."

"Didn't you see it lying on the library floor within a few feet of your father's dead body?"

"No. I didn't see the gun or anything else. I was looking at him."

"You didn't see the gun at all?"

"No." Jeffrey was meeting the district attorney's grim gaze with a scowl. "And since I knew that gun could be traced to me, if I had shot him and had left it there I would have been a bigger boob than I am."

"If you did it, you had to leave it somewhere and there wasn't much time. Then your contention is that the murderer got the gun from the seat of your car."

"I'm not making any contention. I'm just telling where I left the gun."

"Haven't you returned to your car at all since ten o'clock this morning?"

"Yes. I went there this afternoon about four o'clock to see if the gun was still there and it wasn't."

"After Colonel Brissenden had finished his interview with you?"

"Yes."

"You didn't mention that gun to Colonel Brissenden, did you?"

"No."

"You didn't mention that you had borrowed it, or that it was in your possession this morning, or that you had left it on the seat of your car?"

"No."

"Didn't the possibility occur to you that it was that gun that had killed your father?"

"Yes."

"And that it might therefore be an important clue. So you were willing to hamper the investigation of your father's murder?"

"No. I wasn't hampering it. I knew you had the

gun that had killed him, because I heard Colonel Brissenden say it was there on the floor, though I hadn't seen it. If it was the gun I had left in my car and the murderer had got it from there it wouldn't have helped you any to know that, because any one who was around could have got it. As a matter of fact, I would probably have told you about it if it hadn't been that sap Brissenden that was questioning me. And I would have told even him, if he had had the brains to show me the gun and ask me if I had ever seen it. I was expecting he would——"

"He couldn't, at that time. It was away being tested. We had to establish that that gun had fired the bullet—What is it, Colonel?"

"We ought to get him out of here! Take him to the courthouse!"

Inspector Damon caught Derwin's eye and, barely perceptibly, shook his head. The district attorney hesitated a moment and then returned to Jeffrey:

"If you object to the audience, Mr. Thorpe——"

"Not at all," Jeffrey declared. "I'm not going to your damned courthouse as long as I have any alternative."

"Very well. After you learned from your sister that we had identified the gun as the property of Tecumseh Fox, why didn't you come forward and tell us about it?"

"I was making up my mind to. I knew then I'd have to. She only told me a little before dinner started."

"Oh." Derwin sounded sceptical. "That made you decide to tell, did it?"

"Yes."

"But you weren't in any hurry. You had to have dinner first. A vital piece of information for the inquiry into the murder of your father, but any time this week would do."

"I said I was making up my mind." Jeffrey's color had heightened. "I deny it was a vital piece of information. I didn't say 'any time this week.' You can leave the sneers for the colonel."

"I wasn't sneering, Mr. Thorpe, I was commenting, I think not improperly, on your attitude—or rather, your actions. It seems to me reasonable to say that if they were not actuated by a sense of guilt, they displayed a remarkable apathy towards the object of our investigation. If you resent my remark, I resent your failure to impart information in your possession. It costs us, at the least, much valuable time. I should think Fox would also resent it, since he narrowly escaped arrest as a material witness. And speaking of the motivation of your actions, what did you borrow the gun for? What were you going to do with it?"

Jeffrey nodded gloomily. "Uh-huh. That's where you've got me."

"Why have I got you?"

"Because the only explanation I can give for borrowing the gun will sound loony. It was loony. I'll have to drag Miss Grant in again. Do you remember that photograph of her you showed me yesterday?"

"Yes."

"And later you showed it to my father and he didn't deny it had been given to him?"

"Yes."

"All right. When you showed it to him and he didn't deny it was his, I wished in my heart he had been killed instead of that fellow at the bungalow. I wanted him dead. I wanted——"

"Jeffrey!" Fuller's voice was sharply warning. "You don't need to——"

"Let me alone," said Jeffrey impatiently. "I'm all right. I wanted to kill him myself and by God, if I found—I would have. But last evening at Fox's place I learned that that was bunk. My father had never even seen Miss Grant. So when I left there I was feeling exuberant. Call it that or call it loony. Anyhow I had a reaction and I was feeling better toward my father than I ever had in my life, and I was ashamed because I had wanted to kill him, and the reaction to that was that I wanted to protect him——"

"Tchah!" Brissenden snorted.

Jeffrey ignored it. "I knew the man in the bungalow had been killed by someone who wanted to kill my father. I thought he wouldn't stop with one attempt and he might make another one any minute, even that very night. I felt like protecting him. When I saw him —Pavey—there on the porch with a gun as we went out, on an impulse I asked to borrow it. By the time I got home, I was already feeling silly, because I was so seldom where my father was that my chances of protecting him were practically non-existent. When I dressed this morning, I put the gun in my pocket, because I expected to drive over to Fox's place during the morning and return it, and then Miss Grant and her uncle suddenly arrived and put that out of my mind."

He looked at Nancy. "I hope you'll forgive me for dragging you in so often."

"You can't help it," she replied. "I dragged myself in by taking Uncle Andy to that bungalow." She moved her eyes to the district attorney and spoke to him: "Anyway, this is all stupid. I didn't interrupt before because I thought Mr. Thorpe would want to explain about the gun in any case. But he couldn't possibly have killed his father, because at the moment the shot was fired he was on the other side of the house behind the rose trellis and I was looking straight at him."

She might as well have lit the fuse of a giant firecracker and tossed it under their feet.

Miranda stared at her an instant and then jumped and threw her arms around her. Jeffrey goggled at her. Tecumseh Fox threw up his hands. Brissenden and Derwin were speechless. Inspector Damon gazed at her pessimistically.

"Nancy! You lovely Nancy!" Miranda cried, squeezing her.

Jeffrey said in a tone of solemn awe, "By God. But you weren't. I didn't kill my father and that will be all right somehow, but you know damn well you didn't see me."

Nancy nodded not at him but at Derwin. "Yes, I did. I was looking straight at him when I heard that shot."

Brissenden started a bark, "You have stated—you have absolutely stated——"

"I know what I've stated." Nancy's tone was spirited. "I said I didn't see him. I wasn't going to give him the satisfaction of knowing that all the time I was sitting on the terrace I knew he was there behind the trellis watching me. I did know it. I saw him. The reason I didn't get up and go somewhere else was that I was tired and didn't want to move, and it was cool there. I'm telling the truth about it now because —all this about the gun—I couldn't very well let an innocent man be accused of murder—not even him——"

"Why did you run to the swimming pool?" Derwin demanded.

"Because I thought that was where the shot came from."

"You have stated that you had been with Jeffrey Thorpe at the swimming pool and you thought he was still there."

"I had been with him at the swimming pool. Or he had been with me. He followed me. I said I thought he was still there because I wasn't admitting that I knew he was behind the rose trellis."

"But if you knew he wasn't at the pool, why did you think the shot came from there?"

"Because," said Nancy patiently, "it sounded like it. I'm not an expert on acoustics, but no doubt——"

"I said all along to get him out of here," Brissenden blurted savagely. "She would never have been able to play that trick if you hadn't let him——"

"Shut up!" Derwin told him.

Another voice broke in. "May I make a request?" It was Tecumseh Fox. "You fellows are about played out. It's getting on your nerves and I don't blame you. Every fish you make a grab for slips right out of your hands. I've had it happen to me. Haven't you, Inspector?"

Damon nodded. "Too often for comfort."

"What's your request?" Derwin demanded.

"Nothing very momentous," Fox assured him.

"I agree with the colonel that it's sort of crowded in here and I suppose, with this snag you've struck, you'll be starting another series of interviews. Won't you?"

"If I'm here all night——" Derwin began grimly.

"Sure." Fox nodded sympathetically. "But before you begin, I request permission to finish a little game I was proposing when that shot interrupted us. It'll only take a few minutes."

"What kind of a game?"

"I'll show you. Just a foolish idea of mine." Fox turned brusquely. "Have you got the pads and pencils, Bellows? There, on the table. Pass them around—here, give me some. Only those who were in here at the time—Here, Mrs. Pemberton, Miss Grant—Take it, Mr. Fuller, you won't have to write what I say if you don't like it——"

"Write what?" Brissenden spluttered. "What are you trying to get away with? Let me see one of those pads!"

"I can't allow this, Fox——" Derwin began; but Inspector Damon muttered at him, "Let him alone, I would. With him you never know."

Fox tossed him a smile. "Thanks, Inspector. I didn't know either, but it's a bright idea." His eyes swept the group. "For Mr. Jordan, Bellows. That's right. Now. Each one of you will write what I dictate and put your name beneath it, or your initials will do. As I have said before, it will be a sentence from the Declaration of Independence."

"Tschah!" Brissenden snorted.

"Certainly," Fox went on, "there is no compulsion on any of you to humor me, but Mrs. Pemberton kindly consented, so I hope you will. Here's the sentence——"

"Print it or write it?" Kester inquired.

"Either one, whichever you please. Writing would be faster. Here it is: 'We mutually pledge to each other our lives . . .'" He paused. A glance showed him that all eight of the pencils had started to move. He waited a moment. "Got that? 'We mutually pledge to each other our lives, our fortunes, and our sacred honor.'" He waited again. The last of the pencils to stop movement was Luke Wheer's. "That's all. Now

please put your name or initials at the bottom—
what's that, Mr. Fuller? That's all right, here, give it
to me, I'll initial it for you."

"Give me that pad!" Derwin was at his elbow.
"Give me all of them!"

"You won't know what to do with it, Mr. Derwin,"
Fox objected; but after one swift glance at the chirog-
raphy of Mr. Fuller, he surrendered the pad; and then
did the same with each of the others. He moved so
swiftly and glanced so briefly at each pad as he
handed it over to the district attorney, that before
Derwin knew it he was standing there with the stack
of pads in his hand and Fox was telling him with a
smile:

"You'd better take care of them; they may be
needed as evidence." He encompassed the group with
a glance: "Thank you very much." He spoke again to
Derwin, "I'll be out on the terrace if you want me,"
turned on his heel and marched from the room with
twenty pairs of eyes staring at him.

Brissenden growled to Inspector Damon, "He's
plain batty."

Damon shook his head. "Not plain. Very fancy,
Fox is. Listen to him."

As Fox was crossing the hall, his baritone could be
heard, just loud enough to reach them: "Lah-de-dah,
dum dum, lah-de-dah, dum dum . . ."

Chapter 21

An hour later, halfway between eleven and midnight, Dan Pavey emerged from the library
and favored the two troopers in the side hall
with a ferocious scowl. All he got in return was a pair
of yawns. He adjusted his left arm to a more comfortable position in its support, a makeshift sling con-
trived of a folded strip of white muslin, and passed
into the music room. Several persons were seated
there, but not Tecumseh Fox, so he proceeded towards the main hall. As he entered it, Bellows appeared from somewhere and informed him that Mr.
Fox would like to see him upstairs—if he would
please follow——

"I'll show him, Bellows."

It was Nancy Grant, somehow there. Bellows
thanked her and made off. Nancy led the way, with
Dan following, up the broad winding stair, down half
the length of the wide carpeted corridor, and indicated a door.

"In there," she said.

"Thanks."

Nancy stood. He stood. Her mouth opened and
closed again.

Dan asked, "What is it?"

"Your arm."

"What about it?"

Her finger nearly touched it. "Does it hurt?"

"Nothing to brag about."

They stood. Dan's mouth opened and closed again. Nancy asked, "What is it?"

"Something I might as well say," Dan rumbled, his bass pitched lower even than usual. "I'll get it out. That playboy of yours. I really did think he had shot his father. Since I understand you have alibied him, I was wrong. Congrat——"

"He is not my playboy."

"Well, your whatever you want to call him. Anyhow, what I want to say, on account of my accusing him in public of being a murderer, I owe you a laugh. I dreamed about you yesterday. I dreamed I was picking flowers for you. Red flowers. With these hands—ouch. Draw any conclusion you want to and you'll probably be right."

"But I——" Nancy stopped, then went on, "Whatever conclusion did you draw?"

"I didn't draw any. I didn't have to. You wouldn't either, if you had a dream like that. Picking red flowers and arranging them to look nice. Kindly postpone the laugh until you are out of hearing."

He strode to the door she had indicated, opened it without knocking, passed through and closed it.

Tecumseh Fox, there alone, faced him and inquired:

"Well?"

The vice-president nodded. "Okay," he declared. "They wanted me to sign a statement and identify the gun, that's all. It's my gun all right. You know, it kind of gives you the creeps to realize that your own gun was used to shoot——"

"It's not your gun, it's mine." Fox compressed his lips. "You know, Dan, this is past the limit. We won't discuss it now——"

"We might as well. That is, if we've got to discuss it at all. It won't do any good. We've been over it all before and what good does it do? You have your ideas and I have mine."

"It might do some good if I made it impossible for you to put your ideas in practice in my business and with my property."

Dan shook his head. "You mean kick me out?" He extended an enormous paw in an appeal to reason. "What do you say things like that for? To begin with, you couldn't kick anybody out. Particularly not me. Six years ago last May, you saved my life. If you hadn't butted in, that Arizona jury would have hung me higher than a kite, as sure as a duck quacks. If it wasn't for you I wouldn't be here. Then in the last analysis, who's responsible for my actions? You are— All right, I've admitted before that I got that argument from Pokorny, but that doesn't keep it from being a good argument. You saved my life and here I am. Whatever I do, brilliant or the contrary as you seem to think, it's up to you. As far as that gun is concerned, common sense ought to tell you that if that one hadn't been handy——"

"I said we won't discuss it now!"

"We might as well if we're going to."

"No. I'm busy."

"I know you are. You've found out who murdered Thorpe. I can tell that by the way your eyes look. But if we've got to discuss my lending that gun—I don't want to be worrying about it all night——"

"You never worried about anything for five minutes in your life. Please go downstairs and ask Vaughn Kester to come up here, and to bring Luke Wheer and Henry Jordan with him."

Dan stared a second, grunted, rumbled, "I thought it was him all along," and started for the door; and paused not for Fox's challenge:

"Wait a minute, I'll call that! Ten to one you can't name him——"

The vice-president was gone. Fox made a face at the door, then crossed to an open window and leaned out for a breath of the cooler night air. Apparently Dan was having trouble finding Kester, or Kester was having difficulty locating the other pair, for ten minutes passed before footsteps were heard, muffled on the carpet of the corridor.

Fox faced the door as it opened. Luke Wheer was in the van, his face sullen, his eyes bloodshot. Vaughn Kester's backbone was stiff and he walked with nervous jerky steps. Henry Jordan looked completely miserable, with the corners of his mouth drooping, his shoulders sagging, his feet dragging. There were only three chairs in the room. Fox invited the others to take them and, for himself, brought over the bench from the dressing table, then spoke to Dan.

"Stay out in the hall, will you, please? By the door. Sit on the floor and don't go to sleep. If any one comes, give us a tap."

Dan rumbled, not resentfully, "That's one thing I've never done, I've never gone to sleep," on his way out.

Fox turned to Kester: "Can we be heard in an adjoining room if we keep our voices down?"

The secretary shook his head. "The house is soundproofed. What's this all about?"

"Murder," said Fox curtly. "That's what we're going to discuss. But the precautions for secrecy are for the purpose of preserving the reputation of Ridley Thorpe. It's his secret we're trying to keep. You and Luke want to, I know. Jordan has his own reason for wanting the same thing and so have I. I'd hate to have to return this check to the Thorpe estate. I earned it and I want to keep it."

"In any event," Kester observed dryly, "you couldn't be compelled to return it."

"Oh, yes, I could, by my scruples—or my vanity. No matter what you call it, it's the most effective compulsion there is."

Kester didn't look impressed. "What is it you want to discuss about the murder?"

Luke Wheer broke in, in a hoarse squeak, "I do not want to discuss any more about murder. I tell you, gentlemen, with all respect, I don't want to!"

"I don't blame you, Luke," Fox sympathized. "But we four share the secret we want to keep and that's why I asked all of you to come up here." He turned and said abruptly, "The discussion will be mostly between you and me, Mr. Jordan."

The wiry little man looked wearily surprised. "I don't know what you think I can discuss about it," he declared.

"Well," Fox conceded, "I expect I'll do most of the discussing myself. The fact is, I want to apply a test to you. I did it with Kester this afternoon; I built up an inference that he had killed both Arnold and Thorpe, and I did a pretty good job of it. Now I'm going to do the same thing with you."

Jordan frowned at him. "I don't understand. What is it you're going to do?"

"I'm going to build up an inference that you killed

Arnold, Sunday night, and Thorpe here today, and see what you think of it."

The sag left Jordan's shoulders, his chin stiffened and a flash came from his deep-set grey eyes. His voice was an angry growl: "I can tell you right now what I think of it."

"Sure you can," Fox agreed quietly, "but you'd just have to tell me all over again when I get through. To save time and avoid misunderstanding, I'll put it this way: you're going to sit there and listen right through to the end. If you start any motions I don't like I'll be on you and don't think I can't handle you. If you bust up the discussion, I'll leave you in charge of Luke and Kester, and I'll go downstairs and give the district attorney all the information I have, including the detail of Ridley Thorpe's real weekend."

"Not that," Kester snapped.

"Yes, that," Fox snapped back. "What about it, Jordan?"

"It's ridiculous." Jordan wet his lips. "It's illegal. You can't force me to sit and listen to this scurrilous——"

"I'm not forcing you. I'm merely telling you what will happen if you don't."

Jordan's deep-set eyes were barely visible behind their ramparts. The palms of his hands slid down his legs and cupped over his knees and gripped there, as though he would hold himself down. "It's blackmail," he said. "I've suspected you from the beginning. Go ahead. Let me hear it."

Fox nodded. "That's sensible. I'll make it as brief as I can, but there's a lot to it."

Luke, his bloodshot eyes wide at Jordan, squeaked, "He was on the boat!"

"Sure he was on the boat. Don't start butting in,

Luke, let's get it over." Fox's eyes had not left Jordan. "Here are the bald details of the inference. Ten days ago, your plans being perfected, you sent an anonymous letter to Thorpe, threatening his life. You worded it so as to make it appear that it had been sent by a man who had been financially ruined by Thorpe, a man who lunched at the club he did. You did that to guide suspicion in that direction and also to establish the supposition that the man who killed Arnold thought he was killing Thorpe. You mailed the letter on Monday. The following Thursday you went for a trip on your boat. You knew of course that Thorpe would spend the weekend at the cottage in New Jersey with your daughter. Sunday night you anchored your boat at some deserted strip of beach on the Connecticut shore—I wouldn't be surprised if it was the same spot where I embarked Luke and Kester and Thorpe yesterday—rowed ashore, stole a car somewhere and drove to the bungalow—probably on the road along the woods back of it, since Grant and his niece saw no car—sneaked through the woods, shot Arnold through the window, drove back to where your boat was, or near there, went back on board, crossed the sound to the Long Island shore, anchored, got into your bunk and slept. Maybe you slept; sometimes they do and sometimes they don't. Any comment?"

"No," said Jordan contemptuously. "I wouldn't know where to begin."

"I think myself," Fox agreed, "it would be better to wait till I've finished. Before proceeding to more bald details, I'll turn some light on a few of those. You had no desire or intention of harming Thorpe; it was Arnold you were after. You had no expectation of ever being remotely associated with the affair in the

mind of any one. There were only four people in the
world who knew that there was any connection whatever between you and Ridley Thorpe; Luke Wheer,
Vaughn Kester, your daughter and Thorpe himself;
and they were all people who would not divulge that
connection. So your natural expectation was that all
you would ever hear about the murder of Corey Arnold would be what you would read in the papers
whenever you saw fit to go ashore and get some. It
must have been the nastiest shock of your life, yesterday afternoon, when I floated alongside and you saw
who was sitting in my boat. Wasn't it?"

Fox shook his head. "Excuse me. Don't try to answer yet. You handled that situation marvelously. To
be sure, I wasn't expecting anything suspicious, but I
always have my eyes open and you didn't betray
yourself by the slightest flicker. The negotiations
were completed, and Luke and Kester and I left.
Then, at some moment prior to the time when it had
been agreed you and Thorpe would go ashore, you
had a second shock. Probably, I imagine, while you
were steering the boat to Port Jefferson. Thorpe
emerged from the cabin with a revolver in his hand.
'Look here, Jordan,' he said—I can hear him saying
it—'I was poking around in there and found this in a
drawer. I hate guns and I never carry one, but good
gracious, somebody's trying to kill me and I'm going
to protect myself. I'll just borrow this until I get one
of my own.' And he stuck it in his pocket. Wasn't that
the way it happened?"

Fox shook his head again. "Excuse me. That shock
must have been almost as bad as the first one. It was
the gun you had killed Arnold with. You had seen no
necessity for disposing of it, since there hadn't been
one chance in a million that you would ever be con-

nected with the crime and after our arrival with
Thorpe you had had no opportunity to ditch the gun.
Of course you tried to talk him out of taking it, but
what Thorpe wanted he took and you couldn't make
your objections too strong for fear of arousing suspicion.

"But you were certainly on a spot. If any faint
suspicion should arise, Thorpe had in his possession
evidence that would convict you like that"—Fox
snapped his fingers—"of murder. You must have been
very uncomfortable at my house last night. With the
fears of a guilty conscience aroused, some remark I
made may even have led you to think that I already
suspected you, though I certainly didn't. I'm not very
proud of the fact that I didn't really suspect you at all
until I looked at the writing on those pads downstairs.
Your best defense against the threat of disaster was
to get the gun back from Thorpe, but you didn't know
how to go about it. But your fear forced you to do
something, to erect some barrier against suspicion
and you had devised a pretty good one. I admit you
fooled me completely with that early morning trip to
your daughter's apartment. I should have suspected
you then, hearing you tell about her giving you a biscuit and tea, but your calculations were sound. You
figured that by running away from my place before
sunrise, ostensibly for the purpose of talking with
your daughter in order to make sure that Thorpe
hadn't committed the murder himself—to make sure
that you weren't furnishing an alibi for a murderer—
you would render yourself immune to suspicion; and it
worked. I underestimated you. After that trick, I
even passed over your remark about a biscuit and tea
—What is it, Kester?"

"Nothing," said the secretary shortly. "Only the

inference you're building against Jordan seems to be more elaborate than the one you tried on me and a good deal more mystifying. What the devil have a biscuit and tea got to do with it?"

"Everything," Fox declared. "No American would ever speak of a biscuit and tea, but an Englishman would. Before that even, I should have known that Jordan's an Englishman, since I heard him say he had been purser on the *Cedric*, which is a British ship, but he had himself insulated."

Fox's eyes were not leaving Jordan. Jordan apparently was meeting them, but his own were so deep under the jutting brows, so narrow behind the crinkled leathery lids, that they left their expression to be guessed at.

"Then," Fox told him, "I brought you here to Maple Hill myself. I suppose you were on the edge of panic. You had expected to be quietly on your boat, untroubled and utterly unsuspected, during the hullabaloo over Arnold's murder and here you were right in the thick of it. You had begun to be afraid of me. My sudden appearance at your daughter's apartment, so soon after your own arrival there, had alarmed you—quite needlessly, for I hadn't expected to see you there. Worst of all, Thorpe still had the gun and he knew it was yours. That was your most acute danger, Thorpe's knowledge that that gun belonged to you, and circumstances conspired to tempt you with an opportunity of removing that danger. You were sitting on the side terrace and men came and disturbed you. You wanted to be alone, to decide whether to take any action and if so, what. You went to the back of the house where the cars were parked and the gun lying on the seat of Jeffrey Thorpe's car caught your eye.

"The sight of that gun made your blood pump. You

knew Thorpe was in the library on the opposite side of the house from the side terrace, for I had told you so. The windows would certainly be open and the notion of shooting through an open window wasn't a new one for you. You knew there were plenty of available suspects around—the son and daughter, Luke and Kester, Grant and his niece, a group of business associates. But you were not in enough of a panic to abandon caution. You thought it over before touching the gun. A man firing a gun seldom leaves recognizable fingerprints, but particles of burnt powder lodge in his skin and can invariably be detected. It wouldn't do to use your own handkerchief. You looked around and on the seat of my sedan you found the blue scarf which Miss Grant had left there. Making sure that you were not observed, you took it, and then you took the gun. You were clever enough to wipe the metal parts of the gun, for if any fingerprints were found on it suspicion would be directed against one person and it might be that that one person would have an unshakable alibi; besides, suspicion should be dispersed. Equipped, you strolled to the other side——"

Fox stopped at the sound of a tapping at the door, the pecking of a fingernail. Barely audible footsteps were heard without, on the carpet of the hall. After a moment the door opened wide enough for the insertion of Dan Pavey's head, and his hoarse whisper came:

"A woman with a big nose and a squint! Went into a room!"

"Knudsen, Mrs. Pemberton's maid," Kester said.

"All right, shut the door," said Fox, with his eyes steady at Jordan. He went on, "You strolled to the other side of the house and from behind a ring of shrubbery you heard voices—those of Colonel Brissenden and Ridley Thorpe. You wriggled into the shrubbery and saw them in the library through the open French windows. Your cover was perfect. You maneuvered into position and waited, with the scarf around your hand holding the gun. Kester was there too, or he was summoned by Thorpe, and then he went out with Brissenden. Thorpe was alone. When his back was turned you darted from your cover, shot him in the back, tossed the gun and scarf into the room, ran back through the shrubbery to a spot under a tree at the back of the house, and adopted the role of a man who had been sitting on the grass and had been suddenly startled by hearing the sound of a shot. A gardener appeared from somewhere and you followed him as he was guided by Kester's yells in the direction of the library. You showed good presence of mind following the gardener through the shrubbery you had just used for your cover; that was the natural thing to do, but it took nerve, since it placed you on that side of the house."

Fox stopped. Still gazing steadily at Jordan, he pulled at the lobe of his ear. No one spoke.

"Well," Fox said, "those are the bald details."

Jordan's lips twisted. His palms were still cupped over his knees, gripping them, holding them down. "Come on, out with it," he demanded.

"With what, Mr. Jordan? What more do you want?"

"I want you to put it in words. In front of these chaps. You must take me for a bloody idiot, if you think I won't defend myself against a false charge of murder to keep it from coming out about Thorpe and my daughter. That dirty game won't work."

Fox shook his head. "It's not a game. If I've given you the impression that it's only a game, I apologize.

I'm accusing you of the premeditated murder of Corey Arnold and the more briefly premeditated murder of Ridley Thorpe."

"Bah. I thought you had better sense. Why would I want to kill Arnold? I had never seen him. I knew Thorpe had a man at that bungalow impersonating him, but I didn't even know the man's name."

"Sure," Fox agreed. "That was part of your immunity to suspicion. Absence of motive. I'll take that last. First I'll mention a couple of other points, both to my own discredit. When Derwin told me today that the gun that shot Arnold was found in Thorpe's safe, I should have suspected you immediately. Where could it have come from? I won't go through the process by which all other possibilities could have been demonstrated as highly improbable; it's enough to say that the one place Thorpe had been where it was plausible to suppose he had got hold of that gun was on your boat. At least I should have suspected it and I was dumb not to. By the way, I doubt if you're right in supposing that by killing Thorpe you destroyed the evidence of the gun. There must be someone who can recognize it as yours—for instance, that woman who is your next door neighbor—I'll bet she can."

Jordan wet his lips. "No," he said huskily. He wet his lips again. "No, she can't. Not the gun that killed Arnold. I had no motive."

"I'll take that last." Fox's gaze was relentless. "You see, you're springing leaks. Another one is that letter you wrote. It was obvious it had been written by a Briton or someone with a British education and background. It said, 'You will meet me on the pavement.' An American would say, 'You will meet me on the sidewalk,' or 'You will meet me on the street.' But in England they never say sidewalk, they say pavement. No American ever does, in that sense. Also you mentioned your word of honor and you spelled honor with a u. No American does that; all Britons do. That was all there was to that sentence downstairs; it had the word honor in it. You were the only one who spelled it with a u."

Luke Wheer was whispering to himself, "H, O, N, O . . ."

Kester, his colorless eyes leaving Jordan for Fox, muttered, "I'll be damned."

Fox nodded. "That's all there was to that. It ought to be a pretty fair piece of evidence."

Apparently Jordan's lips were dry; he kept wetting them. The muscles of his hands, still cupped over his knees, were slowly and rhythmically tensing and relaxing; he said nothing.

"But I have an idea," Fox resumed, "that the evidence that will clinch it is your motive for murdering Arnold. That's another thing I'm not very proud of. Since traditional morality left its cradle thousands of years ago, so many outraged fathers have killed the men who were weekending with their daughters without benefit of clergy! That was the outstanding ostentatious fact of your connection with Thorpe: you were the father of his weekend companion. Such fathers have immemorially fallen into one of two categories: one is the enraged defender of the family honor who kills the man if he can; the other is the complacent sharer in the proceeds of his daughter's degradation. Obviously you were not in the second category, since you refused even to accept any gift either from Thorpe or your daughter. Apparently you were not in the first category either, since your expressed attitude was that it was her life she was living; and even if you had been, that would have supplied no motive for your killing the man in the bungalow, since you knew it wasn't Thorpe. Those considerations seemed to put you out of the running, but they shouldn't have, since there was one other point to consider. Particularly I should have considered it, but like a fool I didn't. Thorpe himself had told me that you were a comparatively poor man, that you lived on a little income from your savings and that the one thing in the world you wanted was a new boat of a certain design that would cost twenty thousand dollars."

Jordan blurted, as if involuntarily, "He wanted to give me the money himself and I wouldn't take it!"

Fox nodded. "I know. He told me about that. Your pride wouldn't let you. You wouldn't have been able to look yourself in the face if you had accepted money from Thorpe, but you wanted that boat and there wasn't the remotest chance that you would ever be able to acquire it. So you made a plan and you carried it out. It's a dismal commentary on the limitations of the human mind, at least of my mind, that I considered the likelihood that Arnold had been murdered by someone who wanted to buy Thorpe Control at 40 and sell it at 80—I considered that possibility in connection with Kester and Thorpe himself and any number of unknown financiers, but not in connection with you. I was too grandiose. I thought of someone doing it to clean up a couple of million profit, but not of you doing it to get a boat. Of course I have no evidence of that, but it will be easy to get if it exists. If it is found that you recently turned your savings into cash, and that Thorpe Control was bought for you Monday on the drop, that will be conclusive."

"I didn't——" Jordan's tongue was struggling heroically against the dizzy and horrible panic of his brain. His hands, still on his knees, no longer had a firm grip; they were flaccid, quivering, useless to hold anything down. His eyes, withdrawn under the jutting brows, were dark little slits of terror.

"Pull yourself together," Fox told him in a hard, metallic voice. "You had a boat, didn't you? If you were tough enough to kill a man to get a new boat, you can be tough enough to take what's coming to you. You haven't even got the excuse——"

Fox stopped because the door of the room was opening. As he frowned at it, it swung wide enough to admit the breadth of Dan Pavey; then it was closed again, softly. Dan approached, glanced at the little man in the chair, no longer wiry, and announced to Fox:

"Not just a boat."

"Why not?" Fox demanded. "I'll handle this, Dan, if you'll——"

"You can't handle what I've got in my pocket unless you get it out. With this bum arm I can't get at it —here in my jacket—no, the other side——"

Fox's fingers, inserted into the inner pocket of Dan's jacket, came out again clutching a folded sheaf of papers. He unfolded them, fingered through them with a glance at each, screwed up his lips and looked at Dan.

"Where the devil did you get these?"

"On Jordan's boat."

"This morning?"

"Sure." Dan ignored an inarticulate cry of rage from Jordan, behind him. "I thought I might as well look around. They were in a metal box I had to pry open. There's a box of cartridges there too, a kind I never saw before, in a drawer in the galley. I left them there——"

"It might interest you to know," Fox said dryly, "that if you had given these to me this morning it would have saved a life."

"You mean Ridley Thorpe."

"Yes."

"You mean there in the rose trellis."

"Yes."

"Right. I should have. After you finished laughing. You sent me home before I had a chance——"

"It can't be helped now." Fox glanced at the papers again, then returned his gaze to Henry Jordan. "So," he observed quietly, "it wasn't just a boat. Thorpe told me he doubted if you profited by the market tips he gave you, but you must have, to get enough capital to swing fifteen thousand shares of Thorpe Control. What in the name of God were you going to do with a million dollars when you got it, at your age? But that's none of my business. My only purpose in bringing you up here to talk it over was to let you know that Luke and Kester and I will say nothing about Thorpe and your daughter if you don't. It's up to you. Your motive for murder is valid without that. Stand up!"

Jordan came up from his chair. Technically, he was standing, but he could scarcely have been called erect. He was shaking all over and his mouth was hanging open. "I d-d-didn't——" he stammered. "I—I didn't—you c-c-can't——"

"He's going to have hysterics," Vaughn Kester said icily.

Fox moved until he was directly in front of Jordan, facing him, and stood there frowning down intently at the suddenly grey and flabby face. Abruptly and swiftly his hand swooped up and its palm flattened against Jordan's cheek-bone with a sharp and staggering smack. Jordan nearly fell, but recovered his balance; and then, slowly and painfully, he straightened. He was erect. A last quiver ran over his body and it was composed. He looked up at Tecumseh Fox and said clearly and firmly:

"Thank you. I'm all right now. What do you want me to do?"

"Go on." Fox inclined his head to the door. "I'll follow. To the library to see Derwin."

As they went out, Jordan with a steady unfaltering step and Fox close behind him, Kester's pale cold eyes followed them. Luke's did not. His head was bent and his eyes closed, like a preacher leading his congregation in prayer.

Chapter 22

A man, with brown cheeks almost smoothly shaven and wearing a blue denim shirt still fairly clean because it was milking time Monday afternoon, was chaperoning his herd of Jerseys across the paved road from the pasture side to the barn side. He saw a car coming and cussed. With any driver whatever the car would make his cows nervous; and if bad luck made it a certain kind of weekend driver from New York there was no telling what might happen. He stood in the middle of the road and glared at the approaching demon, then felt easier as he saw it slowing down and still easier when it crept, circling for a six-foot clearance past Jennifer's indifferent rump. But two other cows rendered the démarche futile, and the car surrendered and came to a full stop directly alongside the man; and, glancing at the two occupants, he recognized the pretty girl who, a week previously, had momentarily taken his mind off of cows. The driver, beside her, was a citified male at least ten years her senior.

She smiled at him through the open window. "Hello! Nice cows."

He squinted at her; she certainly was a promising

heifer. "You don't look as mad as you did last time," he observed.

"I wasn't mad, I was worried."

"You don't look worried."

"I'm not any more."

The road was clear and the car moved forward. In two minutes, having covered another mile of highway, it turned in at the entrance to the Fox place, known locally as The Zoo, and was guided by the curving lane over the little brook and on to the sweeping circle around the house, ending at the broad graveled space which was bounded in the rear by the enormous old barn which had been converted into a garage. From the right came the sound of voices. As the man and girl climbed out three dogs converged upon them for inspection. A man appeared at a small door at the far corner of the barn, decided in one brief glance that he wasn't interested and vanished.

Andrew Grant said to his niece, "They're pitching horseshoes. I didn't know Thorpe and his sister were to be here."

"Neither did I," said Nancy with spots on her cheeks.

Tecumseh Fox, a pair of horseshoes in his left hand, came to greet them, and behind him Jeffrey and Miranda. Dan Pavey returned their salutation from his distance, turned as if to leave the festive scene, then changed his mind and stayed. As Nancy gave Fox her hand she remarked in a tone polite enough but faintly disparaging:

"Oh, I didn't know it was a party."

"It isn't," Fox declared. "Mr. Thorpe dropped in to negotiate for that photograph and I told him you folks were coming for dinner, and Mrs. Pemberton invited me to dine with her at my house instead of hers."

Nancy was frowning. "You don't mean my photograph?"

"That's the one."

"He can't negotiate that from you. It's mine."

"He says it is part of his father's estate. He lays claim to it."

"Look here, Miss Grant." Jeffrey was there facing her, looking resolute. "Has your uncle told you about the talk we had yesterday?"

She nodded reluctantly. "He has."

"Then you know there's going to be a publishing firm called Grant and Thorpe?"

"I do."

"Well. Are you going to hamper the firm's prospects by perpetuating a feud between the junior partner and the senior partner's niece?"

"Our personal relations have nothing to do——"

"You'll see whether they have or not. Have you ever pitched horseshoes?"

"Yes."

"Do you know how hard it is to throw a ringer?"

"It isn't hard, it's impossible."

"That's right. I have a proposition to make. If I throw a ringer with one toss with this shoe, that photograph is mine, you and I become reconciled immediately and you get kissed. What about it?"

Nancy looked contemptuous. "You mean a ringer on the first toss?"

"Yes."

She laughed sneeringly. "Go ahead. It will be you perpetuating the feud, not me."

"Do you accept my proposition?"

"Certainly, why not?"

Jeffrey turned on his heel, marched to the nearest clay box, took position, set his jaw, clutched the horseshoe, glued his eyes to the iron peg forty feet away and let fly. Instead of sailing professionally, the shoe hurtled drunkenly through the air, twisting and wobbling, hit the clay at the extreme corner of the opposite box, staggered across crazily, performed a feeble spin near the center and lazily toppled over into an embrace of the iron peg with its iron arms.

"By God," Jeffrey muttered in incredulous awe, staring at it, "it's fate!" Then he whirled and leaped for Nancy.

She leaped too. It was not a frantic panic-stricken scuttle away from peril, but a purposeful and well-aimed dash for a selected sanctuary; and was so unexpected that its force nearly toppled the sanctuary, which was the brawny form of Dan Pavey, to the ground. He staggered and regained balance. Nancy hung to him and on him, her arms around his neck and told his ear:

"Don't let him!"

Dan's arms, around her, held her there. Jeffrey Thorpe, confronting him, demanded:

"Put her down! Turn her loose! I ask you because I can't make you. You're wounded."

"Oh," cried Nancy, "I forgot! Your arm!" She wriggled.

"My arm's all right," Dan rumbled. "Quit squirming. You can't squirm out of your agreement, either. Don't be a welcher. The deal was that if he threw a ringer you got kissed and you're going to. Are you going to let him kiss you?"

"No."

"Okay, then I'll have to do it myself."

He did so, standing there with her in his arms oblivious to the audience, full on her lips. Ten seconds later he said:

"That was intended to make an impression. Did it?"

"Yes," said Nancy. She got her breath. "Put me down so I can look at your arm."

Tecumseh Fox pitched a horseshoe.

The World of
Rex Stout

Now, for the first time ever, enjoy a peek into the life of Nero Wolfe's creator, Rex Stout, courtesy of the Stout Estate. Pulled from Rex Stout's own archives, here are rarely seen, never-before-published memorabilia. Each title in "The Rex Stout Library" will offer an exclusive look into the life of the man who gave Nero Wolfe life.

Double for Death

With *Double for Death*, Rex Stout introduced a new detective to his readers: Tecumseh Fox. Fox would never gain the popularity of Stout's most famous creation, Nero Wolfe, but Stout himself held *Double for Death* in especially high regard. He told his biographer: "I think it is the best detective story, technically, that I ever wrote." Reproduced here is the original jacket art from the 1939 hardcover edition of *Double for Death*, published by Farrar & Rinehart.

DOUBLE
FOR
DEATH
A TECUMSEH FOX MYSTERY
BY
REX
STOUT
CREATOR OF NERO WOLFE